Michael Christopher Sanders was born in Liverpool, England, in 1953. He has enjoyed a varied career. On leaving school, he worked as a Gasfitter for several years before returning to education to read Drama at Manchester University. Also, he has been awarded a Gold Medal for acting by LAMDA drama school. He worked in professional theatre for many years including running two theatre companies as an Artistic Director. In later life, he worked for the British Civil Service, in social welfare. He is now retired, and he lives on the Salford Quays in Greater Manchester, England. He has had several articles and short stories published as well as two books of short stories: one about the Lake District, called *Fells, Phantoms & Fables*, and a book of romantic short stories, called *Love's Winners and Losers*.

Blood, Passion & Self-Sacrifice

Also by M C Sanders

Fells, Phantoms & Fables – stories of myth, horror and the
supernatural set in the English Lake District.
1st edition 2019
2nd edition 2020.

Love's Winners and Losers – a collection of romantic stories,
some bitter and some sweet.
Published 2020.

M C Sanders

Blood, Passion & Self-Sacrifice

Blood, Passion & Self-Sacrifice

Plays of old sorrow, written in tears and blood.
Eugene O'Neill, 22nd July, 1941

Blood, Passion & Self-Sacrifice

by

Michael Christopher Sanders

6 plays about love, devotion & desire

Blood, Passion & Self-Sacrifice

Blood, Passion & Self-Sacrifice
First published by Amazon 2022

Conditions of Sale

M C Sanders

For Cindy,
many thanks for all your support and advice

Blood, Passion & Self-Sacrifice

Special thanks to:

As always, to Dr Adrienne Jervis, whose advice and generosity of spirit has aided me across the years to bring these plays to publication. Lynette Walkley, for her perceptiveness and intelligent guidance on the plays. The late Cindy Wells, who was a very fine actress and a good friend. Carol Sanders, my sister, for all her support and understanding in helping me to bring this work to fruition. And, Gizmo Sanders, my sister's Jack Russell, for doing the grand job of keeping me sane by taking me for long walks in the park and also for a drink in his favourite dog-friendly pub on the Salford Quays.

Also, a special thanks to: Ces Abbottson, Maureen Boase, Barry Anderson, Diana Fraser and Dianne Frison for coming to the aid of the party.

M C Sanders

Table of Contents:

Introduction

I was introduced to the world of the theatre by a girl friend and I started to do amateur dramatics in north Liverpool, England, at an Amateur Dramatic Society called The Lucilla. Once introduced, I was bitten. I remember three people at The Lucilla who helped me enormously in learning about the theatre. One was Ces Abbottson, a teacher by profession and a fine actor, the second was Mrs Maureen Boase, a kind and understanding lovely lady, and the other was, Barry Anderson, an ex-professional actor and a very good Artistic Director. I thank them all for their kindness and patience in taking the trouble to help an untutored ingenue.

During this time, I started to take drama lessons and I was fortunate enough to be trained by two superb teachers, Mrs Diana Fraser and Mrs Dianne Frison. Both ladies guided and trained me through the trials and landscape of acting and vocal training. I lost my Liverpool accent and through their nurturing gained the LAMDA gold medal for acting, the highest award one can achieve without actually going to the Drama School itself. I thank both ladies unreservedly and I know that a lot of my prospering in drama is due to them. Thank you, Ladies. Thank you.

When it was time to choose a university course, the advice from my tutors was to choose a subject that I was interested in; that subject was, of course, drama. I was fortunate enough to be able to read Drama at Manchester University, England. At university, I appeared in many plays, directed a comedy company that toured to other universities, wrote several plays and chaired the Film Making Club before graduating with honours.

After university, I went into professional theatre, doing small-part acting and Stage Management at The Welsh

National Theatre and Repertory Theatre Companies in Perth, Scotland, and Southend, England. Eventually, I ran my own small theatre company producing plays for schools on the English south coast. Alas, that theatre company closed due to government cut backs and so in my mid-thirties my theatre career ended. I decided that it was time to seek new adventures, but I never lost my interest in drama and I continued to write plays and to see many, many theatrical productions.

Over the years, I discovered a passion for classical Greek drama, with its dramatic intensity and power. Also, I like the plays of the Roman tragedian, Seneca, with their strong characters and exposition. Added to all this is my love of the plays penned by the Italian dramatist, Luigi Pirandello, who explored the human psyche and theatricality in everyday life. My plays display my passion for these dramatic forms. They fuse the tight, dramatic intensity of Greek classical drama with the power and exposition of Seneca, and they explore the psychology behind our beliefs and the theatricality in the way we behave.

This collection consists of three tragedies, two comedies and a dramatic monologue:

The first play is a tragedy called, *Justice and Revenge*. It is a drama about a couple who have to come to terms with the death of their daughter in a hit-and-run accident after the driver receives a very light sentence from the court. It explores the extreme measures they take; are they seeking justice or after revenge?

The second play, *You're Mine Forevermore*, is a tragedy also. It is based on one of my short stories. In the play, a man finds a skeleton clutching a relic. The man keeps the relic, but awful things start to happen to anybody whom he feels affection towards. He seeks advice on what to do to protect his loved ones, only to discover the terrible price he has to pay to ensure their safety.

The third play is a tragedy called, *Scorpions of the Mind*. It is about a man who helps a girl when she is being attacked in a public place. She befriends him, but her attackers where not random thugs, and she has a dark purpose to which she tries to get her rescuer to help her fulfil.

Fortunately, not all of life is tragic and serious. So, the next two plays explore similar themes, but from the funny, lighter side of life.

The first comedy, *Heroes of Yesterday*, was originally performed decades ago at Manchester University when I was a student. Alas, it was a small-scale production performed in one of the university drama studios and there was no theatre programme printed; indeed, it is so long ago that I cannot remember the names of all the students involved in the production to give them any credit, but I thank them all. When I was a student at Manchester University, there was a totally unsubstantiated but amusing rumour circulating the university campus that one of the Drama Faculty professors had once auditioned for the part of James Bond. The particular professor was a formidable intellectual, a nice man, very handsome and an ex-actor. The totally unsubstantiated rumour was so prevalent that if one went into the bar at the Students' Union and said that one was reading Drama, then one was likely to be asked, 'Is it true that one of your professors once auditioned for the part of James Bond?' So, out of that spark of gossip and tittle-tattle came the comedy, *Heroes of Yesterday*; a play which still raises a smile today and has been revised since its original production.

M C Sanders

The next play is a 20-minute comedy entitled, *An Admirer from Afar*. It is about an actress haunted by a fan who cannot accept that the character she plays in a television soap-opera and with whom he is in love, does not exist. Eventually, she agrees to meet him dressed as her character, in the hope of pacifying him.

The final play, *Vissi d'arte*, [meaning, I lived for art] certainly contains both passion and self-sacrifice. It is a one act monologue about Maria Callas, the world-famous soprano. Indeed, Maria is one of the most famous Greeks since Plato. During the piece, a 50-something Maria reflexes on her life and her art. In many ways, Maria's life was as colourful and as exciting as the operas in which she starred. There is no singing in the play; it is purely a dramatic piece. For Maria, fame and love tinged her life with sadness and tragedy as well as success.

Is there a common theme to all the plays? Well, all the plays display love, passion, desire, devotion, commitment and self-sacrifice; I spared you the blood in the last three plays, but even they have a visceral dramatic tension mingled with the laughs.

Enjoy them all, and please look out for them in performance.

Best wishes,

Michael Christopher Sanders.

Justice and Revenge

A tragedy.

To know and not to act is not to know,
Lao Tzu, a Taoist philosopher.

M C Sanders

List of Characters:

John Landsbury - the father, 42, car mechanic & a martial arts enthusiast

Georgina Landsbury- the mother, 35, office manager & amateur actress

Amy Landsbury - their daughter, 16 years old

Narrator - a fifty something martial arts enthusiast

Wayne - a 19 years old boy

[The other minor characters are played by the narrator]

Blood, Passion & Self-Sacrifice

[The scene has an oriental mysticism to it as the audience enter. THE NARRATOR practices sword swipes. THE NARRATOR shouts a 'ki-ai' occasionally. In the background sounds of gongs, bells and chanting. Incense sticks burn on the set. The gongs, bells and chanting return throughout the play at the director's discretion to maintain a mystical air.]

NARRATOR: Blood will have blood. Blood will have blood. Once the judgement was made, even reflecting back over the events with the wisdom and arrogance of retrospect, I cannot see what anybody could change in the choices and actions they pursued. Once the judgement was made, once the judgement was made even with the knowledge and enlightenment of future happenings would – could any single character have made a different choice in the options of action and inaction available to them to change their fate? I desperately need to believe there must have been a point, I am certain – certain that there must have been a point, an instance, a moment when a different decision would have changed the history about to unfold, but reason and contemplation fails my mind-racked obsession to find it. Surely, there must have been a point when the blood fest could have – would have – been avoided.

[JOHN'S house. A living room. There is a sideboard and a telephone. JOHN enters. JOHN goes to the sideboard and pours a large whiskey.]

NARRATOR: John Landsbury, age 42, a car mechanic by profession. John is good at fixing things. Mechanical, technical problems he's good at. But the irrational, the emotional... We meet him going through the mundane motions of living, dealing with the death of his daughter, Amy, and the breakup of his marriage. Dealing with it badly.

[*JOHN picks up the phone and he presses automatic dialling.*]

JOHN: Hello. I would like to order some food, please. A chicken curry and a portion of fried rice. What? Yes, that's right, the usual. Ten minutes. Ok. Thank you, bye.

[*JOHN takes a large swig of whiskey and he puts the glass down. He practices Samurai sword swipes with an invisible Samurai sword. On the last swipe he gives a passionate 'ki-ai'. Then, he gabs the whiskey glass, fills it with more whiskey, takes another swig and he sits in the seiza posture.*]

NARRATOR: Memories. Memories haunt him. So many memories. Ghosts that refuse to stay in the past. The mind plays tricks on you. We remember events how we would like them to be, rather than how they were. Perhaps it is fate being kind to us, acting as a healing balm, or perhaps it is a pernicious God playing games inside our minds.

[*AMY enters. She wears her school uniform and carries a shoulder bag.*]

AMY: Bye, mum, bye, dad, see you both later after school.

[*Enter GEORGINA.*]

GEORGINA: Amy, you have plenty of time to get to school, don't rush. And watch the roads, young lady. Have you done your homework?

AMY: Yes.

GEORGINA: All done?

AMY: Yes, mum, all done.

Blood, Passion & Self-Sacrifice

GEORGINA: Have you got your lunch?

AMY: Mum, yes! It's in my bag.

GEORGINA: The lunches that I prepare for you are nutritionally well balanced to ensure that you eat a good healthy diet. If I find that you have been eating burgers and chips again at school, young lady, there'll be trouble. I know that you think I badger you, but you will thank me for it when you grow up. Now, give mummy a big kiss, sweetheart, and watch when you're crossing the road to school. Remember, I've got amateur dramatics tonight, so your dad will sort out your tea.

[AMY gives GEORGINA a kiss on the cheek. AMY turns to JOHN.]

AMY: Bye, dad.

JOHN: Goodbye, my darling, I love you.

AMY: Love you lots as well, dad.

[AMY gives JOHN a kiss on the cheek and she exits.]

JOHN: That was the last time I saw my daughter alive.

[JOHN swigs the whiskey.]

GEORGINA: There's a lasagne in the fridge for you and Amy. You only have to microwave it. I'm off to my amateur dramatics this evening.

JOHN: *Blood Wedding.*

[GEORGINA busies herself checking her appearance in a mirror.]

GEORGINA: That's right. So, you do listen to me sometimes. I'm playing the part of the mother in a play called *Blood Wedding* by a Spanish playwright, Federico Garcia Lorca. Even though I say it myself, as a production, it threatens to be rather good. You must take a night off from your martial arts obsession and come to see it with Amy when we perform it at the Town Hall. *[She smiles warmly and she pecks him on the cheek.]* Bye, sweetheart, see you later.

[Exit GEORGINA.]

JOHN: *Blood Wedding.* She appears in plays coloured by blood and death and then she taunts me about practicing martial arts. I remember thinking in those final years that perhaps I should just leave, but I didn't. A marriage gone stale. Still, at least we had Amy. We stayed together for Amy.

[JOHN takes a large swig of whiskey. He rises and he takes his drink to the side of the stage. The scene changes to a rehearsal room.

Enter GEORGINA.]

GEORGINA as THE MOTHER: 'It hurts me to the tips of my veins. On the forehead of all of them I see only the hand with which they killed what was mine. Can you really see me? Don't I seem mad to you? Well, it's the madness of not having shrieked out all my breast needs to. Always in my breast there's a shriek standing tiptoe that I have to beat down and hold in under my shawls. But the dead are carried off and one has to keep still. And, then people find fault.

NARRATOR as the FATHER-IN-LAW: 'I want to have lots of children. Lots of sons are needed.

GEORGINA as THE MOTHER: 'And daughters too. Men are like the wind. They're forced to handle weapons. Girls never go out onto the street.

NARRATOR as the FATHER-IN-LAW: 'I think we'll have both. What I'd like is to have all this happen in a day. So that right away we'd have two or three children.

GEORGINA as THE MOTHER: 'But it's not like that. Raring children takes a long time. That's why it's so terrible to see one's own blood spilled out on the ground. A fountain that spurts for a minute but costs us a lift time. When I got to my son, he lay fallen in the middle of the street. I wet my hands with his blood and licked them with my tongue – because it was his blood.'

NARRATOR: Ok. I'm going to stop you there. I think we need to block you further stage centre for that speech. Remember the character is a woman who has repressed for years her rage at the murder of her son and her feelings of injustice for the murderers not being punished properly.

[JOHN phones GEORGINA. A mobile phone rings.]

GEORGINA: Oh, sorry! Sorry! I must have forgotten to turn it off. Sorry!

[GEORGINA goes to answer it. The bleep, bleep, bleep of a life support monitor begins.]

GEORGINA: Hello.

JOHN: Georgina, it's John.

GEORGINA: Hello, John.

JOHN: It's about Amy. There's been a terrible accident.

GEORGINA: Amy, an accident? Oh, God, what kind of accident? What do you mean?

JOHN: A road traffic accident.

GEORGINA: Oh, God, Amy. Is she all right?

JOHN: Just – just come to the hospital right away.

[The heart beat monitor increases in volume and then changes to a steady, single, continuous note.]

JOHN: I couldn't tell her on the phone. It is not the type of information to give to your wife, your daughter's mother, in a telephone call.

GEORGINA: Where is she? Is she all right? My baby, where is she?

JOHN: Georgina, Amy is dead. She was pronounced dead on arrival at the hospital.

[GEORGINA starts shaking and crying. JOHN comforts her.]

GEORGINA: No, no, no, no, no!

[Blackout. JOHN and THE NARRATOR on stage.]

JOHN: The driver did not even stop. If he had stopped then I could have forgiven him. If the driver had stopped, tried to help, then I could have found the strength in my heart to forgive him. I could have forgiven him. I could have forgiven the driver when he killed my little girl if he had stopped and tried to help. Accidents happen; they shouldn't, but they do. If he had stopped and tried to help then I could have forgiven him. I could have found it in my heart to forgive him.

Keep control. The facts. Amy died on the 28th of May. That is a fact. She was walking home from school along a pavement with her friend. That is a fact too. It was verified by two witnesses; a retired policeman who was walking his dog on the opposite side of the road and a mother of two, who had collected her young children from school, Ian, aged eight, and Cathy, aged six. It was 4:21 pm. Another fact. Amy was walking along with her friend. A fact. The day was sunny and dry, warm but not humid. A light rain had fallen that morning but the ground was dry. A fact. There was no other traffic on the road. It was just a side road on an estate with a thirty-miles-per-hour speed limit, just like thousands, even millions of side roads in the country. That is also a fact. It was mentioned in court. The car came racing around the corner in the road; that was an eyewitness description given as evidence to the police. It was a red car, old, noisy, the make was uncertain, but the licence number was clear, the retired policeman noted it down. Another fact. 'Driving at speed,' was how the prosecution described it. 'Driving at speed...' Using the public highway as a racetrack, but that's an opinion, not a fact, that's my opinion. 'Driving at speed,' that was considered to be a fact. The driver lost control of the car as he careered, sorry, opinion, drove at speed around the bend. Both witnesses reported hearing the tyres screeching. The burnt rubber marks on the surface of the road measured by the police gave an estimated speed of sixty-miles-per-hour. The driver lost control. Skidded out of the bend out of control and on to the pavement. 'Driving at speed.' Like a run-away train. Like a run-away train careering at speed. Amy's friend managed to jump out of the path of the two-tonne machine hurtling at them 'at speed'. The driver's barrister described the injuries of Amy's friend as 'minor injuries'. I wonder how many lawyers who have suffered the trauma of a road traffic accident resulting in a fractured leg and a permanent scar at the tender age of sixteen-years-old would describe their injuries as, 'minor injuries'? Amy, my daughter, did not stand a chance. The two-tonne machine hit her full on. The driver never even stopped. Like a run-away train. Hit and run. Like a run-away train… He left two young girls to die in the road; one survived after a fashion and the other died. He left them to die. If he had stopped and tried to help them, I could have forgiven him, after all, accidents happen, they shouldn't but they do, but he never even stopped. The police traced the driver by the car number plate. A nineteen-year-old boy racer. He was not in when the police called at his home. He lived with his parents. He had left home according to his parents. A week later he walked into a police station with his father and he gave himself up. Pleaded guilty in court. He had lost control of the car whilst driving 'at speed'. He knocked down two young girls and he left them to die in the road. He careered a two-tonne machine into two sixteen-year-old girls and then he left them to die in the road. Driving a car as though it were a high-speed train. *[Pause.]* The driver had a good lawyer. She said that he did not stop because he panicked. First offence. Nineteen-years-old. Promising career in architecture. Wore an expensive suit, shirt and tie in court. He cried for the judge. He had given himself up. Pleaded guilty. He said that he was sorry. *[Pause.]* Sorry. He left the two girls to die and he was sorry. The court sentenced him to fourteen weeks in prison. Fourteen weeks for killing one sixteen-year-old girl and ruining the life of another. If he had stopped and tried to help them, accidents happen, they shouldn't but they do, if he had stopped and helped them then I could forgive him. Fourteen weeks. That's all the law court valued the lives of two young girls; one whose life was ruined forever and the other, my young daughter, Amy, who was killed. Fourteen weeks. Fact.

That is a fact. Fourteen weeks. Who is guiltier? The child killer or the law court; the one who doesn't value the lives of two young girls at all or the institution who valued them at only fourteen weeks? [*Pause.*] What do you do when you live in a culture where the rights of the criminal are considered to be more important than the rights of the victim? What do you do?

NARRATOR: There is an old Spanish proverb, 'Revenge is a dish best served cold'. What does one do when the society that one lives in considers the rights of the criminal to be more important than the rights of the victim? When it is perceived by the victim that the rule of law is not applied fairly. When it is perceived that convicted criminals are not punished properly. The moral majority howls in disgust at the criminal justice system. But, what does one do?

[*Enter the WAYNE.*]

WAYNE: I have done my time for the crime. Served my sentence. What more do you want? What more? I passed my driving test first time, not like those losers who muck it up over and over again until they eventually scrape through by a gnat's bollocks. No, first time. That's how good I am behind the wheel. Then, my own pair of wheels before any of my mates. A red, two door, 1600cc, six-year-old, hatchback. My own car. A babe magnet. A pair of wheels. Second hand, but no problem. Bought and paid for by my dad, well, what are dads for, eh? My own pair of wheels. I was on the road. It moves a bit despite its age. A hundred on the motorway. Yeah!! So, what if I do break the speed limit? Everyone does. Only wimps drive within the speed limit. I'm a good driver, I am. I am! Those two girls, it was an accident. It's not as if I meant it. I'm sorry one got injured and the other got killed. But, I'm a good driver. Sure, I took that bend a little fast. It's a tight bend, tricky. Lost the back end of the car. All drivers do that. Besides, I owned up to doing it. All right, not right away, but I did give myself up. Mind you, that lawyer my dad hired was good. She had that judge wrapped around her little finger. Eating out of her hand he was. She said to me wear a nice suit and have a bit of a cry in court. Yeah!!! Got off with a few weeks in prison. The court was right to let me off with it, I mean; nobody drives within the speed limit. I mean, look at any action programme on the tele or the cinema, do any of them drive within the speed limit? Of course, they don't. Nobody does. I'm a good driver and I have paid my debt to society. Fourteen weeks in that doped up loser's institute of a prison. God, it was enough to drive anyone stark raving mad being banged up in that place. But I did my porridge and now I'm free and back behind the wheel. Back down the road again. I've got to move on, put the past behind me. Move like the wind. I'm sorry that those two kids got hurt, well one got killed, but I have paid my debt to society and that is that.

[Exit WAYNE.]

NARRATOR: The moral majority howls in disgust. 'Revenge is a dish best served cold'.

[Enter GEORGINA and AMY. AMY is dressed to go out with her friends.]

JOHN: You look fantastic!

AMY: Thanks, Dad.

GEORGINA: Phone when you're ready to come home and your father will pick you up in the car.

AMY: Mum, there's really no need. I can get a taxi.

Blood, Passion & Self-Sacrifice

GEORGINA: The first time out on your own, I think there is, even if it is just a school disco.

JOHN: I don't think they have disco's anymore, Georgina.

GEORGINA: Whatever.

AMY: Mom, I promise to phone.

[AMY gives GEORGINA a farewell hug. AMY exits.]

JOHN: Memories. Idealised, perhaps, but it's how I choose to remember the events of the past. Georgina, my wife, was always the stern one with Amy, always the sensible one.

[JOHN pours a large glass of whiskey. JOHN drinks and exits. GEORGINA stands alone. GEORGINA takes a teddy bear from the sideboard.]

GEORGINA: It's odd the mementoes you keep as your child grows up. This was always her favourite. She still had it by her bed when she left us, although, of course, she never told any of her friends. And, I remember her favourite song. It was a hymn. I can still hear her singing it from when I went to see her in her first Carol service over eleven years ago; she was only five-years-old then. Eleven years ago, but it is still fresh in my memory.

[GEORGINA sings]:
            'Away in a manger, no crib for his bed,
            the little Lord Jesus laid down his sweet head.
            The stars in the bright sky looked down where he
            lay,
            the little Lord Jesus asleep on the hay.

            Be near me, Lord Jesus; I ask thee to stay

close by me forever, and love me I pray.
Bless all the dear children in thy tender care,
and fit us for heaven to live with thee there.'

[Pause. GEORGINA speaks the next two lines.]
'Bless all the dear children in thy tender care,
and fit us for heaven to live with thee there.'

The memories never leave you. 'Don't be back late.' I shall
always remember saying that to her as she went out of the
door to school on that last day. I remember saying to her,
'Have you done your homework, young lady?' and 'If I find
that you have eaten junk food at school again, there'll be
trouble.' 'Young, lady.' 'Young, lady.' The phrases echo back
at me now that she's gone... I had a good pregnancy. I
actually enjoyed it. It wasn't a difficult birth. Hurt like hell,
but she was such an angel when I held her in my arms. She
cried a lot. A little demanding, but a good baby. And a good
kid. I was always hard on her, making sure that she did her
prep work, her homework, always ensuring that she knew
how to eat properly at the table, how to order in a restaurant
and how to behave in public. 'Remember,' I would say to
her, 'when you grow up, you will thank me for all this one
day, because I gave you the choice, I gave you the choice of
how to behave correctly in society, of getting a good job, a
career. Remember, young lady, I gave you that choice.'
'When you grow up...' It wasn't a difficult birth. John was
with me. He actually held my hand as I gave birth. Bless him.
He was a good husband in those early years and a good dad.
We made a good team. And my mum and dad were superb.
And Amy was such a lovely little thing. *[Pause.]* After Amy
left us, I remember walking into her school to see her
teachers and, in the corridor, I saw the lockers of all her
classmates standing in a row. All the lockers had names on
them save for one. Above the names, the children had put
photos of themselves or their favourite pop group or singer.

Just one locker stood amidst them unadorned, bare and empty. The teachers had emptied it to spare me the pain of seeing Amy's name and photo on it, yet it stood out in its stark bareness and emptiness even louder than if they had left it adorned with her name and her ... The bastard didn't even stop to see if he could help her... My dad had already had one stroke by the time Amy went away and I don't think that he will survive this... The law court didn't seem too bothered over the fact that many, many lives are destroyed when a child is taken away. My marriage to John never survived Amy going away. Heavens above, in the last few years we were only going through the motions a lot of the time in any case, functioning as a couple. Socially, well, he had his martial arts and I had my amateur dramatics. We stayed together as much out of convenience as anything else and, of course, for Amy. We stayed together for Amy. But when Amy went away – I hope that bastard child killer stews in hell! Steady, Georgina, steady. I must move on. Move on now I am off the medication and starting to go out again. I must concentrate my energies on my career. If I work hard, I shall be up for promotion soon. It will mean moving house. *[Long pause.]* Death stops time, ambition, purpose and meaning; they all end.

[GEORGINA exits. Enter JOHN.]

JOHN: To know and not to act is not to know.

NARRATOR: A Samurai lives everyday as though it is his last.

JOHN & NARRATOR: It is the mentality of the warrior code.

JOHN: I am a walking corpse.

NARRATOR: But you eat, sleep and still have feelings.

JOHN: My dreams of my little girl, running, laughing, playing, are more real than the empty functional drudge of day-to-day living. I live in a dark, deep pit of grief, no light, no end, no hope of redemption.

JOHN & NARRATOR: To know and not to act is not to know.

JOHN: Do I become a kind of avenger, a Eumenides, a fury, a divine wind sweeping through to enact justice? The law court valued my sweet girl's life at fourteen weeks. Who is the guiltier, the law court or the child killer?

NARRATOR: Injustice breeds bloodshed. I have known John for some years now through the martial arts Dojo we both belong to. Like myself, he was keen on the subject. Fascinated. Mesmerized by the way of the Samurai and their warrior code. The nobility of thought entwined with neo-Confucian reasoning, 'To know and not to act is not to know'. The way of the Samurai involves a blending of experience, tuition and behaviour that produces a wisdom liberating one from the dilemmas of indecision. In life events the code of the Samurai shows one the right thing to do and the right way to conduct oneself. I should have known what John intended, but we were not close friends, we just shared a common interest; we were not friends, just friendly. The course of action that he pursued I both admired and abhorred in equal measures.

If you live in a culture where the criminal justice system perceives the rights of the criminal to be more important than the rights of the victim, if the criminal is perceived as not being punished for the crime committed, if the punishment is considered to be grossly inadequate by the over-whelming majority of the population, a punishment regarded as morally wrong by society's standards of crime related to punishment, then blood will have blood. For justice can be achieved only through vendetta, the criminalisation of every member of society, an eye for an eye, a tooth for a tooth and a life for a life.

The Greeks have a saying; before embarking on a vendetta always dig two graves.

It is obvious in retrospect what was going to happen. Could I have prevented it? Stopped the blood fest. It is a question that has haunted my thoughts during many, many sleepless nights. However, I know that I could not. I could not change the impersonal force of circumstances, that complex web of human interactions spun out over time, the moving force of life events that we call history. I could not change them. The present comes out of the past and projects into the future. To change the present, I would need to change the past and the past exists in memories only. Once Amy was killed and the killer was not properly punished, then events surged forward and down a precipice with an unstoppable momentum like a runaway train careering down a railway embankment. Justice was not seen to have been satisfied. There was public outrage, private grief, anger not sated.

[Enter GEORGINA]

GEORGINA as THE MOTHER: 'The months pass and the hopelessness of it stings in my eyes and even to the roots of my hair.

NARRATOR as THE BRIDEGROOM: Let's quit this talk.

GEORGINA as THE MOTHER: No. No. Let's not quit this talk. Can anyone bring back my daughter' – sorry, sorry – 'my son? Then there's the jail. What do they mean, jail? They eat there, smoke there, play music there! My kin choking with the weeds, silent, turning to dust. A beautiful flower. The killer in jail, carefree, looking at the mountains.

NARRATOR as THE BRIDEGROOM & JOHN [*both speak together*]: Do you want me to go kill him?'

NARRATOR: I think that I should stop you there.

[*GEORGINA breaks character*]

NARRATOR: Are you sure that you want to continue with this play? I mean *Blood Wedding* and to be playing the part of the mother grieving over the unavenged death of her son. Isn't it a bit too close to home?

GEORGINA: I must do this play. I must do it. For me, it's cathartic, therapeutic. I feel that it will help me deal with my grief.

NARRATOR: I think that the character of the mother wallows in her grief.

GEORGINA: No, that's not true. The mother in the play is trapped by her grief because of her sense of injustice. The murderers of her husband and her son were never punished properly. From her point of view, she has never been given justice. So, she is unable to move on. This play, *Blood Wedding*, is important to me. For me it contains a truth that I can empathise with. I understand the character of the mother and I want to see the production through to the end.

NARRATOR: If you insist.

Blood, Passion & Self-Sacrifice

GEORGINA: Yes. Yes, I do.

[Exit GEORGINA]

JOHN: Do you want me to kill him? Forced by injustice into becoming an avenger, a righter of wrongs.

NARRATOR: Everybody at the Dojo was shocked when we heard the law court's sentence on young Amy's killer. Fourteen weeks! We had all followed the case in the papers. How the driver had been speeding in a built-up area. How he lost control of the car on a bend because he was going too fast. How he hit the two young girls and didn't brother to stop. The papers likened the girls' injuries to the equivalent of being hit by an express train. So, when we read that the sentence was only fourteen weeks, well, most of us thought that it was a misprint, it must be fourteen years; but, no, the papers had reported the sentence accurately, fourteen weeks. The sentence was an insult to the two girls. Also, it sent a message to boy racers that they can get away with knocking people down and even killing them. They can do what they like because they won't be punished properly. Criminals laughing at the police doing the thankless job of trying to enforce a law that has no teeth. Everybody in the Dojo signed a petition of complaint. I volunteered to stand in the town square asking people to sign. They did of course. Hundreds of signatures. Hundreds and hundreds of signatures complaining about the lightness of the sentence. Everyone in the Dojo wrote to his or her Member of Parliament, but, of course, nothing came of all of it. As for the child killer, well, one could hardly blame him; it is not his fault if the law court failed to punish him properly. But, as I practiced my sword cutting swipes with the bokken —a wooden practice sword - during those days following the sentencing, the target that I mentally visualized standing in front of me was the child killer.

[THE NARRATOR mimes a sword swipe and a 'ki-ai'.]

To know and not to act is not to know.

John continued to come to the Dojo, but after Amy's death there was a change. His eyes were cold and dead. There was a grim determination in the way he went through the kendo kata perfecting the use of the sword. Ideally, budo training should be a means to aid the student to realise a stoic constitution, a solid personality and an unshakable sense of right and wrong, but all I saw in John's eyes was a living corpse. The Samurai is always conscious that there is no tomorrow just today. The Samurai always lives in the moment. But was John actually living or just going through the motions, muted by the double blow of Amy's death and the insult of the light sentence? Ironically, and unbeknown to me at the time, I helped things along. Without comprehending, I provided, facilitated, the means to right the moral wrong. I remember it started like any other evening. How often do significant events begin as just another ordinary day? We had finished our training session in the Dojo. I had gone for a drink with some of the other trainees. John did not come. Afterwards, I was walking home when I saw John standing on a railway bridge, just looking out across the track. *[To John.]* John, John, what are you doing?

JOHN: Oh, hi, nothing. Just standing here watching the trains go by.

NARRATOR: Why didn't you come for a drink with the rest of us?

JOHN: Oh, no, no, I didn't fancy that. I just wanted to stand here watching the trains.

NARRATOR: So you said.

JOHN: Don't worry I'm not going to jump over in front of an express train or anything like that. I use to bring Amy here when she was a little girl, you see. We use to walk the dog together up here. We would watch the trains together as they sped along the lines. Amy would wave at the drivers and some of them would wave back. Memories, eh?

NARRATOR: Mmm, memories. It must have been many years ago.

JOHN: Yes, it was. She was just a little girl then; she was only nine. But, now, I come here often, and I just stand here, thinking.

NARRATOR: Thinking? Thinking what?

JOHN: Thinking that revenge is a dish best served cold.

NARRATOR: It's a long way down. They certainly dug deep when they made these railway cuttings, didn't they? Well, look, if you won't come for a drink and you say that you're not thinking of throwing yourself under a train, well, then, do you remember me telling you about the present of a real Samurai sword that I was given during my visit to Japan?

JOHN: Sensei, you tell everybody the story about that sword.

NARRATOR: It was my moment of glory.

JOHN: You prevented three thugs beating up and robbing a wealthy businessman.

NARRATOR: It wasn't just his wallet that they would have taken but his life. If I hadn't intervened, they would have left him dead in the street.

JOHN: Hit and run.

NARRATOR: Yes, I supposed so. He was so grateful for me saving his life, that I had stopped and helped, he made me the generous gift of the sword. I was embarrassed by his generosity, but very grateful. Would you like to see it?

JOHN: That is an honour, Sensei.

NARRATOR: Yes, but, not too great an honour, I hope?

JOHN: I assure you, Sensei, that I was not going to throw myself from the bridge into the path of an oncoming train.

NARRATOR: Good. You can stand here on another evening with your memories and contemplate revenge, the offer still stands. Would you like to see the sword?

JOHN: Yes, Sensei, I would.

[Cross fade to THE NARRATOR'S flat. It is neat and modern with lots of Budo memorabilia around tastefully arrayed in a Japanese style.]

NARRATOR: Most Japanese swords that you see nowadays are not real swords.

JOHN: Not real swords?

Blood, Passion & Self-Sacrifice

NARRATOR: Well, they are real swords, but they are not proper swords.

JOHN: You mean that they are like stage props, they merely look the part?

NARRATOR: Erm, no, not quite. What I mean is that they look good. They would certainly do a lot of damage if they struck you but then any sharp knife would do just as much damage, any pointed instrument if welded with enough force would leave its mark. Most Japanese swords you see nowadays are dress swords. They look good and they certainly look flash, especially in the movies, and they would do damage if stabbed into a body, as any sharp knife would do, but they are imitations. A pastiche of a great sword. A toy compared to the real thing. They are not great swords.

JOHN: What is a great sword?

NARRATOR: Let me show you.

[*THE NARRATOR produces the sword. There is a religious air to his action.*]

NARRATOR: I do not keep it on display. It is too valuable. Also, there is the fear of rust and damage. I keep it away from prying eyes in this scabbard.

JOHN: A Shirasaya.

NARRATOR: That's right. The scabbard is called a Shirasaya.

[*THE NARRATOR removes the covering and hands the sword to JOHN.*]

M C Sanders

NARRATOR: Always ensure that you keep the cutting edge turned inward towards yourself when you are handing a sword to another person. It is part of the Japanese sword code and there are very practical safety reasons for it. One slip and you can slice off a finger or even a leg.

JOHN: It feels so light.

NARRATOR: Perfect balance. The sword is a Seki no Magoroku. That is the name of family of sword smiths who fashioned the blade. It is centuries old and the craftsmanship is of museum quality.

JOHN: It feels good to hold.

NARRATOR: Like an extension of the body.

JOHN: One feels complete.

NARRATOR: Hold the sword horizontal so that the eye gazes along the blade. Notice how the temper line on the blade seems to have a slight haze about it.

JOHN: It is like an aura reflecting off the surface.

NARRATOR: Only great swords of museum quality produce that phenomenon. Only a superior sword smith knows how to achieve that standard.

JOHN: Amazing.

NARRATOR: To me it mirrors the soul of the sword; clarity of thought and directness of action.

JOHN: There is a cold, thorough purity to it.

Blood, Passion & Self-Sacrifice

NARRATOR: The blade was forged in a charcoal furnace heated to the colour of an August moon. The handle wrapping is made from cotton, silk and whale whiskers, -

JOHN: 'whale whiskers'

NARRATOR: - and bamboo to hold the blade to the handle. They used bamboo for its tactile quality to absorb the shock when the blade slices into its enemy. The sword is handmade by experts who spent a lifetime perfecting their art.

JOHN: There is a power in it. One feels an energy surging through the veins as one holds it.

NARRATOR: Certain Sensei believe that a sword contains Kami, a spirit that lives within the blade.

JOHN: A martial weapon that gives one a spiritual experience.

NARRATOR: When an Emperor in old Japan unleashed his Samurai, they acted as a Kamikaze; a divine wind.

JOHN: A divine wind.

NARRATOR: After World War Two the idea of a Kamikaze was that of a crazed maniac who killed himself on the whim of the Generals, and whilst that view holds an undoubted truth, that is not where the concept originated.

JOHN: A divine wind.

NARRATOR: A Samurai warrior, a Kamikaze, a divine wind wielding in his hand a flash of metal that is the pure, sharp wrath of the avenging Gods of retribution.

[JOHN swipes into the air with the sword ending in a 'ki-ai' on his imaged target.]

NARRATOR: Makes you feel good, doesn't it?

JOHN: A spiritual experience. Yes, it makes you feel good.

NARRATOR: I know. I know. You can feel a spiritual energy surging through you.

JOHN: You said that this is a great sword.

NARRATOR: I did.

JOHN: So, has this sword ever been used in combat to kill someone?

NARRATOR: Almost certainly.

JOHN: So, the blade has tasted death.

NARRATOR: Yes, the blade has tasted death. All the great swords of old were tested on dead bodies to assess their cutting capability and to ensure that they did not warp, shatter, splinter or crack when used in action. The dead bodies of convicted criminals were used.

JOHN: This sword has been used on convicted criminals?

NARRATOR: Oh, yes, - after they had been put to death though. The cutting test usually involved using three corpses placed on top of one another. The sword testers were very proficient swordsmen. The blade had to slice through all three dead bodies to be declared a great sword.

Blood, Passion & Self-Sacrifice

JOHN: And this sword has been declared a great sword?

NARRATOR: Yes. Another test – again on the dead body of a convicted criminal – was for the blade to slice right through a specific tough part on the body.

JOHN: Such as the skull?

NARRATOR: Well, the bodies were decapitated already; but the skull is certainly a tough part of the body.

JOHN: Slicing right through the skull of a convicted criminal.

[JOHN does a sword swipe and a 'ki-ai'].

JOHN: What about the sword's ability to carve through living skin and bone?

NARRATOR: The sword's ability to carve through living skin and bone? That, I do not know.

[Enter GEORGINA. She holds a small knife.]

GEORGINA as THE MOTHER:
    'With a knife,
    with a little knife,
    on the appointed day, between two and three -'

NARRATOR: Who is morally more culpable, the law court who regards the rights of the child killer as more important than the rights of the child or the criminal who committed the crime?

JOHN: To know and not to act is not to know. The purity of becoming an avenger, a Eumenides, a fury, a kamikaze, a divine wind sweeping through to enact justice.

GEORGINA as THE MOTHER:
>'With a knife,
>with a tiny knife,
>that barely fits the hand,
>but that slides in clean
>through the astonished flesh
>and stops at the place
>where trembles, enmeshed,
>the dark root of the scream.'

[Exit GEORGINA.]

JOHN: The execution of convicted criminals in old Japan was by beheading?

NARRATOR: Correct. Decapitation was one form of execution. As in Europe at the time, justice was determined by one's rank, the nature of the offence and the preferred method of despatching convicted criminals in the area in which the crime was committed.

JOHN: Is it possible that your sword, Seki no Magoroku, was used to execute a convicted criminal?

NARRATOR: No. It is too great a sword. For a sword of that quality to be used the convicted criminal would have to be of great rank and nobility – a Samurai, a high-ranking bureaucrat or a high political figure such as a Shogunate.

JOHN: I see.

Blood, Passion & Self-Sacrifice

NARRATOR: Anyway, a personage of such status would not be executed; they would be expected to commit Seppuku.

JOHN: Of course, Seppuku.

NARRATOR: Belly cutting; it is suicide, but performed by the act of ritual disembowelment. Hara Kiri, as it is more commonly known in the West. In ancient Japan to be executed as a convicted criminal would have brought disgrace upon the convict and his entire family. The classes of wealth and rank were expected to commit Seppuku: the ritual of taking one's own life. That way there was no disgrace. In the western world in the eighteenth century and the nineteenth century there was much the same idea, one's best friend handed the disgraced gentleman a loaded pistol and the gentleman was expected to take his own life – to take the honourable way out.

JOHN: The honourable way out?

NARRATOR: Yes.

JOHN: And Seki no Magoroku was used for belly cutting – Seppuku?

NARRATOR: No. Not quite. Let me explain. The blade used for Seppuku is a short blade about five or six inches long. Often one used a short sword, either a tanto or a Yoroi-dōshi, an armour-piercing sword. This kind of sword. *[THE NARRATOR shows JOHN a short sword.]* One pushes the blade into the stomach – so. *[In mime, THE NARRATOR stabs the left side of his stomach.]* Only about two inches, no more. To cut deeper makes one's body lurch forward making any further cutting difficult. Next, one starts to push the blade across the body - so. *[THE NARRATOR demonstrates in mime.]* Ideally, one aims at an 'L' shaped cut severing across the stomach and up towards the rib cage. However, the pain is excruciating and the blood pouring out of the gash and the bodily fluids and the excrement clog up the path of the blade. So, the practice was to recruit a second called a 'Kaishakunin' from the Japanese verb to assist. The job of the Kaishakunin was to decapitate the person committing Seppuku. As soon as the blade tip penetrated the flesh, then honour was deemed to have been satisfied and the Kaishakunin would cleave off the suicide's head. So, belly slitting was not the actual cause of death. Death was by decapitation, the slicing off of the head by the Kaishakunin.

JOHN: Who were these Kaishakunin?

NARRATOR: The Second, as in sword and pistol duels of honour in the West, was usually a friend. He had to be a proficient swordsman, of course. There is a Kata that practices it. In Japan martial culture there is a Kata for everything.

JOHN: A Kata is a series of moves choreographed into a set sequence that is practiced and practiced and practiced to perfection. So, when called upon to perform the move in reality then one should be as near perfect as possible.

NARRATOR: Exactly. It is a little macabre, but we could practice the Kaishaku Kata at the Dojo, if you like?

JOHN: *[He gives a visceral but formal bow.]* Thank you, Sensei.

[Enter GEORGINA.]

GEORGINA as THE MOTHER: 'Is anybody home? My son ought to answer me. But now my son is an armful of shrivelled flowers. My son is a fading voice beyond the mountains. When I'm alone my tears will come, from the soles of my feet, from my roots and they'll burn hotter than blood.'

[*Exit GEORGINA.*
Scene – the Dojo. JOHN and THE NARRATOR kneel in the seiza posture at right angles to each other. JOHN has his neck stretched out prominently. THE NARRATOR holds a practice sword.]

NARRATOR: Each Kata has a rhythm of its own. It is never a question simply of repetition. One strives to achieve the rhythm within the action. Always give one hundred percent of yourself as one moves through the rehearsed actions. Always remember that an individual who merely practices an art is not even an artist yet alone a Samurai - live the moment.

JOHN: When do we begin the rehearsal?

NARRATOR: We have already begun –

[*THE NARRATOR mimes the actions during the following speech.*]

NARRATOR: The Kaishaku kata is intended to help one perfect the art of rising from a sitting position on the floor whilst drawing a sword and striking. One sits ready for when the tip of the knife penetrates the flesh of the suicide.

JOHN: I insert the knife just two inches and no more or it inhibits the belly cut?

NARRATOR: Correct. The Kaishakunin rises onto his toes commencing to draw the sword from the scabbard. Stand slightly behind the suicide to avoid being sprayed by the fountain of blood throbbing out from the neck arteries after decapitation. Stand steady, well balanced. Complete the sword draw. Move the right foot back taking the body weight with it. Stay well balanced. Keep the centre of gravity low. Bring up the sword to a position well behind your head. Ensure that the blade is pointed down. Grip the sword with the right hand only. Pause. Focus. Now move forward slicing at a slight angle to the suicide's neck. Halt the swing just before slicing right through the neck. The objective is to leave the skin intact under the suicide's chin. You achieve this by bringing up the left hand to the handle during the downward swish of the cut and so halting the swing of the sword before it slices completely through the neck. A 'ki-ai' may be given to help focus the cut.

JOHN: Why is the head not severed off completely?

NARRATOR: For the head to be cut off totally allowing it to roll across the room like a discarded football would be considered improper. The skill is to stop the blade so as to leave the skin under the chin untouched and still connecting the head with the torso. This enables the severed head to fall down with dignity onto the chest of the suicide.

JOHN: Difficult.

NARRATOR: Very difficult but, with practice and providing the suicide can keep their neck still, quite possible.

JOHN: Let's practice.

NARRATOR: We will take turns.

JOHN: We shall practice, practice, practice to strive for perfection.

[They practice the move. There is a blackout as the sword swipe is made. We hear a shout of 'ki-ai' from THE NARRATOR.

Lights up. Enter GEORGINA. She holds three mementoes: a miniature portrait of Amy, Amy's teddy and Amy's hospital identification tag.]

GEORGINA: Moving on. I am moving on, but not without sorrow and not without regret for all those 'if-onlys' and 'might-have-beens'. I realise that wherever I go Amy will always be there with me. I am learning, slowly, to accept that what little time I had with Amy was a bonus, to cherish it, to value it, to rejoice in it. I am not a philosophical person, but even I know that things heal very, very slowly and that precious memories return and should be enjoyed time and time again. Warm comforting memories to smile over and to be cried over. *[AMY enters and she stands by GEORGINA.]* Yet, as I weep, I see Amy walking towards me laughing and giggling, always laughing and giggling. And I smile a warm smile at her. She is always with me, always there to brighten up my day. *[Pause]*. I kept these. They are things a mum keeps. Her hospital identification tag when she was born, bless her. This is her favourite teddy. She had lots of toys but this is her favourite. And her portrait. The portrait of a wonderful, lovely young girl who will never grow old. Not a day goes by that I don't think of her. Not a day. Not one day. Not one day. *[GEORGINA hugs AMY to her.]*

[Exit GEORGINA and AMY. Blackout.

There is the noise of hammering a metal spike into the ground. The noise stops. The lights come up. WAYNE lies on the ground between a set of railway tracks. He has a blindfold on. JOHN stands next to him holding a lump hammer. JOHN removes the blindfold. JOHN stands between the tracks a little away from WAYNE.]

WAYNE: Where am I?

JOHN: You are connected to a metal spike in the middle of a railway track. It is five thirty in the morning, just a little after daybreak. There is still a slight chill in the air and morning dew on the ground. Your home is eleven miles to the South East; mine is three miles to the North West. *[JOHN looks at his watch.]* The Airport Express is due in ten minutes and forty-six seconds.

[WAYNE realizes his predicament and he rattles the handcuffs in a futile attempt to free himself.]

WAYNE: What the Fuck! What the fuck do you think you are doing, you dipstick? Let me go!

JOHN: I use to bring Amy down here when she was a little girl to watch the trains go by. We would wave to the drivers from that bridge over there. She loved it here. She had a fascination with trains – strange for a girl, but, still, there you are.

WAYNE: What the fuck are you talking about?

JOHN: What happens to a body when it is struck at sixty miles per hour?

WAYNE: What?

JOHN: What happens to a body when it is struck at sixty miles per hour?

WAYNE: Fuck knows. Let me go!

JOHN: Then, I shall tell you by quoting to you from the post mortem report on Amy, that's the sixteen-year-old girl you killed going at sixty miles per hour in an area with a thirty miles per hour speed limit. The young girl you left to die in the street because you chose not to stop. Allow me to read to you from the post mortem report detailing what you did. I have a copy of it here.

[JOHN produces the report.]

WAYNE: I don't care. Do you hear me? I don't fucking care.

JOHN: I know you don't, but when that train careers along here in - *[JOHN looks at his watch.]* - ten minutes precisely at sixty miles per hour and you realise that you are secured to a metal spike in the middle of the railway tracks that that particular train will be flying along, then, perhaps you will start to care.

WAYNE: You're mad. You're fucking mad! Let me go!

JOHN: I probably am mad. You're right. Perhaps I'll use that as my mitigation plea in court in the hope that the law court will let me off with your death by giving me a few weeks in jail - just as the law court did for you with Amy. Anyway, to the effects of a two-tonne metal machine hitting a human body at sixty miles per hour. Now, according to Amy's post mortem report —

WAYNE: That was an accident. I didn't mean it.

JOHN: We can't unring a bell. You see, if you had stopped and tried to help then I could have forgiven you. If you had just stopped and helped, I could have forgiven you, but, you didn't, you chose to continue speeding down the road. Not caring that you left two young girls to die. You only gave yourself up because you couldn't get your car fixed without being caught.

WAYNE: It was an accident, all right. I panicked. I'm sorry. I'm sorry!

JOHN: You are now. Yes, I believe that sitting here secured to a railway line with only - *[JOHN looks at his watch.]* - eight minutes forty-one seconds to live that you are sorry or, at least, feeling sorry for yourself. Contrary to popular opinion, English railway trains usually do run on time.

WAYNE: You're fucking mad. Look, I paid my debt to society. I'm sorry about your kid, all right?

JOHN: "Paid your debt to society". When a law court considers that the rights of the criminal are more important than the rights of the victim or the safety of every other human being living in our society, then who is the more culpable? I actually considered whether I should secure the judge to this spike in the railway line in your stead. After all, it is not your fault if the law courts regard convicted criminals as having more rights than the victim. Anyway, I digress, the affect on a body of being hit at sixty miles per hour – *[JOHN flips through the pages as he reads snippets.]* 'There were transverse fractures of the upper right humerus and comminuted fractures to the wrist and the elbow... ...fractures to the right femur, left patella smashed and severed arteries... Also, a displaced fibular fracture. ...The abdomen was full of blood. The hit tore the inferior vena cava. Internal bleeding would have been very fast... ...The back was broken at L1 and S1... ...The superior gluteal artery was severed... ...shattered upper torso and a blunt head injury.' This is interesting – 'When struck, the subject would have acquired the velocity of the vehicle, estimated at 62 miles per hour, only to be thrown against the adjacent garden wall by the violent braking of the vehicle…' You created quite a mess. All this doesn't mean much to you, does it? Allow me to explain, because you couldn't drive your car properly, one sixteen-year-old girl's life was taken away and the other young girl you crippled for life. Crippled for life at sixteen-years-old. And you didn't even bother to stop. The report goes on to explain that primary trace evidence of paint from your car was found on Amy's skin. Found on Amy's skin. That's why you couldn't get your car fixed without being caught. That's why you gave yourself up. You never felt sorry for anybody else except yourself.

[The sound of the train can be heard in the distance. It increases in volume to the end of the scene.]

JOHN: Ah, you hear that, Wayne, the sound of the airport express. It's a few seconds late, but we can forgive it.

WAYNE: Mister, please, I gave myself up. I've served my sentence.

JOHN: An eye for an eye. A tooth for a tooth. The old-world Christian philosophy is very different to that of the law courts and my God you're lucky that you don't live in a Muslin state. You've served your sentence, but I haven't finished serving mine. Amy, you sentenced to death. The other young girl that you crippled for life, she hasn't finished serving her sentence. Her parents haven't finished serving their sentences of rearing a disabled daughter. My wife hasn't finished serving her sentence. You're the criminal; yet you're the only one that got off lightly!

WAYNE: Please, mister, look, I'm sorry, it was an accident. I didn't mean it! I - I didn't mean it! I didn't mean it!

JOHN: 'I didn't mean it.' And that's your mitigation plea? Show me mercy because I didn't mean it. Mercy? There are Arabic states where it is the next-of-kin who decides the fate of the convicted criminal within the boundaries set by the law. Mercy. Now, let me see... if you had stopped, tried to help then I could have forgiven you. After all, people make mistakes, accidents happen. They shouldn't, but they do. Mercy. Sitting there perhaps you are also a victim of the criminal justice system and its failure to punish convicted criminals properly. Mercy. Well, now, let me see, what kind of mercy can I offer to someone who is about to be hit by a vehicle careering at them at sixty miles an hour in just over - *[JOHN looks at his watch.]-* four minutes and twenty seconds?

WAYNE: If you leave me here to die, it's murder. You're just a fucking murdering bastard!

JOHN: 'Murdering bastard?' Me!

WAYNE: You're worst then me. You're worst then me! At least mine was an accident and I'm sorry, all right? I'm sorry about your kid, both kids. I'm fucking sorry!

JOHN: Me, a 'murdering bastard'?

WAYNE *[WAYNE is crying.]*: Please, mister, please, I'm sorry, all right? I'm sorry.

JOHN: 'Murdering bastard'? You – you see me as a 'murdering bastard'? Me! Me, an avenging angel, a Eumenides, a fury, an Ancient Greek avenger swooping down like a divine wind to right a moral wrong. And you of all people regard me as a 'murdering bastard'!

WAYNE: Everybody will, you stupid cunt!

Blood, Passion & Self-Sacrifice

JOHN: Why, that would make me worse than you. How quickly the veneer of civilisation falls away degenerating us back to savages once we lose the rule of law and justice is no longer fairly given.

WAYNE: What?

JOHN: I'm here for justice! Here to right a wrong. Here to meet out punishment. Here to... Here to ... I'm not a murderer! I'm not a savage! You! You're - you're the criminal. You're the one who did wrong. You're a ... You're a... You are just an obnoxious little scumbag, aren't you; yes, you're certainly that. A boy racer; yes, you're that also. A little gobshite; yes, you're certainly that! But, not a murderer. I'm here to... I'm here...

[Enter AMY running to JOHN. We hear WAYNE saying 'Sorry' and pleading for his life in the background.]

AMY: Dad! Dad!

JOHN: Amy? Amy, my little darling, what are you doing here and at this hour in the morning?

AMY: This is our favourite place, Dad. You know that! We've always happy when we come here. This place is very special to us.

JOHN: Yes. Yes, we are always happy when we come here, my darling. You're right, yes, we are. This place is special to us. Lots of happy memories. Our private, special place.

[There is a pause. WAYNE continues to plead. JOHN gently touches AMY on the head.]

AMY: Don't spoil our special place, Dad. Don't sully it with bad memories.

JOHN: No, my darling, no, I promise that I won't. You must go home now, my darling. And, thank you. Don't worry about me, I'll come and join you soon; I won't leave you waiting long.

AMY: Bye, Dad, bye, see you later.

JOHN: Goodbye, my darling. I will see you later.

[AMY exits.]

WAYNE: Mister, please, it was an accident, I made a mistake, I admit it, please! Please, I'm sorry!

JOHN: To sully this sacred place by degenerating myself to something lower than that I despise. It was an accident. You're not a murderer; it was an accident. If you had stopped and tried to help, if you had stopped and tried to help then I could have forgiven you, but, no, you're just a little boy who could not face up to his moral responsibilities; you're definitely that, but nothing else. Nothing else. Just a pathetic little boy who hasn't finished growing up. *[Pause.]* To sully this special place, this private place for Amy and me. Amy deserves better than that. It makes me even worse than you. Amy deserves better.

WAYNE: Mister, please, I made a mistake!

JOHN: I accept your mitigation plea and I will show you mercy. After all, 'the quality of mercy is not strained, it droppeth as the gentle rain from heaven upon the place beneath'.

Blood, Passion & Self-Sacrifice

WAYNE: Will you cut this fucking shit and let me go!

JOHN: I shall be merciful. *[JOHN produces a knife.]* Yoroi-dōshi, an armour-piercing sword. It will not cut through the metal handcuffs and I don't have the key.

WAYNE: What!!

JOHN: But this knife will cut through flesh, soft tissue and, I think, through bone quickly.

[JOHN moves in one action between WAYNE'S torso and his handcuffed wrist trapping the handcuffed arm in an arm-lock. The sound of the train increases.]

WAYNE: What! Please! No! No! No! No! No!

[JOHN begins to sever WAYNE'S wrist. The sound of the train grows very loud. Blackout.

Lights up. GEORGINA is on stage.]

GEORGINA: We never quite move on, ever. The past exists in memories. They control and govern everything we do. In that sense, there is no past and there is no future; but there is memory. Fortunately, we have choices, and there is always hope.

[Cross fade to THE NARRATOR'S flat. Enter JOHN and THE NARRATOR.]

NARRATOR: I'm glad you didn't kill him.

JOHN: I dropped him off at the hospital and I went home.

NARRATOR: At least you did not descend into the moral cesspit that he wallows in.

JOHN: I wanted to rid society of a chill killer; I wanted to avenge Amy's death, yet when I had him all I could see was a pathetic, foolish and sad excuse for a human being. A foolish little boy who was allowed to drive a killing machine called a car. To execute him would make me worse than him and sully the memory of Amy. So, I dropped off my child's killer at the hospital, minus his hand, and then I went home and I showered and I shaved.

NARRATOR: John, do you want me to go to the police with you?

JOHN: And subject myself to state justice? If a law court valued the life of a sixteen-year-old girl at fourteen weeks then what value would it place on the abortive murder of her killer? No, I have had my belly full of state justice.

NARRATOR: Do you want me to help you to flee the country?

JOHN: And become a fugitive for the rest of my life? No, that is not the path that I have chosen.

Narrative: Then, what do you want to do, John?

JOHN: It is odd how once one has decided on a course of action how calmness descends on one. A Samurai always treats today as though it is the last day of his life.

NARRATOR: John, where is this leading?

JOHN: You once told me that there are many forms of Seppuku.

Blood, Passion & Self-Sacrifice

NARRATOR: Yes, yes there are, but what of it?

JOHN: Junshi – the suicide of the faithful servants joining their Lord in death.

NARRATOR: Yes, many cultures, the Pharaohs of Ancient Egypt as well as the ancient Japanese had the tradition that when a great Lord died then his household and his retinue were expected to die with him.

JOHN: Kanshi – to show the strength of one's disapproval with a great Lord's actions.

NARRATOR: Again, an out-dated, old-world idea, but it was meant to embarrass or shock the Lord into repentance and a change of mind.

JOHN: Inseki-jisatsu – a way a showing that one has taken full responsibility for an error that has resulted in a totally unsatisfactory conclusion. Perhaps I should suggest that course of action to the law court who decided Amy's life was worth only fourteen weeks.

NARRATOR: We would all say 'Amen' to that.

JOHN: And, finally Funshi – suicide as a protest to display anger and disgust at an injustice. The strongest way to show one's protest at injustice is to support one's words by the ritual taking of one's own life.

NARRATOR: John, you are talking of the actions of men who existed in cultures hundreds of years ago. We are not in a Japanese Noh play or an ancient Greek tragedy. This is the real world; times have changed.

JOHN: Not as much as you think. Honour, a sense of justice, fair play, no matter what age one lives in, no matter how far back into human existence one probes, one finds that human beings have always craved these concepts. When Amy died, I died with her. I am a walking corpse. I ask that you show me compassion and that you let me end my life with honour.

NARRATOR: John, no!

JOHN: A man of true sincerity will be an example to the world, even after death. There is one thing about honour; it survives you when you die. I ask you out of friendship to grant me this one act of compassion. I want to commit Seppuku as an act of protest at the injustice of the light sentence given to Amy's killer.

NARRATOR: John, this is madness.

JOHN: Then, I am mad, mad with anger, mad with moral outrage, mad with my impotence to right a wrong. But my death this way shall have more significance than a sad existence.

NARRATOR: John, you are wrong. This is wrong!

JOHN: I will not allow Amy's death to be considered insignificant. Seppuku as an act of protest at injustice. It will make the front pages of all the newspapers and the top story on all the news programmes.

NARRATOR: It will certainly be news worthy.

JOHN: The ancients knew what they were doing. It is all that I have left to give to Amy, please don't deny me this.

Blood, Passion & Self-Sacrifice

NARRATOR: Death is not part of life; it is the end, merely the end.

JOHN: For the Samurai death hovers every day in the mind. It is important to die strong. It is important to die beautiful.

NARRATOR: John, this is the reasoning of a military class that lived centuries ago. The Samurai evolved a means of proving their manhood, their military prowess, by inventing a ritualised way of self-destruction justified by the socially defined protocols and the etiquette of their era. It is an age gone by. It is no longer the way. Even in Japan it is no longer the way. John, please, stop.

JOHN: I die for Amy, nothing more. I intend to commit Seppuku whether you act as my assistant, my Kaishakunin, or not.

NARRATOR: You will commit Seppuku without a Kaishakunin to assist?

JOHN: If necessary.

NARRATOR: Disembowelment is a slow, painful and horrible way to die.

JOHN: I know. I have read the descriptions of ritual disembowelment without the luxury of a Kaishakunin. One begins by winding a white bandage around the blade of a short sword, leaving two inches of naked steel showing at the point. Massage the abdomen muscles to relax them. Then rise slightly onto the hips and lean over the sword point. Muster strength by breathing in three times in quick succession then exhaling fully. Pull the sword back. Aim to strike into the left side of the stomach. Stab fast and sure.

M C Sanders

The blade pierces the stomach wall. The naked point vanishes into the bare flesh and the white bandage presses against the stomach. A cry of pain cannot be avoided. Breathing becomes difficult. The chest thumps violently. Both the hand and the bandage around the blade are dyed deep red with blood. With fists clenched about the sword pull the blade from left to right through the stomach. The blade gets snarled up in muscle, stomach parts, blood and grease. Both hands are needed to keep the blade pushed deep into your body as it cuts through your stomach. When the blade cuts through the navel the pain makes the stomach shudder. A volcano of blood and entrails spurt from the wound. Blood pours out by the pint. The blade is coated in blood and grease. It is difficult to handle. The body pushes the blade out of the wound along with your blood and guts. Keep pushing the blade into the stomach with both hands; keep propelling it to the right. Then, the vomiting starts. The retching allows your stomach to open wide and spew out its innards into your crotch. The pain is fierce. A smell of entrails and blood fills the room. Between the retching, you watch your own blood pouring out of the gash in your stomach. If a merciful blackout into painless unconsciousness has not claimed you, then thrust the blade back into the stomach, turn the blade to face upwards and cut up the torso to complete the 'L' shape flap. You lie amidst your blood and organs flowing out around you as you wait for the release of pain-free death. All this I know, but I still intend to do it. Will you help me?

NARRATOR: To watch you die horribly? I cannot do that, but, then, to deny you your death by protest. I cannot do that either.

JOHN: I ask for a decision.

Blood, Passion & Self-Sacrifice

NARRATOR: Out of friendship and compassion, I shall act as your Kaishakunin. I shall not watch you suffer. You shall have your ritual death as protest against the injustice shown to Amy. I shall not deny you your wish. Out of friendship and compassion I shall assist you.

[They bow formally out of friendship and respect for each other.]

JOHN: If you assist me then the police will arrest you for murder.

NARRATOR: If the law courts valued Amy's life at only fourteen weeks, then how much value will they place on the life of a suicide? I will take my chances. I make my choice knowingly.

JOHN: Then, it is time to begin. You will be performing an act of compassion.

NARRATOR: I act out of compassion for you.

[THE NARRATOR takes the sword, Seki no Magoroku and sheaths it.]

JOHN: Seki no Magoroku. A great sword used only for persons of the highest nobility. I am honoured.

NARRATOR: No. It is totally right and it is I who feels honoured.

[They bow to each other. THE NARRATOR sits at right angles to JOHN in the seiza posture. JOHN produces the short sword, Yoroi-dōshi. He wraps a white cloth around the blade to give him a better grip.]

NARRATOR: Remember, cut no deeper than two inches.

JOHN: No deeper than two inches.

[Enter AMY and GEORGINA. GEORGINA holds Amy's teddy.]

GEORGINA:
       'With a knife,
       with a tiny knife,
       that barely fits the hand,
       but that slides in clean
       through the astonished flesh
       and stops at the place
       where trembles, enmeshed,
       the dark root of the scream.'

[JOHN braces himself with the short sword held to the left side of his stomach.]

JOHN: Clarity of thought and directness of action, this is the promised retribution of the Gods. Amy, all I asked for was justice.

[JOHN raises slightly on his hips. He breathes sharply three times in quick succession, then he exhales fully before pulling the blade into his stomach. There is obvious pain. He gives a sharp cry. He stretches, straining his neck as far forward as he can. THE NARRATOR stands drawing the sword. THE NARRATOR pauses with the sword held high and then swipes downward. We hear THE NARRATOR shout a "ki-ai" as the stage goes to a Blackout.]

You're Mine Forevermore

A tragedy.

M C Sanders

List of Characters:

John Cavendish - a forty-something who enjoys walking holidays in the mountains

Alison Cavendish - his wife

Sharon Cavendish - their 13 years old daughter

Caius Marcius Brutus - a Roman land owner

Priestess - a mystic

Dr Jocasta Sterling - an academic

[All other minor parts can be played by members of the cast.]

{The invisible Goddess – I leave open to directorial interpretation whether or not to have an actress portraying this rôle.}

Blood, Passion & Self-Sacrifice

Act I

[There is a long haunting howl off stage.]

OFF STAGE VOICE: There be spirits that are created for vengeance, which in their fury lay on sore strokes; in the time of destruction, they pour out their force and appease the wrath of him that made them.

[Enter Dr JOCASTA STERLING. She carries a scroll. She is dialling on her mobile phone.]

Dr STERLING: Hello, Mr Cavendish, this is Dr Jocasta Sterling speaking. When you pick up this message, please, please, return the call immediately on autodial. It is imperative I talk to you urgently.

[Dr STERLING finishes the phone call and she retires to the side of the stage reading the scroll. Enter CAIUS MARCIUS BRUTUS and the PRIESTESS; her hands and arms are covered in blood.]

CAIUS: Priestess, learned in the mysteries -

PRIESTESS: The Gods cursed me with the gift of prophecy long, long ago. My fate is to see the future for people who then try to change it.

CAIUS: - tell me what you see. Tell me who is this Goddess whom only I can see and hear?

PRIESTESS: You hear voices too?

CAIUS: I have heard the voices of the dead since I was young, but I have never heard a voice like this one. For this is a Goddess who appears only to me and only I hear her seductive entreaties.

PRIESTESS: You too are cursed by the Gods. I also hear the voices of the Gods and the dead. Always talking, never, never ending. Voices! Constantly talking at me without end, always in my head, but when I say your name, when I speak the name, Caius Marcius Brutus, they scream. They scream terror. They scream blood. They scream images that haunt my dreams.

CAIUS: Priestess, tell me what your voices say about me.

PRIESTESS: It was a bull, a black bull, and the best of your herd that was sacrificed?

CAIUS: The beast's blood covers your hands.

PRIESTESS: My fingers tremble from its cold, fresh blood. Cold, fresh blood is unnatural.

CAIUS: It is unnatural, but what does it signify?

PRIESTESS: Remember Caius Marcius Brutus, man is not destined to know his fate. Do not make me foretell.

CAIUS: I am paying you to foretell. I command you to tell me!

PRIESTESS: Voices screaming in my head! My mind aches from the boom of their cries. This is not good. The Gods give life and death to all. They measure existence in centuries. We are ephemeral to them. Unnatural, cold, fresh blood covers my fingers. My voices are screaming at me, a tsunami of sound sweeping through my skull. The Gods will not be silent. This is bad. This is very bad! The Gods do not speak calmly but shout their warnings for you, Caius Marcius Brutus. They howl for you to beware.

Blood, Passion & Self-Sacrifice

CAIUS: Beware?

PRIESTESS: The worst is yet to come. The future springs out of the past through the present and forward and onward. What has happened here? Tell me, you who commune with the Gods and the dead, tell me the past events that chill the sour air we breathe.

CAIUS: If it will help, Priestess, then I shall tell you my story and you will see why I need your help. It started less than one year ago. It was then this Goddess made herself known to me. Before then she did not visit me. I did not hear her sweet, seductive voice demanding all my attention. It began when I stumbled upon the skeleton of a man who had hidden in a pit.

PRIESTESS: In a pit? In a deep, dark pit?

CAIUS: In a pit hewed out by miners before time began high up in the mountains above my estate. The man had stolen away from his known world to secret himself out of sight of his fellow human beings for all eternity.

PRIESTESS: For all eternity.

CAIUS: I fell into the pit and this Goddess embraced me. On that fresh, spring morning, I led a hunting party high into the mountains. The wild boars that roam the region are a good source of meat. Chasing one wild boar through thick undergrowth I trod on a mesh of roots and grass concealing a hole in the ground. I fell through the tangled covering and I tumbled down into the pit.

PRIESTESS: Down, down through the earth. Down into the underworld.

CAIUS: Down I rolled into the darkness until I crashed passed some stones.

PRIESTESS: Through a circle of stones?

CAIUS: Possibly, it was dark, I do not know. I collided with a halt by, well – I knew not what in the darkness.

PRIESTESS: Something hiding in the darkness. Something deep, down in the pit. It felt cold?

CAIUS: Yes, it felt cold, oh, so, cold, a deep penetrating cold, chilling the bones beneath my skin.

PRIESTESS: A dark coldness burrowing deep beneath the skin. As unnatural as cold, fresh blood.

CAIUS: I shuddered either from fear, or from fright, or from the cold, or from I know not what but, as I shuddered, I heard a distinct voice, old, very old, and faint.

PRIESTESS: Beware! Beware!

CAIUS: It spoke an ancient tongue I did not understand; then, there was silence.

PRIESTESS: A cold and silent sepulchre.

CAIUS: I could not stop shuddering. Then, the concerned shouts of my kinsmen from above greeted my ears. I returned their anxious calls assuring them that I was all right. A lighted torch fell by my side, thrown down to me by my kinsmen. I grabbed it and as I turned, I saw in the flicking light of the flame a skeleton.

Blood, Passion & Self-Sacrifice

PRIESTESS: A man like you.

CAIUS: I screamed in fright and scrambled away from the wretched soul. A remnant of humanity long ago reduced by the centuries to just bones and rags.

PRIESTESS: He was a man like you.

CAIUS: I stared into the dark sockets of his skull.

PRIESTESS: Beware! Beware!

CAIUS: More shouting from above. A rope appeared in the light of the flame. I grabbed it, wrapped it around my arm and screamed for them to pull me up. The rope grew taught, the strain on my arm was immense but up I rose out of the pit, out of the darkness, out of the cold and to safety.

PRIESTESS: Safety? No, you are not safe.

CAIUS: My anxious kinsmen ensured I was not injured. Then, my young son asked -

PRIESTESS: Father, what is that in your hand?

CAIUS [He produces a small skull.]: I held a skull. I did not realise until that moment that I held it.

PRIESTESS: Is it human? Or is it inhuman?

CAIUS: It was not part of the skeleton down in the pit.

PRIESTESS: In the pit. Something human and inhuman.

CAIUS: This skull is different from anything I have ever seen. It is strange and I feel it is very old. A trophy, something to be treasured from the day's hunt or so I thought at the time. It would have been better for all, if my kinsmen had left me in the pit to rot.

PRIESTESS: The skull, the skull is inhuman.

CAIUS: That is my belief. I thought, at the time, I thought that it was quite harmless. After all, before finding the skull, the Gods had smiled upon me. My estate prospered and my family enjoyed good health. Then, the Goddess started to visit me and that summer the mood in my villa turned to one of tension and strife. I became so fascinated with her I started to neglect the estate. For the first time in living memory our crops failed and in order to pay our way I was forced to sell my better slaves, those who were well trained and industrious. Nevertheless, I cared little for fiscal matters, for my fascination with my new friend was so intense. She dwells within the skull and she is a beautiful Goddess who makes herself known only to me.

PRIESTESS: A beautiful Goddess?

CAIUS: Yes, and she speaks to me; only I can hear her voice. It is a seductive, beautiful voice whispering soft, sweet words, wooing me, guiding me, telling me what to do and what to think. She is always in my thoughts, always in my mind, absorbing all my interest.

PRIESTESS: A jealous lover.

CAIUS: That may well be so, for my wife begged me to throw the skull away, but I ignored her entreaties. Then, one day my wife, a rival for my affections with the Goddess, my wife stood directing the servants in the preparation of a meal to celebrate our twentieth year of betrothal. It was to be a day of great joy for my family, when a cooking pot slipped from the fire pouring scolding hot fat over my wife's face and arms. She survived the incident but with gross disfigurement.

PRIESTESS: The Goddess of the skull is a possessive lover; she will brook no rivals.

CAIUS: I adored my daughter, fifteen years old and so fair and charming. She enjoyed playing the Cithara, from whose strings she could pluck mellifluous tunes so pleasing on the ear. One day, she sat in one of my carts. We were going to the games at Lyons. It was a great celebration to commemorate the living god, our Emperor Claudius. The cart stood loaded and ready to begin our journey. It was to be a great holiday; all was smiles and laughter, a day full of happiness and excitement.

PRIESTESS: Beware, for the Goddess of the skull will not have a rival.

CAIUS: My lovely daughter sat in the cart laughing and giggling. Then, one of the cartwheels collapsed. The cart toppled over trapping my girl's hands under it. Her beautiful delicate fingers crushed to lumps of bone, blood and flesh. How could the Gods be so cruel? Yet, even then, I did not learn the lesson and so further horror followed.

PRIESTESS: It is a jealous lover whom embraces you.

CAIUS: I could not help myself. Like a drug-possessed glutton, I graved the Goddess more than anything else, more than life. My eighteen-year-old boy and I both loved hunting with the dogs. It was a sport that bonded us as father and son. He loved the hounds I kept at the villa. He mastered them better than I. Strange, but once I brought the skull home, the dogs would never settle when I approached them.

They tensed, rose up on their front legs, growled and barked with their hair standing up in fear. But my son, oh, my son ruled those dogs. He loved them and they loved him. After a hunt, he would bate his favourite hound with a leg of wild boar. The boy often played this game. Yet, after one hunt when I had been especially proud of a kill my son had made, the hound, instead of grabbing at the leg of meat as the lad bated the beast, it jumped at my boy instead. The beast savaged his hand, ripped at his face and tore at his neck before my servants subdued and killed it. My boy, my brave, brave boy, screamed in agony from his wounds for three whole days before the mighty Emperor of the Gods, Jupiter, was merciful and granted him peaceful death.

PRIESTESS: The blessing of silence and peace.

CAIUS: As I stared into the flames of his funeral pyre, I heard his voice asking -

PRIESTESS: Father, what is that in your hand?

CAIUS: I held the skull! Without realising, I had brought the skull to my son's funeral! As on the accursed day of the hunt in the mountains when I had discovered it, I did not realise until that moment I held it. Suddenly, thanks to my son's love, in that momentary release from the magic spell of the Goddess, I understood all the misfortune had started since I had found the skull. At last, despite the voice of the Goddess raging at me, I came to my senses. I sought out a Priestess learned in the Mysteries. I sought out you!

PRIESTESS: Jupiter, Emperor of the Gods, send me one spark of fire from one of your mighty thunderbolts to grant me the light of perception!

CAIUS: I sought out you to help me, Priestess.

PRIESTESS: Voices! The voices in my head speak of a dreadful shade, a shadow moving in the darkness. We cannot change fate but we can prepare ourselves for it. A shadow? No, a jealous, gluttonous Goddess covets your soul. All whom you love are in great danger. My voices help us! I beg you to help us! Tell me what must be done! Caius Marcius Brutus your loved ones are not free from further harm. Answer me - What is love?

CAIUS: I do not understand you, Priestess. However, I understand when one knows one's fate that the mind becomes calm. Tell me what to do.

PRIESTESS: What is love?

CAIUS: I do not understand what you mean. Priestess you must help me to see what is happening to me.

PRIESTESS: You wish to protect your loved ones?

CAIUS: By all the Gods I do.

PRIESTESS: It is by all the Gods that I direct you, for it is they who decide the road on which we tread, but I warn you that you may think it was better you had never been born!

[Exit CAIUS and the PRIESTESS. Dr STERLING stops reading the scroll. She makes a call on her mobile phone. A mobile phone rings off stage.]

Dr STERLING: Mr Cavendish, my name is Dr Jocasta Sterling. I work for the Antiquarian Society to whom you very kindly presented the scroll you found. I really could do with talking to you about it quite urgently. The scroll is original. The ink and parchment are typical of their kind. It actually dates from the first century AD. I'm afraid it is not really worth much, except as an historical curio.

[*Enter JOHN CAVENDISH, his wife, ALISON CAVENDISH, and their daughter, SHARON CAVENDISH. JOHN is talking into his mobile phone to Dr STERLING.*]

JOHN: I am not interested in the money, doctor. Your society may keep the scroll.

Dr STERLING: I say that's very descent of you, old chap. I know our branch of the Antiquarian Society in Aberdeenshire, where you found the scroll, will be very appreciative of your kind gesture. Perhaps I could repay you by telling you something about the person who wrote the scroll. It is written in Latin by a Roman. The text is unusual for its time. It is in the form of a final statement. Indeed, it is intended to serve as a warning to others.

JOHN: A warning?

Dr STERLING: Yes. Did you find anything else in the cave next to the skeleton?

JOHN: Such as?

Dr STERLING: Such as an unusually shaped skull that was not part of the human remains.

JOHN [*Producing the skull*]: No.

Dr STERLING: Definitely not.

JOHN: Doctor, I told you, no. Look, doctor, this isn't a good time to speak. I have just returned from burying my son, Peter. We held his funeral earlier today.

Blood, Passion & Self-Sacrifice

Dr STERLING: I'm sorry to hear of your loss. However, hearing of your bereavement I now consider it vital I talk to you urgently.

JOHN: Not at the moment, thank you, doctor.

Dr STERLING: Then, I shall send you a copy of the scroll in English for your perusal. Please promise to read it immediately and ring me to discuss it.

JOHN: Very well, thank you, doctor.

Dr STERLING: Mr Cavendish, you promise.

JOHN: Doctor, I'll read it and I shall call you if I need you. Now, goodbye.

[They end the phone call. JOHN places the skull back in his pocket. Exit Dr STERLING.]

ALISON: Who was that?

JOHN: Dr Jocasta Sterling.

ALISON: Who?

JOHN: She's some old fossil from the British Museum calling me about the scroll I found by the skeleton up in the Cairngorm Mountains.

ALISON: 'Jocasta', what an odd name to call your child. The poor girl must have been taunted terribly at school. What did she want with you?

JOHN: She's going to send me a copy of the scroll in English for my "perusal".

ALISON: What's so funny? John you're always so dismissive of anything you personally do not find interesting. It might be a fascinating piece of Scotland's history.

JOHN: She said it was Roman.

ALISON: Roman? In the Highlands of Scotland? What would a Roman be doing high up in the Cairngorm Mountains?

JOHN: I don't know, he probably got lost whilst building Hadrian's Wall or something. It sounds as interesting as watching paint dry.

ALISON: With you, other than football and women is there anything that sounds more interesting than watching paint dry?

JOHN: Alison, please, let's not start this backbiting, not today. Not today of all days.

ALISON: I'm merely saying that as you found the scroll then why aren't you interested in what it says?

SHARON: Skeletons and old scrolls, it all sounds spooky.

ALISON: Ghosts and ghouls, there are no such things.

SHARON: If you say so, mum.

ALISON: I do say so, young lady.

Blood, Passion & Self-Sacrifice

SHARON: Mum at the funeral Wendy asked me if I wanted to stay over at her house tonight. Can I?

ALISON: As long as her parents don't mind, I think it's an excellent idea.

SHARON: They were with us when she asked. Can I, mum?

ALISON: Yes, Sharon, my darling, I think it's a great idea.

SHARON: Thanks mum.

[ALISON *kisses* SHARON *gently on the forehead.*]

JOHN: Here, the pair of you get a pizza or something.

[JOHN *gives* SHARON *some money.*]

SHARON: Thanks dad! You're the best.

[JOHN *and* SHARON do a high five. *Exit* SHARON.]

ALISON: It will take her mind off Peter's death. She's gone subdued and quiet since his death. They were very close. Always together... John, have you taken your medication today?

JOHN: I'll take now, ok? Please, let's not start on that again.

ALISON: Let's not start on what? Being sensible. Thank God one of us is. All you seem to do these days is to argue with me. Life must go on. Remember, we still have Sharon to think about. We have to be strong for her sake. Now that Peter's gone nothing is more important than her, nothing.

JOHN: You think I don't know that?

ALISON: John, please, I - I know you love Sharon. We're all a little on edge. I'll go and sort out your medication for you.

[ALISON exits.]

JOHN *[Talking to the invisible being.]*: How can she say that to me about Sharon? How can she say that? You heard what she said? You were listening, right? Of course, Sharon's important to me. You know she is, don't you? Yes, we have had this conversation before and how many times have I said to you, I would give my life for my kids. Yes, yes, I know, I know, I'm sorry; I know you understand the way I feel. Thank God, somebody does. Thank God I have somebody who is on my side, who will listen to me, who understands me.

[Enter ALISON. She holds a glass of water, some pills and a letter.]

ALISON: John, you were talking to yourself again.

JOHN: I wasn't.

ALISON: You were. You've got Sharon frightened. I had to tell her that dad is just upset because of Peter's death. Here, take these.

[She gives him the medication and water. He takes it whilst she reads the letter.]

JOHN: What's that?

ALISON: It's a letter from the solicitor. It says that the lorry driver admits that he wasn't paying full attention to the motorway traffic because he was using his mobile phone at the time. *[She becomes weepy.]*

JOHN: Let me see. Let me see. *[He takes the letter off her and he reads it quickly.]* But we know all this... that he did not brake in time... he drove the lorry into Peter's car which was stationary in the motorway traffic jam...squashing Peter's car into the stationary lorry in front...we know all this. We know all this.

ALISON: At least it avoids a messy trial if the lorry driver is admitting guilt. It's spared us that.

JOHN: It won't bring Peter back. It was my fault. I suggested to Peter that he take the car. He was going to get the train, but I suggested to him he took the car. I don't know why I suggested it; it just came into my head. *[He looks sharply round at the invisible being.]*

ALISON *[who has not noticed John's reaction.]*: It was not a bad suggestion. Peter loved it. Going down by car instead of getting the train to see the university he would study at after leaving college. He loved the idea. It seemed to him very sophisticated, grown up; at eighteen he was quite the young man. *[She is about to cry again but she stops herself.]* You forgot to turn the dishwasher on again yesterday when it was full. How many times have I got to tell you to turn it on once it is full or it will start to smell from the dirty dishes?

JOHN: Sorry, I'll try to remember next time.

ALISON: Every time you forget and every time you say you will try to remember next time.

JOHN: It's just that it was four o'clock and well...

ALISON: Your mother died at four o'clock, your father was in ward 4 when he died and the car accident happened at four o'clock in the afternoon. I know, darling, I know. I'll go and help Sharon pack an over-night bag. Going to Wendy's will give her a break from all this.

[Exit ALISON.]

JOHN *[Talking to the invisible being.]*: Tell me and answer me truthfully, did you put that suggestion into my head to let Peter use the car? Well, did you? OK, ok, if you say that you did not then I accept that. I believe you; I know that you're on my side. I know that you are my friend, yes, my best friend, my only friend and my confident. If I didn't have you to talk to, to discuss things with, I don't know what I would have done, probably gone mad ages ago. I had to know if you were involved in the suggestion about the car. I have to be clear in my mind about that. Sorry. It's just, well, my children – I - I have done my best for both my children. I always have. I suggested that Peter go in the car rather than take the train. I suggested it. It was my fault, all my fault. If there is some power punishing me for doing something wrong, then what was my crime and why was Peter punished as well, he was an innocent? It was my suggestion that he used the car, not his. I am to blame, not him. You do your best to rare your kids properly, to look after them, to prepare them for life, to give them a good start, to give them a good future, to give them a future. Peter was only eighteen. Nothing really, is it? Just eighteen. He was a good driver; he passed his driving test at the first attempt, inexperienced, after all, he was only eighteen, but good. I suggested that he take the car; it is my fault that he is dead. I am to blame and if I am being punished for doing something wrong, then why also punish an innocent like Peter? Why? My children are my life. I gave up everything for them: my career, I could have focused more on work than on them, my happiness, I stayed in the marriage despite the arguments with Alison, I gave up my life for them. To outlive your children; it is a fate that is dread by most parents. What? Yes, yes, you're right, I have to move on now and think of the future. I shall think of Sharon. I thank you for all your sensible advice and kind words. I don't know what I'd have done without you to talk to, to console me. However, even you must admit that surely something is wrong when the young die before the old.

[Enter SHARON.]

SHARON *[She is talking into a mobile phone.]*: Hi, Wendy, it's Sharon. Look, I'll bring over my iPod. It's got some great songs on it. We can share my headphones by having an earpiece each. Will your mum let us order a pizza? She will! Great! My dad's paying. He's given me the money. I'll see you at seven. My mum's going to drop me off with my overnight bag. Bye. See you later, bye.

[SHARON runs to JOHN.]

SHARON *[kisses him on the cheek]*: Bye, dad, see you later.

JOHN: Bye, dear. Oh, Sharon, make sure you wear a warm pullover, it's cold out.

SHARON: Dad, I'm not a child anymore; I'm thirteen. I will, dad, OK?

JOHN: I love you, Sharon.

SHARON: I love you too, dad.

[They do a high five. JOHN and SHARON exit. Enter Dr STERLING. She is talking on her mobile phone.]

Dr STERLING: Mr Cavendish, this is Dr Sterling calling you again. I have rung you every day now for the past week to see if you have read the transcript of the scroll that I sent to you over seven days ago. I assure you I am only going to this trouble because I regard it as absolutely vital that we talk in order to protect your family from harm. When you pick up this message, please, please return the call; I beg you.

[Exit Dr STERLING. Enter ALISON talking into her mobile phone.]

ALISON: Marion? It's Alison. Sorry for not getting in touch with you sooner but I've been busy what with the funeral and all. I just wanted to thank you for letting Sharon stay over with your Wendy the other night. It was a great help. Sharon was full of it when she returned. The stay has really lifted her spirits. Being with Wendy is helping her to get through all this. Thank you. That's right, when they were young Sharon and Peter were inseparable. That is kind of you; she would love to stay again. You must let Wendy stay over at our house some time. Me? Well, you know, I'm all right. I have to be. Someone has to keep the family together. You saw John the other day? If he passed you without saying, 'Hello' it is because he is too preoccupied with his own thoughts to notice anybody else. Don't worry he wouldn't have meant to insult you. Indeed, he would be upset if he thought that he had insulted you. It's just that he seems to live in a world of his own these days; his own private dream world. In an odd sort of way, I quite envy him. You know he's on medication? Well, with Peter's death I'm trying to get him to go to his doctor for a stronger dose but he won't do it. Anyway, if you're going to the Health Club this Friday we must get together afterwards and have a drink and a good chinwag. Let's see if we can get some of the other girls to join us. Great talking to you. Bye for now, luv, bye.

Blood, Passion & Self-Sacrifice

[Exit ALISON. Enter JOHN. He is laughing as with a lover.]

JOHN *[Talking to the invisible being.]*: What? No, no, you're wrong, there's nothing wrong with Sharon; she's fine. She's just a lovely, intelligent, young girl. Look, you know I like you very much but I'm a married man with a young daughter. Yes, it's true I don't get on well with Alison. In fact, I don't get on with her at all. Nowadays, she seems to relate to me through nothing more than argument. She always seems to be against me, everything I do and everything I say is wrong. Look, you're a lovely, lovely lady and I'm very flatted you find me attractive, but my family comes first. Yes, even Alison, the old witch, warts and all. Please, just think about it. What would happen if my wife found out or my daughter saw us together? Sure, it would be the end of my marriage, but, more important, it would wreak our friendship also. Why? Because of us, my daughter's faith in me would be destroyed forever. It would sour our friendship. Things could never be the same between you and I again. It would be the end of our relationship. Now you don't want that, do you? Exactly. Exactly. You know I don't want to lose you, so we have to be discreet. *[His mobile phone rings.]* Hello.

[Enter Dr STERLING talking into her mobile phone.]

Dr STERLING: Mr Cavendish, it's Dr Sterling. Thank God I've managed to get hold of you at last. Have you read the translated copy of the scroll I sent to you yet?

JOHN: I've read part of it. A story about a Roman who found an old skull.

Dr STERLING: It is not a story. It's a chronicle of past events.

JOHN: Whatever.

Dr STERLING: Did you find anything else in that cave with the scroll and the skeleton?

JOHN: Dr Sterling, we have already had this conversation.

Dr STERLING: The author of the scroll was the man whose body you discovered in the cave.

JOHN: The Roman?

Dr STERLING: Yes, the Roman. He scribed the scroll as a warning, as a warning for you.

JOHN: A thousand years ago! Oh, really, doctor.

Dr STERLING: I know, it sounds strange.

JOHN: Dr Sterling, I appreciate you mean well, but –

Dr STERLING: Mr Cavendish, I am very concerned for you and your family.

JOHN: I thank you for your concern, but I don't think an old story about ghosts written a thousand years ago has anything to teach me.

Dr STERLING: I beg to differ.

JOHN: Frankly, doctor, I think in a thousand years we have progressed somewhat, don't you?

Dr STERLING: Mr Cavendish, I assure you, you are quite incorrect on that point. Evolution does not mean improvement of the species. As we move from one generation to another, we do not find better philosophers or artists, and it is the philosophers and artists of our species who encompass the higher aspirations of us all. Therefore, if our artists and philosophers do not improve through time there is no meaningful evolutionary progression. One cannot say the philosophers of today are better than Plato or Confucius, or the artists of today are superior to Shakespeare or Leonardo De Vinci. Humankind, like any other species, survives by adapting; but it is the superior lout who survives, not the higher specimens of humanity. The humankind whom we aspire to emulate and admire, the philosopher and the artist, merely emerge unpredictably and arbitrarily from time to time regardless of culture, race, colour, sex, creed or country. They are scattered and accidental existences spread out over time. Nobody can foretell when or where these superior specimens of our species will be born or who they will be. Also, the superior specimens of humankind do not pass on their DNA pool of genius to their progeny. The genius dies with the individual and leaves us to wait for the next superior individual to emerge in another culture in another part of the world in another time. It is not proven that nature improves a species through generations, civilisations rise and fall, skills are learnt and lost as the needs of each civilisation dictate, and who is to say one particular civilisation is superior to another? There is no evolutionary arc of improvement stretching from the cave man to the present day. The wisdom and artistic genius the ancients strived to achieve is still the same wisdom and artistic genius we strive for today. It is highly improbable humankind today is more intelligent and perceptive than Socrates or Herodotus, or, indeed, any of our ancestors. So, if there has been no improvement in the species in the generations spanning the last five thousand years then it is fallacious to believe improvement will occur in the future generations spanning the next five thousand years and beyond. The cultures of classical Greece, or of the Italian Renaissance or of ancient China are not inferior to our own. So, why should one assume our civilisation or future civilisations will be better? I shall merely assert: the goal of humanity lies not in its end but in its highest individuals.

JOHN: Finish?

Dr STERLING: Sorry, a bit of hobbyhorse of mine, got carried away, but I beg you, Mr Cavendish, please, take the scroll seriously, finish reading it and call me.

[They end the phone call. Exit Dr STERLING. JOHN'S mobile phone rings. Enter ALISON.]

ALISON *[talking to him on her phone]*: Whom have you been talking to? I've been trying to get you for ages.

JOHN: I've had that fossil from the British Museum pestering me again about the scroll.

ALISON: Never mind that now. It's Sharon. There's been a terrible accident. She's badly injured. I'm at the hospital now. Just come right away.

[They end the phone call. Exit ALISON.]

JOHN: Oh, no. Oh, no. Oh, please, God, no. Please, no, please. Anything but this. What crime have we committed to deserve this? Please, please, please, God, not Sharon, please God, no, please.

> Our Father, which art in heaven;
> Hallowed be Thy name,
> Thy kingdom come,
> Thy will be done,

In earth as it is in heaven.
Give us this day our daily bread;
And forgive us our trespasses,
As we forgive them that trespass against us;
And lead us not into temptation,
But deliver us from evil.
For Thine is the kingdom, the power, and the glory,
Forever and ever.
Amen.

Lord, I beg you if anything horrible has to happen, please, please, let it happen to me, not to Sharon. She's an innocent.

[Exit JOHN. Enter SHARON. She wears a veil.]

SHARON: I was walking home from school with Wendy my best friend. Wendy had just got a new mobile phone and we were listening to music on it. We saw three boys messing about in the street. We didn't take much notice of them at first. They were just larking around on the pavement further up the road. We had to pass them but we didn't think much about it. They were about the same age as Wendy and I. They were laughing and giggling as they taunted each other. The boys were playing with a canister; squirting it at each other. One of the boys had a box of matches. He struck a match and when the flame flared up, he sprayed the canister across the flame. A spray of gas projected out of the tiny nozzle of the canister and it ignited into a belching cloud of fire as it met the flame. The cloudburst of yellow burnt and disappeared in seconds. The boys laughed and jumped around with lots of nervous energy. The boy with the canister struck another match and sprayed the canister at his mates. The boys jumped back giggling as the flame flared into life when the spray spurted across the lighted match. They were laughing, larking around, and having fun. Wendy and I caught up to them as we walked along the pavement.

One of the boys shouted, "Do it to them! Do it to them!" His mate grabbed at Wendy and I. Wendy pulled free and ran but he caught me by my pullover and I couldn't get away. His friend with the canister ran up to me. He lit the match. I could smell the phosphorus stench as the flame burst into life. He brought the spray canister up to my face. I heard the hiss of the nozzle. I saw the jet of fine sticky liquid ejecting as a veil of mist in front of my face. I closed my eyes. I felt the cool, droplets clinging to my skin. The vile, sweet-smelling odour clung to my features. He placed the lighted match to the hissing canister as he sprayed the odious liquid. The liquid flared into a flame. It burnt. And it burnt. And it burnt. I could feel the heat. It burnt. I could smell the sweet scent on my skin. It burnt. I sensed my skin burning. The liquid on my skin was burning. My face was on fire. I screamed and I screamed and I screamed. The boys released my arms. I heard the boys running away beyond my screams. They ran away. I screamed in pain for help and they ran away! I felt my skin burning. I heard myself screaming. I heard Wendy crying and calling, "Sharon! Oh, God, Sharon!" I kept my eyes closed. I could feel the heat, nasty, horrible heat, and I felt the fire. I screamed. I could feel the skin on my face melting! I could feel my features distorting under the flames. I screamed. I could feel my features distorting. My hands held my face patting desperately to stop the hurt. I heard Wendy by me. She smothered my face with her hands to stop the flames, to stop the hurt, to stop the flames, to stop the hurt, to stop the damage to my face, to stop the distortion, to stop the hurt, to put out the flames, to make the hurt go away. Then, all was silent. I had collapsed. No more pain. The next thing I remember is gaining consciousness in hospital. [SHARON *lifts the veil to show the damage done to her face.*] There is no pain now; at least, not physical pain.

[*Blackout.*]

INTERVAL.

Act II

[Enter Dr STERLING reading the scroll.]

Dr STERLING *[Reading.]*:   'The primal motivation of a species is not survival but self-interest. Self-interest is a desire that suffuses all of humankind's actions from the greedy speculator focused on the acquisition of wealth, to the dictator focused on domination, to the parent who ensures the survival of their bloodline through the protection of their children. Self-interest gives our species purpose and spurs us on to do noble actions far beyond the necessity of personal survival.'

[Enter CAIUS and the PRIESTESS.]

CAIUS: I am in your hands Priestess. Tell me what I must do to save my wife and child from this jealous lover.

PRIESTESS: Each person's fate is a destiny drawn by the Gods. I can only advise.

CAIUS: Then advise.

PRIESTESS: My voices tell me the Goddess who processes you will brook no rivals for your affection and attention. Your family will never be safe.

CAIUS: Then, what must I do?

PRIESTESS: You must disappear.

CAIUS: I must destroy myself?

PRIESTESS: That would allow the Goddess to re-enter the skull and she would soon find another lover-victim. No, you must go away. You must travel far, far away.

CAIUS: To the very edge of the Empire?

PRIESTESS: Beyond civilization.

CAIUS: To live with barbarians? Savages?

PRIESTESS: Human beings like us. You must travel far away from humanity.

CAIUS: And live alone? I must live all alone with this Goddess, like - like the skeleton I found.

PRIESTESS: Once he was a human being like you.

CAIUS: A brave and noble soul.

PRIESTESS: Yet, even then, each time you think of your family you would render them in danger from the wrath of this monstrous Goddess, for she demands absolute devotion, absolute attention.

CAIUS: I cannot stop my thoughts.

PRIESTESS: I shall tell you how to construct an invisible sphere in which you can contain her. A magic circle made from plain stones, but a prison from which she will not escape unless it be penetrated from outside by another person.

CAIUS: To save my family I must live alone forever with my jealous lover?

Blood, Passion & Self-Sacrifice

PRIESTESS: The wise ones teach us nothing remains the same forever. The centuries will past and then another person will free you to join your ancestors. Your sacrifice will protect humankind for many ages to come.

CAIUS: But, Priestess, what if I destroy the skull? I shall have it pulverised to dust and cast to the four winds. That, surely, will kill the Goddess and eliminate any danger. It would mean I would lose a friend who has been my companion and confidant, but it is a sacrifice I am willing to make to save my family.

PRIESTESS: The skull is merely a vessel, a container in which she dwells, her home. The Goddess haunts you. If the skull were destroyed then she would haunt your skull instead. It is you who must disappear.

CAIUS: Was I doomed to this fate before I was even born? Was I chosen by destiny to carry this burden? Am I merely an actor in a tragedy written thousands of years before I was conceived?

PRIESTESS: It is for you to choose to give your life to save others. It must be your choice.

CAIUS: For my wife and my daughter, then I choose to disappear.

PRIESTESS: You are a brave and noble man. You fully understand your choice?

CAIUS: Yes, to live in the darkness with my jealous lover at the edge of doom until another soul finds me.

PRIESTESS: To live in the darkness at the edge of doom with a monster of jealousy until Jupiter, Emperor of the Gods, releases you.

[Exit CAIUS and the PRIESTESS.]

Dr STERLING *[Reading.]*: 'Humankind, like any species, will sacrifice their lives for a cause they consider worthwhile, be it an ideal or the safety of their loved ones.' *[She stops reading and looks up.]* I shall merely assert: there is much that life esteems more highly than life itself.

[Exit Dr STERLING. Enter JOHN and ALISON. JOHN holds some papers.]

JOHN: The police have caught the boys responsible.

ALISON: God knows what good that is to us. I spoke to the Consultant at the hospital. Sharon's face can be reconstructed with cosmetic surgery.

JOHN: That's a blessing, but it will take years and she will have to endure a lot of pain. The boys caught her by her pullover and she couldn't get away.

ALISON: Yes, the bastards.

JOHN: I had said to Sharon, "make sure you wear a warm pullover because it's cold outside". I said it to her almost every time she left the house. It was my fault. She wore the pullover because I told her to wear it. It was my fault.

ALISON: John, what are you saying?

JOHN: Alison, I read the translation of the scroll the academic from the British Museum sent to me.

Blood, Passion & Self-Sacrifice

ALISON: John, it's a story.

JOHN: The accidents are now happening to us, just as foretold.

ALISON: It's a story. You're letting it play on your mind. I should never have persuaded you to read it.

JOHN: No, you were right; the academic is right. Examine the facts. I suggested to Peter to take the car.

ALISON: John, don't start this!

JOHN: Just listen, and I told Sharon to wear a pullover, which resulted in the boys being able to grab hold of her. It's all coming true.

ALISON: John, the scroll takes coincidences and connects them together as though they are all part of some grand diabolical plot. It's nonsense! *[ALISON takes the papers off JOHN and she rips them up.]* It's a story, a fiction and a nonsense! You're letting this thing play on your mind. For Christ's sake take some stronger medication, go back to your doctor, do something, but for heaven's sake pull yourself together, I can't deal with you like this, not at the moment, not now! I'm - I'm going to get ready to go to the hospital. One of us has to remain sensible, if only for Sharon's sake.

[Exit ALISON.]

JOHN *[Talking to the invisible being.]*: Damn! You saw what she is like? How she treats me. Well, after what's happened to Sharon how can I leave her now? She needs my support. You saw that for yourself. Why are horrendous things happening to my loved ones when I think about them?

What? I did not say that you had anything to do with the accidents to Peter or Sharon. I accept what you have told me. I accept that you are innocent. Yes, I know you love me. Yes, I know Alison constantly undermines me, belittles me, but she is not evil. She is being influenced by some malicious power that wishes me harm. But who? And why? What have I done wrong that merits me being punished like this? What sin have I committed that demands retribution? If only I knew what I have done wrong? Why am I being punished? What? I know you are on my side. I know you will protect me; you are my friend. Well, I do enjoy your company; I enjoy it very much.

[Exit JOHN. Enter Dr STERLING and ALISON; they are talking to each other on their mobile phones.]

Dr STERLING: Hello, Mrs Cavendish, this is Dr Sterling speaking.

ALISON: Dr Sterling, from the Antiquarian Society?

Dr STERLING: That's right, I've been trying to meet with your husband for some time now to discuss the scroll, but he refuses to see me.

ALISON: What about the scroll?

Dr STERLING: I need to talk to him about the danger it prophesied.

ALISON: Danger? What danger?

Dr STERLING: Well, have you read it yourself?

ALISON: Yes.

Blood, Passion & Self-Sacrifice

Dr STERLING: Then, you must be aware of the danger it warns against?

ALISON: That's a load of superstitious rubbish.

Dr STERLING: I accept you think it is all hocus-pocus, but do you want to take the risk of ignoring its warnings?

ALISON: Warnings?

Dr STERLING: Yes, I think it would be fallacious, especially as the scroll's purpose is to help to avoid harm befalling, yourself, your daughter, relatives and friends.

ALISON: It is a bit late for that.

Dr STERLING: You mean regarding your late son, Peter?

ALISON: No, I mean regarding Sharon, my daughter. She is in hospital at present due to a terrible accident.

Dr STERLING: What?

ALISON: Some boys squirted an inflammable liquid at her and set it on fire.

Dr STERLING: Oh, my God!

ALISON: Her face is terribly disfigured.

Dr STERLING: Oh, my God, that's awful! Mrs Cavendish, I am sincerely concerned for you and your daughter's safety, did your husband find anything else in that cave?

ALISON: He found an old skull that he kept. He seems to think more of it than his family these days.

Dr STERLING: He found the skull. Please, just humour me on this one; if he will not meet me, then I need to see you urgently. I appreciate you find all this hokum, however, please accept I'm acting as much for you and your family's safety as out of academic interest. I firmly believe this is just the start of your troubles; it is certainly not the end.

ALISON: Dr Sterling, I know you mean well, but my husband is very ill. He was taking medication due to his mental health before all this started. The events of the last few months are making him worse. All this talk of spirits and Daemons is not helping him. I've actually caught John talking to himself.

Dr STERLING: Talking to himself?

ALISON: Yes, having whole conservations with someone who is not there.

Dr STERLING: You mean an invisible person or spirit we cannot see?

ALISON: No, I mean someone who is not there, non-existent. Dr Sterling, John is not a well man. I'm worried for his sanity.

Dr STERLING: Which is why I need to meet him. If he will give me the skull, I can get the Daemon banished, or, at least, confined within the skull regardless of what the scroll says.

ALISON: Doctor, he's a sick man!

Dr STERLING: Then, once his mind is settled on that point, you will find with the help of medication, John will be all right again and things will return to normal. Now, will you let me help you?

ALISON: I'm home at present. John managed to smash a pane of glass in the door. He insisted on repairing it himself rather than get it done professionally. Well, I am not risking him handling glass and chisels in his present state of mind, so I said I would replace it. I am in the middle of doing the job now.

Dr STERLING: It will take me a few hours to reach you.

ALISON: I'm going to the hospital later.

Dr STERLING: How about after you visit Sharon? I can meet you at the hospital.

ALISON: Ok, it's the Royal Victoria Hospital, Ward 4, about eight o'clock.

Dr STERLING: Excellent. I'll see you there.

[Exit Dr STERLING.

ALISON carries a pane of glass across the stage and off. She returns and she collects a hammer and a chisel. She places them in a tool box, which contains other tools.]

ALISON: All this talk of Daemons, what nonsense.

[ALISON exits, carrying the tool box.

Off stage, we hear noises as ALISON prepares to fix the window pane and then we hear glass shattering. ALISON screams in pain.

ALISON enters holding a white towel to her arm. The towel is red with blood. She pulls a shard of glass from her arm. She hugs the towel to her arm. The towel is turning bright red with blood.

ALISON takes her mobile phone and she dials for an ambulance.]

ALISON: Operator, my name is Alison Cavendish. I live at 46 Windsor Drive, postcode M50 33Z. I've had a terrible accident; blood is pouring from my hand. I've severed an artery. 46 Windsor Drive, M50 33Z. I shall go to the front door and open it. Please, please hurry.

[ALISON'S body and limbs shake with violent uncontrollable spasms. Near to collapsing, she staggers off stage.

Pause.

Enter JOHN.]

JOHN *[He is laughing as he enters the stage. He talks to the invisible being.]*: Your right, I suppose one of the advantages of all the accidents is that at least we can be together, alone with nobody to disturb us. I shouldn't be so happy after everything that's happened, but I can't help myself. When I'm with you my spirits lift. It's as if – as if I've had too much oxygen or something. At present we can spend all day together, Sharon and Alison are not a threat to us being together, you understand that? They are not a threat to us. I know you love me. I love you too. I can't stop thinking about you.

[There is a knock at the front door.]

JOHN: Who on earth can be calling at this hour? Now remember, we must be discreet.

Blood, Passion & Self-Sacrifice

[JOHN goes off stage to answer the door.]

JOHN *[off stage]*: Dr Sterling. Come in, come in, what are you doing here?

[Enter JOHN and Dr STERLING.]

Dr STERLING: Your wife said I would find you here. She is very worried about you.

JOHN: My wife? She would have me committed as insane if I'm not careful. At least she believes all the disasters striking my family are not my fault. She dismisses them as a run of bad luck.

Dr STERLING: Frankly, I doubt if luck had anything to do them.

JOHN: Nothing happens by chance, eh, doctor? We are fate's puppets and everything has a purpose and a meaning; everything is planned with objectives to be achieved. Is that what you're saying, doctor?

Dr STERLING: I have just come from visiting your wife in hospital, Mr Cavendish; the same hospital in which your daughter, Sharon, is staying due to her disfigurement. We have both read the scroll. We both know why these disasters are befalling your family and we both know they will persist if you choose to do nothing about them.

[JOHN is about to say something to her, but Dr STERLING cautions him with her finger to be silent.]

Dr STERLING: Allow me to perform a simple, but very effective, ceremony of protection around both of us.

[Dr STERLING produces a phial containing a liquid.]

Dr STERLING: Holy Water. It will afford us protection and privacy within its circle.

[Dr STERLING sprinkles the water around them in a circle. As she performs the ritual, she incants the following prayer -]

Dr STERLING: In the name which is above every other name, and in the power of the Father and of the Son and of the Holy Ghost, I exorcise all influences and seeds of evil; I lay upon them the spell of Christ's Holy Church, that they may be bound fast as with chains and cast into outer darkness, that they trouble not the servants of God.

[Pause.]

Dr STERLING: We can talk freely now. Providing that we remain within this magic circle the entity cannot hear or harm us. It cannot pass either in or out of the circle.

JOHN: The air does feel lighter. *[He looks around and speaks furtively.]* I am haunted by the fact I could have saved my son's life, prevented the horrendous disfigurement of Sharon and the traumatic accident to Alison. I, John Cavendish, could have changed fate. If only I had read the scroll and took it seriously. It is all my fault.

Dr STERLING: Nonsense, you are a victim of the curse residing within the skull. The dreadful incidents that have occurred are not your fault.

JOHN: I thought I could control her. I am so happy with her. I thought I could balance my time between her and my family. I refused to believe she was capable of harm. She lied to me, of course, telling me she was innocent of any involvement of harming Peter, Sharon or Alison. She lied to me, and I willingly accepted everything she told me because I wanted to believe in her innocence. I realise now if I am to avoid a fourth catastrophe then I need to leave.

Dr STERLING: No, Mr Cavendish, I think we can lift this curse without you having to disappear.

JOHN: That is not what the scroll instructs.

Dr STERLING: Trust me on this one. May I see the skull you found? Oh, please, don't deny the skull's existence for I know you have it.

JOHN: I shall not deny it this time, doctor, here it is.

[JOHN produces the skull.]

Dr STERLING: I realise it is very personal to you, but may I examine it?

JOHN: Of course.

[JOHN hands the skull to Dr STERLING. She takes out a jeweller's eye loupe and she examines the skull.]

JOHN: You will notice, doctor, there are symbols inscribed on it.

Dr STERLING: They are idea-o-grams. Not in a language I recognise. They are old, very old. These symbols are not part of an extant language either living or dead. I doubt if anybody knows what these idea-o-grams signify. They are from a civilisation far older than Icelandic, or the hieroglyphics of the Egyptians, or even, indeed, possibly older then the I Ching, which, if that's the case, makes this skull priceless.

JOHN: Can you guess at their meaning, doctor?

Dr STERLING: No, or, at least, not without further research, indeed, if they can be translated at all. This is actually not a human skull. It must be thousands of years old. Carbon dating would give us a precise date, but that would take time, and, frankly, I don't think we can afford to wait. Look at this on the cranium. This creature did not die a natural death and it was burnt. Whether the creature was consumed by fire as part of a religious sacrifice or a burial ritual, we can only guess.

JOHN: That's all very interesting, doctor, but, frankly, how does it help me?

Dr STERLING: Do you believe in evil? I mean absolute evil, Devils and Daemons that type of thing?

JOHN: I used to assign all that to the same category as The Tooth Fairy, but now…

Dr STERLING: Exactly, how else do you explain what has happened to you and your family. The greatest achievement in our age by the Devil is to convince people it does not exist. Scepticism is your worse enemy. This entity who has bewitched you, I mean your friend whom only you can see or hear, she is here now, isn't she? Here, now, with us.

JOHN: She is always here; she is always with me.

Dr STERLING: She whispers to you, telling you what to do, telling you what to think.

Blood, Passion & Self-Sacrifice

JOHN: I cannot get her out of my mind. Any thought I have but of her is an anathema to her. Any feeling of affection I have for anyone else renders the object of my affection in extreme danger. I am trying to control her by controlling my thoughts and feelings, for she can read my mind. The effort is tiring, constantly controlling one's thoughts, constantly hiding one's true feelings, but I will; I will prevent her from harming anyone else! I will not allow a fourth catastrophe to happen.

Dr STERLING: I shall help you banish this Daemon.

JOHN: Banish her? Without further harm to my family, or, indeed, endangering yourself?

Dr STERLING: Of course. I warn you your friend may tell you I am wrong in my advice, even evil, malicious, and equivocating.

JOHN: My friend is always talking to me, but I will try, no, I shall, shall contain her for as long as I can. I will not let her harm you; I will not let her harm anyone. There will not be a fourth catastrophe. Four has always been a significant number in my life, perhaps the reason was to guide me to an understanding of my present dilemma; to help me to realise the harm I'm inflicting on innocents by my thoughts and feelings. In that case, the purpose of the actions of my entire life was to guide me to the decision I must now make. Quick, doctor, return the skull to me before the Spirit threatens your life.

Dr STERLING: Here it is, it is yours, not mine.

[Dr STERLING hands the skull back to JOHN. He hugs it to him.]

JOHN: Thank you. Thank you.

Dr STERLING: You must be strong. Stand up to her. I assure you together we will defeat her and give you back a normal life.

JOHN: How, Dr Sterling?

Dr STERLING: May I call you John?

JOHN: Certainly.

Dr STERLING: John, I shall perform a series of magic rituals. I believe I can set up a magic circle that will surround the skull and keep this Daemon at bay, as the Priestess in the scroll directed the Roman to do. The difference, and this is very, very important, John, is you do not need to be trapped in the magic circle of stones with the Daemon. I firmly believe the Priestess was completely incorrect on this point. There are rituals that will exorcise the Daemon, make it return to the skull, and then we shall ensnare it for a millennium inside the skull within a magic circle. You will be free. You and your family will be safe.

JOHN: She is laughing at you, doctor, laughing at your arrogance.

Dr STERLING: It is because it is frightened of me, John.

JOHN: Frightened of you! Oh, doctor, I see, now.

Dr STERLING: See? See what?

JOHN: I see you do not believe in the Spirit, any more than my wife does. You think I am sick and I should be in hospital.

Blood, Passion & Self-Sacrifice

Dr STERLING: On the contrary, I can assure you I do believe in it. I firmly believe she exists; however, I firmly believe also that together we can defeat her. Certainly, I suggest you may need some medication after all this is over to help you to recover from the traumatic experience of exorcising this Daemon.

JOHN: No more innocent people must suffer. I cannot have a fourth catastrophe on my conscience.

Dr STERLING: Agreed.

JOHN: You have the practical knowledge of what to do? Do you know how to construct the magic circle mentioned by the Priestess?

Dr STERLING: I do.

JOHN: Prove it to me. Let me see.

Dr STERLING: The rituals of the ancients are explained in full in this manuscript I have penned.

[Dr STERLING hands JOHN a manuscript. JOHN reads.]

JOHN: It has been written on a word processor.

Dr STERLING: Well, I use the word 'penned' in its generic sense. You may keep that copy and peruse it.

JOHN: 'Peruse it.' Yes, yes, I shall.

Dr STERLING: Note the first chapter, John.

JOHN: 'The exorcising of Daemons.'

Dr STERLING: It is a ritual most religions have practised across the centuries.

JOHN: I suppose for an exorcism to work completely the host is required to want to be rid of their Spirit?

Dr STERLING: But, John, surely you do, don't you?

JOHN: She is reading my thoughts, doctor, and she is circling you. She covets you. Can you see her? There! There she is! What? No, please, you must not! She is plotting against you, doctor. Listen to her. Can you not hear her? Stop this! Stop! She is plotting your death. You were right, doctor, she is frightened of you. Come back to me. You are making me angry with you. Come back to me, now! I shall protect you, doctor; I shall protect you from harm!

Dr STERLING: John, listen to me. I assure you together we can defeat this Daemon.

JOHN: Yes, I believe she can be out-witted. For even though she knows my thoughts and feelings, there is still a part within my mind where secret ideas and emotions can be hidden. Where private thoughts, private feelings and private plans can be concealed from anybody. Yes. Yes, you are right, but we must act quickly. Decision made. Now, for clarity of purpose and directness of action. Act before she realises what is happening. But, to create the magic circle of stones, how is it done?

Dr STERLING: It is all explained within the manuscript. Stone circles have been used by civilisations across time as a means of protecting the interns in the circle from evil or as a means to prevent evil from escaping from the circle.

Blood, Passion & Self-Sacrifice

JOHN: But nothing lasts forever. Eventually, the spell would be broken and the Spirit will escape to find another victim. How many other people must have walked that path high in the Cairngorm Mountains where the skull lay hidden and had not been chosen by destiny to carry this burden?

Dr STERLING: Your aura was fragile due to your mental illness; that is why it chose you. The dead Roman you found in the cave almost certainly had the same fragile aura and mental health condition as yourself; that is why the spirit chose him and then a thousand years later when the magic of the circle was weak it was able to choose another victim with similar mental health problems - you. As to the stone circle, one theory runs that stones are used for magic circles because the energy stored in the stones can last for thousands of years, as proven by the Roman and his predecessor. John, we can protect humankind for a millennium from this Daemon, just as your two predecessors did. I shall help you to do it.

JOHN: You have helped me, doctor, by furnishing me with the knowledge I need. We were fated to have this meeting.

Dr STERLING: It is possible we are merely actors playing our parts in a destiny plotted out before time began, but I choose to help you resolve this. Will you trust me and choose to let me perform these rituals to free you of your Daemon?

JOHN: Decision made. Charity of purpose; directness of action. When? When will we do it?

Dr STERLING: I need to mentally prepare myself. So, tomorrow morning, bring the skull to me at the British Museum at eleven o'clock and I shall be ready to perform the rituals.

JOHN: The ritual the Roman used is the same one you have described in this manuscript?

Dr STERLING: Regarding the stone circle, yes, the very one in every detail. John, you must trust me.

JOHN: I do trust you, Dr Sterling, and I thank you. You must take care tonight, doctor, there is a powerful, dark force abroad wishing to harm you. I will keep it trapped by controlling my thoughts and emotions for as long as I can. Take care, Dr Sterling.

[They shake hands.]

Dr STERLING: I have my protections. Until tomorrow, John, goodbye. *[Exit JOHN. During the next speech, Dr Sterling makes a circle of stones around her moving clockwise and she performs a simple ritual.]* Nature's method of improving a species, indeed, if it exits, is at best slow and meandering. However, humankind's effort to improve its species has often faired far worse. We fall from hubris because we arrogantly think we are capable of rationally understanding our universe. We assume we know more about our world than in fact we do. Perhaps, fortunately, as a species we tend to be creatures of habit preferring what we know from repetition and familiarity. We tend to be suspicious of change. We try to understand change by comparing and assessing it with what we are use to in our lives, by what we find comfortable though usage. Often, these are not rational assessments, our actions and judgements are controlled equally by our sense of right and wrong as by our reason. It is a moral judgement we make and morality always involves self-control of one's desires and emotions. Ultimately, we are still frightened by the shadows we believe to be hiding in the darkness. *[She has completed the magic circle. She makes a sign in the air to the east.]*

Blood, Passion & Self-Sacrifice

May the almighty archangel Raphael protect me from all evil approaching from the east. *[She turns to the south and she makes another sign.]* May the almighty archangel Michael protect me from all evil approaching from the south. *[She turns to the west and she makes another sign.]* May the almighty archangel Gabriel protect me from all evil approaching from the west. *[She turns to the north and she makes another sign.]* May the almighty archangel Uriel protect me from all evil approaching from the north. My protection is complete. I exorcise thee, creatures of air, by the living God, by the holy God, by the omnipotent God that thou mayest be purified of all evil influences in the name of Adonai, who is Lord of Angels and of Men. *[Dr STERLING sits in the lotus position. She meditates. Suddenly, she looks to her left and she follows something around with her eyes.]* I know you're here outside the circle. I feel your coldness, your hate. We will defeat you! You have done enough harm for one millennium. You have gluttoned on the desire, pain and agony of too many innocent souls already. You may be invisible but I can sense you stalking around me, assessing the opportunity to hurt me, desperate to feed off my pain. *[Dr STERLING shudders.]* The coldness of your hatred may penetrate the circle but you cannot harm me. *[Dr STERLING'S mobile phone rings. She jumps. She answers her mobile phone.]* Hello?

[Enter ALISON. ALISON is talking on her mobile phone to Dr STERLING.]

ALISON: Dr Sterling, it's Alison Cavendish.

Dr STERLING: Good morning, Mrs Cavendish

ALISON: Did you see John last night?

Dr STERLING: Yes, and it was a very successful interview. In fact, he is coming to see me today at eleven o'clock.

ALISON: Dr Sterling, are you sure?

Dr STERLING: Of course, why? Why? What's happened?

ALISON: I have received a text from John. It's very, very disturbing. I'm going to call the police.

Dr STERLING: The police? John was fine when I left him yesterday evening.

ALISON: Let me read you this text message from him. I got it a few minutes ago. I have tried to ring him but he will not answer his phone.

Dr STERLING: Please, read the message to me.

ALISON: He says, 'Dear, Alison, I know you may consider me insane to do this, but sometimes love can drive a person to many strange actions. Although we have not got on well over the last few years, I still worry over your welfare and I love Sharon with all my life. Only by following the wisdom contained within the scroll can I ensure no further harm will come to you both. I have tidied up my affairs. I have left a letter for Sharon with our solicitor and a new Will ensuring everything goes to both of you. I ask only for you to raise Sharon with fond memories of me and to remember the happy times we had together as part of those precious moments that makes life worth living, all my love, John.'

Dr STERLING: 'Following the wisdom contained within the scroll' was not what we agreed to do last night.

ALISON: I'm calling the police. I'm worried for his safety.

Blood, Passion & Self-Sacrifice

Dr STERLING: And I shall try to get him on the phone. He may talk to me. Goodbye, Mrs Cavendish, and may your Gods go with you.

ALISON: Oh, for heaven's sake, goodbye!

[ALISON exits. Dr STERLING moves to the side of the stage and dials JOHN on autodial. A mobile phone rings. Enter JOHN answering his mobile phone. He sits in the magic circle made by Dr STERLING.]

JOHN: Ah, Dr Sterling, I have been waiting for your call. Please forgive my deception last night, but I had to know the ritual for making the magic stone circle.

Dr STERLING: John, where are you?

JOHN: Thousands of miles away.

Dr STERLING: Where?

JOHN: Oh, look for the second star on the left and travel straight on until morning. I can hardly tell you the place I have chosen to secret myself away far, far from human beings.

Dr STERLING: We had an agreement, why are you doing this?

JOHN: One thing the Priestess understood was the Roman loved his Goddess; he wanted to protect his loved ones, nothing more.

Dr STERLING: You do not want to be free from this entity?

JOHN: No. It's keeping her under control that racks me with anguish. She pounds at my skull to know my thoughts and feelings, to know whom to hurt. You need to be careful, Dr Sterling, for you would have been her fourth victim.

Dr STERLING: I have my protections. She came to me last night but she could not harm me.

JOHN: She came to you because I had you in mind as I read your manuscript. You are safe now because I have managed to keep her under control. She is caged with me within the magic circle. She is angry with me for keeping the prison door closed. She burns with rage. Her screams make the blood pound in my ears but, thanks to your manuscript, doctor, I understand her now. She is old magic, spawned from the face of chaos in Hell's fire long before time began and weaned on Devil's blood, yet I, I, John Cavendish, can control her. I prevented the fourth catastrophe; I am satisfied.

Dr STERLING: Listen to me, John, return, come back, let me exorcise this Daemon and free your mind.

JOHN: And risk further harm to Sharon, to Alison or to you if your exorcism does not work? No, doctor, by making this sacrifice, I can ensure nobody else I care for will ever be hurt by her.

Dr STERLING: John, there is another way. Please, please, please, come home and let me help you!

JOHN: Dr Sterling, you are trying to save someone who does not need saving.

Dr STERLING: I accept I have inadvertently given you the means to follow the fate of the other two men.

JOHN: No, doctor, you fulfilled your destiny. Here within the magic circle, I can live with my Spirit in harmony because she cannot escape this cage to hurt a fourth soul. I am free to think and to feel what I please without fear of harming anybody. The mental strain of keeping my thoughts and feelings under control until the magic circle was sealed and the prison door closed was worth it, for now I am free, free in the comfort and knowledge that my thoughts and feelings cannot hurt others.

Dr STERLING: But trapped for the rest of your life in the darkness.

JOHN: It is my choice. Before I knew what I had to do, I was being crushed by my anguish, destroyed by the knowledge my thoughts and feelings harmed Peter, Sharon, Alison and the fourth victim would have been you. Seemingly innocent but dangerous thoughts such as take the car instead of using the train or concerns about wearing a warm pullover going to school because it is cold outside or insisting on replacing a broken window pane. But, once I understood, once I knew what to do, I realised I had power over these events providing I could control my thoughts and feelings. Now, within this magic circle where thoughts and feelings can fly freely without harm, I am both mentally and spiritually calm. Yes, calm, it is a wonderful sensation, a type of contentment I have never known before; all uncertainty and emotional anguish have gone. I feel in control. I am in control of my passions and my emotions. I feel mentally tranquil. I have actually found the peace of mind I desire. Oh, doctor, this is the right decision.

Dr STERLING: Then, you are resolved?

JOHN: I am fully resolved, Dr Sterling. Here, I can live purely in the present, not constantly planning for future happenings or regretting past events. I have actually attained a tranquil presence of mind. I am - happy.

Dr STERLING: I envy you your happiness, John, and if angels observe our deeds from heaven may they carry news of your nobility to the seat of God.

JOHN: Thank you, doctor. Thank you for your help. Now, I must complete my isolation from the world. It is time to say goodbye. After I have destroyed this phone, I shall record my story for posterity as a warning and an aid to others just as my previous two soul-mates had done. Goodbye, Dr Sterling and thank you.

Dr STERLING: Goodbye, John, and may your Gods protect you.

[They end the phone call. JOHN dismantles the mobile phone and then he sits in the lotus position. Enter ALISON. ALISON is talking to the police on her mobile phone.]

ALISON: Constable, my husband's name is John Cavendish. He's not a danger to other people, but he is a danger to himself. He's gone quite mad. He thinks his thoughts are physically harming other people. I'm terrified he will self-harm. You must help me to find him! The poor man's going through a personal Hell. He needs to be in an asylum on medication. Don't tell me to calm down, Officer! I need you to find my husband urgently! Yes, he is a missing person. A danger to himself. There's a doctor involved, Dr Jocasta Sterling. She's not a physician, but she knows about his insanity. Please, please ring her; she may know where he is. Her phone number? Yes, hold on I can get it for you.

Blood, Passion & Self-Sacrifice

[Exit ALISON. Dr STERLING'S phone starts to ring. Dr STERLING checks to see who is ringing her and she lets the phone continue to ring.]

Dr STERLING: The police, looking for a man who does not want to be found; a man who lost the world to find peace of mind. *[Dr STERLING decides to switch off the phone. It stops ringing.]* As human beings we labour to transcend our best efforts, and suffering invariably is part of the quest for self-improvement. One can go as far as to say, without suffering a person cannot achieve the peace of mind that comforts them in their belief that they did their best. Both pleasure and pain are part of this ordeal. Indeed, they are essential ingredients in the process to the achievement of happiness. I merely assert a person who has overcome their Daemons and found contentment is truly a happy individual, is truly a superior human being.

[Exit Dr STERLING. JOHN sits alone on the stage in the lotus position. The lights fade to a blackout.]

M C Sanders

Scorpions of the Mind

A tragedy.

Blood, Passion & Self-Sacrifice

List of Characters:

Don - a 60 something man

Dulcinea - a 20 something young woman

Ballerina - a 20 something young woman

Newsreader - BBC received English accent

Off-stage voice of a 4 years old girl

On film – three 8 years old girls and a policeman.

[All other minor parts can be played by members of the cast.]

M C Sanders

{Coup de Théâtre – If the play is performed on an end stage that is large enough, the Artistic Director may consider using this 19th century coup de théâtre: a mannequin of the BALLERINA is behind a gauge curtain painted the same colour as the wall behind the mannequin. When a light is shone behind the gauge the mannequin appears. When the light behind the gauge on the mannequin fades down and light is shone onto the audience side of the gauge the mannequin 'disappears' and the painted wall on the gauge is seen. The BALLERINA enters through the gauge as the light on the mannequin fades down and she exits through the gauge as the light on the mannequin behind the gauge fades up. If this effect is used, please note that the costume change for the BALLERINA partway through the play also means a costume change for the mannequin, probably requiring a second mannequin for the second costume.}

[*Music plays. A BALLERINA dances in a tutu. DON is on stage. This scene continues whilst the audience enters and for the first few minutes of the play whilst they settle. The BALLERINA goes to DON, takes his hand and she gently kisses it. The music fades. Exit the BALLERINA. DON takes a gun from his pocket.*]

DON: Eloi, Eloi, lama sabachthani? My God, my God, why have you forsaken me? I have been banished to outer darkness. My soul exists in a blackness that cannot be lifted. For me, the sun is veiled in a mourning shroud. Not one candle of hope twinkles in the darkness. I drift through life, an unimportant speck floating in a black formless void. I beg for help but nobody listens. I plead for aid, but nobody comes. God never says a word. The years pass without meaning. I implore heaven for one ray of light. I cry to the Universe for one sign of hope, but God will not talk to me, will not even strike me down as a punishment for my sin. So, day follows day, interrupted by sleepless nights. All my thoughts, and all my feelings, gnaw at my soul. I desire a peace I cannot find. I yearn for a spark of salvation, but there is only never-ending darkness and silence. So, I cry alone, praying for a celestial messenger to deliver me, but I know it would be an easier task to search for lost tears scattered across the oceans of the world than to find the redemption I crave; for God has exiled me to outer darkness, far, far from heaven.

[Blackout. Exit DON. There are three loud gunshots. Lights up. DON's flat. A living room with a settee and a coffee table. A large screen projects the television news. DULCINEA is onstage alone. She is lying on the settee, next to the coffee table. She gains consciousness and she sits up.]

NEWSREADER *[on the TV]*: Good evening, this is London and here are the news headlines. In the capital earlier tonight, three men were found shot dead on the Thames Embankment. As yet the motive for the shootings is not clear or whether they are linked to the series of serial killer executions taking place in the capital at present. We will bring you more on that story as we get it. Other news. In South Africa, three of the world's most valuable diamonds have been stolen in a daring robbery from the Johansen Foundation's head office in the capital, Cape Town. Police say the thieves broke into the high security bank two nights ago and took the three gems, each worth an estimated £11 million.

DULCINEA: Hello. Hello. Is anybody there?

NEWSREADER *[on the TV]*: Also, in Africa, police in Ghana say they have uncovered a child prostitution ring that was selling children to brothels in Europe. Several arrests have been made in the capital of Accra and further arrests are expected to follow.

[Enter DON. He switches off the television.]

DON: Hello. At last, you're conscious. Would you like a cup of tea or coffee?

DULCINEA: Coffee. No. Water.

DON: Water, right.

DULCINEA: No, on second thoughts don't bother, I'm all right. Where am I?

DON: You're in my flat.

DULCINEA: In your flat?

DON: Yes, I had to bring you somewhere. Or would you have preferred me to leave you lying on the Embankment with those men and to have called for the police?

DULCINEA: No! No, not the police, please; I don't want the police.

DON: Very well, then, no police.

DULCINEA: I remember, oh, those three men! They were abusing me.

DON: No longer. You are quite safe. They are all dead.

DULCINEA: All dead? How?

[DON: shows her a gun. DON holds it in a handkerchief stained in blood.]

DON: With this.

Blood, Passion & Self-Sacrifice

DULCINEA: It's not mine. Is it yours?

DON: No. You were holding it when I found you.

DULCINEA: It's not mine; it's theirs, I mean the three men. I was just out walking. They grabbed me, forced me to the ground. One of them was on top of me. I grabbed the gun he placed at my side as he lay on top of me. I picked it up with him on top of me. I pressed the trigger. The other two men came towards me. I just kept squeezing the trigger. Those men, all dead? Definitely, all dead?

DON: Yes, definitely all dead.

DULCINEA: Is that blood on that handkerchief?

DON: Yes. You do not have any facial injuries, but you had some blood on your cheek so I wiped it off.

DULCINEA: It must be the blood of one of those men. His blood on me! How awful! Is it all off? Please tell me! Is it all off?

DON: Yes. It is all off. Your face is clean now. I can assure you I have wiped it all off.

DULCINEA: Thank you. But, the blood of one of them on me, how vile. It is all off, definitely?

DON: Definitely. Those men certainly had a lot of blood in them. When I found you, there was a river of the stuff running down into the gutter. Sorry, that was callous of me. There is no blood on your face now, I assure you, absolutely none.

DULCINEA: Good. Look, I really don't want to face police questioning. I would like to just go home.

DON: Of course. I can take you home and throw the gun and the handkerchief into the river Thames.

DULCINEA: Thank you. I was just out walking.

DON: So you said.

DULCINEA: Doing nothing.

DON: As you explained, you were just out walking.

DULCINEA: I know it seems strange for a woman alone to be just out walking late at night, but I was. I –I just want to go home and take a bath, I feel dirty.

DON: Alas, all the perfumes of Paris will not mask the stench of those men from your mind or aid you to forget the smell of their blood, but a bath might help you to relax. If you wish, I will escort you home.

DULCINEA: You are kind. What is your name?

DON: Don Quixoté.

DULCINEA: No, seriously, what is your name?

DON: Don Quixoté.

DULCINEA: Then, my name will be Dulcinea, your fair damsel in distress.

[DON makes a theatrical bow to her. DULCINEA smiles. Lights fade down. The screen projects a television news item.]

NEWSREADER [on the TV]: Good morning, this is London and here are the news headlines. Police have revealed that the three men who were found shot dead last night on the Thames Embankment were all killed by a single shot to the head in the manner of an execution. The shootings have all the hallmarks of the serial killer stalking the capital at present. Police are appealing for anyone to contact them with information about the killings.

[End of the news item. Lights fade up.]

DULCINEA: I had to come back.

DON: You're very welcome.

DULCINEA: Those men.

DON: The ones who were attempting to rape you?

DULCINEA: The ones who attacked me, yes.

DON: What about them?

DULCINEA: Did you see the news?

DON: No, should I?

DULCINEA: They were all shot in the head.

DON: I know, I saw them.

DULCINEA: Did you see me kill them?

DON: No. I reacted to the sound of the shots. They were all dead when I got to you.

DULCINEA: They were executed. I did not execute them. I shot at random. You must believe me.

DON: Well, all three of them are dead, whatever the chain of events.

DULCINEA: I shot the gun at random. I panicked.

DON: So, you shot at random, as you explained.

DULCINEA: Did you go to the police to report the killings?

DON: No, you asked me not to.

DULCINEA: Yes, I did. I did, didn't I? And the gun and the handkerchief?

DON: I threw them into the river, as I promised I would.

DULCINEA: Do you think we did the right thing?

DON: Relative concept. The right thing by whose rules? No doubt the police would not think that we did the right thing.

DULCINEA: Why are you helping me?

DON: I have an old world, penchant for chivalry. You were a damsel in distress, so I rushed to your aid.

DULCINEA: A Don Quixoté, a knight gallant like in the tales of old?

[DON *makes a theatrical bow to her.*]

DON: I freely admit I live in a world of fantasy.

DULCINEA: To a point don't we all? That explanation, I told you last night, about just being out walking, well it was just a story.

DON: I assumed it was.

DULCINEA: You assumed that? I was out - well, I have to get money from somewhere. I mean, it's a living. I did proposition those men. Before they attacked me. I must have been mad, but I need the money. Do you believe me?

DON: The reason you were there and the way you behaved is not important to me. You were in trouble so I helped you. It did not matter to me what you were doing on the Embankment. As it happened, I did not believe your story, but that is not important. You were in trouble, so I helped you.

DULCINEA: I was fortunate you were there. You are a good man. I have not led a good life, but I am a good person. I need the money because someone is blackmailing me. I don't want to go into details, but this man has important information about me that I cannot afford the authorities to find out; at least, not yet. I came back here tonight to ask you for a favour.

DON: A favour?

DULCINEA: Oh, don't worry, it is nothing illegal or dangerous, but you have been so kind to me, kinder than anybody for a long time. I just need you to follow him, the Blackmailer, to see where he lives, where he goes, after he leaves me, that's all. I don't need you to approach him or anything like that; don't do anything dangerous. I just thought that if I can find out where he lives then, perhaps, I could find something on him to stop him pestering me. You have been so kind to me and I wouldn't ask if I wasn't desperate, but I need your help.

DON: You need my help?

DULCINEA: I have nobody else to turn to.

DON: Frankly, I'm not a private detective.

DULCINEA: Please, I am desperate.

DON: If it is just to follow him.

DULCINEA: That is all I want you to do, I promise, and you must phone me immediately afterwards to tell me where he lives.

DON: Very well. I will go and it will be done as you request.

DULCINEA [*Weepy.*]: Thank you. Thank you.

[*DULCINEA goes to DON and he hugs her. It is a filial hug of father to daughter. DULCINEA exits. The screen projects a television news item.*]

NEWSREADER [*on the TV*]: Good evening, this is London and here are the news headlines. The serial killer has struck again in London. This time the victim was a convicted child killer who was released from custody after serving his sentence of four months in jail. The man, Norman Massington, aged 35, had been killed with a single shot to the head. Police are appealing for witnesses. Including the three men who were shot dead in the same fashion on the Thames Embankment last night, this is the 12th execution of this kind in the capital in the last six months.

[DON turns off the television.]

DON: Six months and two days to be precise. Fifteen years, six months and two days ago, it was my granddaughter's fifth birthday. All those years ago, she was five years old and all those years ago, I use to drive a delivery truck. I drove a large delivery truck. It was her 5th birthday and I decided to make a special journey to see her, right across town I drove, miles out of my way, but I wanted to see my granddaughter on her 5th birthday. It was the rush hour, the traffic was heavy, it took me hours to get there, but I had promised her that I would be at her birthday party and I wanted to see her. All her little friends from school were there at her party. All running around. All racing around having fun. I parked the lorry outside the house and I breezed in with my present. I purposely made a grand entrance, playing the kindly, generous grandfather. I kissed my daughter on the cheek and I hugged my granddaughter. She wanted a white ballet tutu for her birthday. Her mum, my daughter, said that it was far too expensive a present for a birthday, but what did I care? I would spoil my granddaughter by buying it for her, even if I did annoy my daughter with my largess. When my granddaughter opened her present, her little eyes lit up. She insisted on wearing the ballet tutu right away and her mummy helped her change into it. She looked so lovely. I held my granddaughter in my arms. I gave her a big hug, a great big hug. I even ate some jelly and I drank some lemonade with the little angel. Oh, I played the kindly, generous grandfather to the hilt. I made a big point that I had driven right out of my way, right across town, to be with her on her special day. After half an hour, it was time for me to leave. Breeze in and breeze out, hit and run, leaving the joyous impression of the generous grandfather in my wake. I smiled to myself as I got into my lorry. I was so happy that I had made the effort to drive all that way, hours right across town, to be with my granddaughter on her birthday. What a good grandfather I was. I donned my seatbelt and I started the engine. I had to reverse back a bit. I had parked too close to the car in front of me to pull straight out. I depressed the clutch, put the lorry into reverse gear and, so full of myself for being such a wonderful grandfather, I reversed without bothering to look into the mirrors to see if anything, or anybody, was behind the lorry. I felt the back wheels bump over something. I thought, 'What the hell was that?' So, I wound down the window, I looked out, and there she was, under the back wheels. My granddaughter had run out to wave goodbye to me. I undid the seatbelt and I climbed down out of the cab feeling the blood straining from my face and hands. 'No, oh, no, please, God, no,' raced through my thoughts. She lay motionless. I held her inert little body in my arms. She looked so lovely in her white ballet tutu. I gave her a big hug, a great big hug. I had driven out of my way, hours out of my way, right across town in rush hour traffic, to see my granddaughter on her 5th birthday so I could give her a great, big hug, right across town I had driven. My daughter insisted to me that it was an accident and not my fault, but I knew better. I did not see my daughter much after that. My fault, not hers. All my fault. How do you look a mother in the face after you have killed her child?

[Don turns on the television. The screen projects a television news item.]

NEWSREADER *[on the TV]*: Good morning, this is London and here are the news headlines. The serial killer stalking the capital has killed again. Police say the victim was a man in his late thirties. He was shot through the skull. The police have not been able to identify him at present, but it is known that he was a foreign national recently arrived from Africa.

[Enter DULCINEA.]

DULCINEA: You followed him?

DON: Yes.

DULCINEA: What happened?

DON: I told you on the phone. After he left you, he went home and so I telephoned you to tell you where he lived.

DULCINEA: He went straight home?

DON: Yes.

DULCINEA: And now he is dead. A victim of the serial killer.

DON: A victim certainly. Are you sorry?

DULCINEA: Sorry? I wanted him to stop blackmailing me that is true.

DON: And now he has.

DULCINEA: The body count is mounting. I'm frightened.

DON: What is it you have or know that is so important that people are being killed for it?

DULCINEA: I cannot tell you yet, but please believe me that if you will help me for just the next two days then I will be able to explain everything to you, I promise. It's important; it's vital you give me a few days more. I promise you will be doing a great good. I need your help again, just for two days. I need you to hide me here in your flat. I cannot stay at my flat in case it is being watched. It is not safe for me there anymore. Can I stay here, for just two days, and then I will be safe and I shall explain everything to you? I am all alone and frightened. There is nobody else I can turn to. You saved me once and I do feel secure here with you. Will you help me? Please, I need you to trust me for just two days more.

DON: Trust you? Is any of what you have told me so far true?

DULCINEA: Yes, it is all true. Well, ok, some of it is true. A little of it is true. I told you, I have not led a good life, but I am a good person.

DON: Exactly, you told me that yesterday with the same pathos in your voice and the same clipped intonation. It's a speech you have given many times before; false face hides a false heart.

DULCINEA: Very well, don't trust me, call the police, and feed me to the wolves. I ask for you to shelter me for just two days, nothing more. Then, I can explain everything to you. Will you protect me for just two days? Don Quixoté, will you help your damsel in distress, your Dulcinea?

DON: You need my help again?

DULCINEA: I promise you that you will be doing a great good. Please, please, will you help me?

DON: Very well, I shall give you sanctuary for two days.

Blood, Passion & Self-Sacrifice

DULCINEA: Thank you. I'm so lucky to have found you. You are a lovely, lovely friend.

[DULCINEA embraces DON warmly and then DULCINEA exits. The screen projects a television news item.]

NEWSREADER *[on the TV]*: Good evening, this is London and here are the news headlines. There has been a further killing in the capital last night. This time the victim was a 52-years-old man police have named as Steven Windermere. He was found near his home in South London. The man was shot in the head. The man, who last year was convicted for two months in jail for killing a child in a hit and run accident, is the 14th victim of the serial killer. The police are asking for witnesses to come forward.

DON *[He turns off the TV]*: The thick darkness of night hides our dark deeds.

[Lights fade down and then up. Enter DULCINEA. She holds some newspaper cuttings.]

DULCINEA: I was just looking for some writing paper in the writing bureau, honestly. I did not mean to pry, but I found these.

DON: Writing paper?

DULCINEA: Yes, I wanted to make some notes.

DON: Top drawer of the writing bureau.

DULCINEA: I did not mean to pry.

DON: You must tell me what you are really thinking?

DULCINEA: Really thinking? Nothing.

DON: You found those newspaper cuttings in the desk drawer. You recognized the pictures as some of the victims of the serial killer.

DULCINEA: I didn't mean to pry, honestly.

DON: Do you think that I am the serial killer?

DULCINEA: No.

DON: Why not?

DULCINEA: You're nice and you're kind.

DON: And you believe serial killers are not nice and kind?

DULCINEA: No, of course not. Well, yes, I suppose some of them are, I mean, well, erm, well, frankly, I'm not sure what I mean.

DON: You mean serial killers are human like the rest of us?

DULCINEA: Yes, well, no; no, they are not like the rest of us, they're murderers.

DON: Murderers are human, perhaps all too human. Would it surprise you if I told you that I am the serial killer?

DULCINEA: You! Are you?

DON: Yes.

DULCINEA: What? You killed that man last night?

Blood, Passion & Self-Sacrifice

DON: Yes.

DULCINEA: Why?

DON: He killed a 9 years old child in a hit and run accident, left her dying in the street whilst he ran away and the court punished him with only two months in jail. At the trial, he did not even say, 'sorry' to the parents.

DULCINEA: And that gives you the right to kill him?

DON: Killing someone is not a right; it's an act, an action.

DULCINEA: He was poor and from a dysfunctional family.

DON: Being poor and from a dysfunctional family does not make you a killer. What about all the other thousands even millions of people from the same kind of backgrounds that live perfectly ordinary lives?

DULCINEA: But to kill him.

DON: What would you have me do?

DULCINEA: Not kill him.

DON: Then, what would you do to him?

DULCINEA: I - I don't know.

DON: Do you agree that to commit the criminal act of knocking down a child and failing to stop thus leaving the child to die in the road is worth a punishment of only two months in jail?

DULCINEA: Of course not.

DON: To know and not to act is not to know.

DULCINEA: But to act in this manner.

DON: For evil to succeed all that is required is for good men to do nothing.

DULCINEA: So, you choose to do something and you killed him!

DON: I made a rational decision. Our basic desires are controlled by our reason, which directs our spirit to channel those basic desires in a positive, constructive manner. I do not commit arbitrary acts. Reason rules and focuses the spirit so that one's appetites are directed in a specific way. I made a rational decision and I executed him. I chose to give the victim justice.

DULCINEA: Is that the reason behind all the other people you have killed?

DON: Yes. One, a hit and run driver who left an eleven years old girl to die in the road after dragging her body one hundred yards under the wheels of his car was given by a court of law three months in jail; three months for leaving a child to die in the road after dragging the child one hundred yards because he decided not to stop his car. I decided on a harsher sentence for the sake of the child and her family. Another driver, paralysed a two-years-old child and his sentence was so light that he got out of jail before the child got out of hospital. A third driver knocked down a schoolboy. The boy suffered a nervous breakdown after being forced to give evidence against the driver in court. When the driver appealed against his four months sentence, the boy committed suicide because he was afraid of meeting the driver again. If you think that I am wrong? I ask you this question. Do you agree with the judgements those convicted criminals received from the courts?

DULCINEA: Of course not. Of course, I don't agree with those judgements. The judgements were wrong. So, you feel you are righting wrongs, doing good?

DON: A deed regarded as good by one person will be considered bad by another person. Any act of help given to one person will invariably harm another. I fight an evil. I act as an avenger for victims of crime, who, in my world-view, do not receive justice.

DULCINEA: Do you intend to continue to 'avenge' perceived miscarriages of justice by execution?

DON: Yes. Why not? In a perfect society reason would reign and criminals would be punished correctly, but, then, in a perfect society there would be no crime. However, our society is based on an aristocracy retained in power by a wealthy oligarchy and legitimised by a veneer of democracy. Wealth and position are everything; money and property rule. So, rob a bank and a judge will give the convict ten years or more in prison, whilst if the crime is murder, manslaughter or rape then the convict is sentenced to only a few years if that. I disagree with the courts' morality and I choose to do something about it. If I set myself up as the whole of the law, it is because I firmly believe justice is one of the highest forms of happiness. It satisfies a primal desire deep within us. It is welcomed for its own sake and its consequences are to provide a well-balanced, fair society, but I firmly believe also that we do not live in a just, well-balanced, fair society and I choose to act to correct that fault. I accept my morality is part of an old-world chivalry where honour, duty and human life are valued above all else and not measured in gold. I accept I am out-of-kilter with the contemporary view of society and, therefore, I am forced to behave like a tyrant acting as jury, judge and executioner. I am forced to become a monster, to be considered mad. So, are you going to try and stop me? *[Pause.]* One of life's big questions, quo vadis?

DULCINEA: Quo vadis? Latin for, 'Where are you going'?

DON: Yes.

DULCINEA: Tomorrow, to conclude by business, I'm going to the airport, but for the moment, I'm staying here. Listen to me, keeping these records is foolish. It expresses a desire to be caught. Do you want to be caught? Well, do you?

DON: No. No, being incarcerated would not serve my purpose.

DULCINEA: Then, these newspaper clippings must go. Do you agree?

DON: Yes, it was sentimental of me to keep them. I did not want the children forgotten. It was foolish keeping them, I agree.

DULCINEA: Then, I'm going to destroy them. I shall burn them, agreed?

DON: Yes, please, burn them. You are right. Commit them to the flames.

DULCINEA: I shall leave the moral dilemma over whether I am going to do a good deed or a bad one to you; I'll go and destroy these papers. Rest assured, Don Quixoté, while I am here, I shall take care of you better than you do yourself.

[Exit DULCINEA. DON holds his head as pictures are flashed on to the television screen of cars braking hard, children crying, people screaming.]

DON: The memories remain. You cannot destroy the memories even by the cleansing gent of fire. The imagines imprinted in my mind cannot be wiped away so easily. They remain regardless of how many pieces of newspaper have been destroyed. The memories remain.

[Enter DULCINEA carrying a waste paper bin and a photograph in a frame.]

DULCINEA: There, all gone. See. Just a pile of ashes now, nothing more.

[DULCINEA shows DON the bin.]

DON: The evidence?

DULCINEA: Yes, the evidence, all gone.

[DULCINEA places the bin to the side of the stage.]

DULCINEA: However, I found this amongst the newspaper clippings. It's a photograph of a little child, about five years old, wearing a white ballet tutu.

[DULCINEA shows DON the framed photograph of his deceased granddaughter.]

DON: Sanctum sanctorum.

DULCINEA: More Latin, 'The holy of holies'?

DON: It is a picture of my granddaughter. I purposely kept it with them. She would have been your age if she had lived. 'Death lies on her like an untimely frost on the best flower in the field.' 'If only we could look into the seeds of time and say which grain will grow and which will not.'

DULCINEA: Another road accident victim?

DON: Yes.

DULCINEA: And the driver?

DON: I give him Hell.

DULCINEA: I bet you do. Don, please make me a promise.

DON: If I can.

DULCINEA: Promise me not to kill anybody else, at least not until tomorrow, just whilst I am here.

DON: I don't kill criminals I execute them.

DULCINEA: Then, promise me not to execute anybody else until this business of mine is concluded.

DON: I am immersed too deep in blood to stop now and start playing the ordinary citizen.

DULCINEA: I shall be gone tomorrow. Please, give me your word you will stop fighting windmills, at least until I have gone.

DON: I would prefer not to give my word, 'for words are dangerous.'

DULCINEA: Another piece of rhetoric. Pray, who are you citing this time?

DON: It is a line from a play by Christopher Marlow called, *Dr. Faustus*, which is about a man who also gave his word.

DULCINEA: I'm not asking you to sell your soul to the Devil, just to promise not to execute anybody else until I have gone tomorrow.

DON: Very well, by all the Gods and suns that shine, I promise.

DULCINEA: Thank you, Don Quixoté.

DON: My pleasure, Dulcinea.

[DON makes a theatrical bow. DULCINEA stands the photograph on the coffee table.]

DULCINEA: I can't keep calling you Don Quixoté.

DON: Pray, tell me, why not?

DULCINEA: It's not your name and it's silly.

DON: No sillier than Dulcinea.

DULCINEA: But, that's my name.

DON: No, it is not.

DULCINEA: Actually, my name is Dulcinea.

DON: Then, mine is Don Quixoté.

DULCINEA: If that is the truth, then I shall call you Don. Just trust me for one more day, Don, and I promise I will tell you what I am involved in.

DON: As your knight errant, I promise I shall.

[DULCINEA exits. The screen projects the television news.]

NEWSREADER *[on the TV]*: Good evening, this is London and here are the news headlines. Police have revealed that the three men who were found shot dead three nights ago on the Thames Embankment had all recently arrived from the African continent. Why the serial killer chose these three men to execute and the fourth man executed in his flat who had also recently arrived from Africa is still not clear. The police are urging anyone to contact them with information about the killings.

VOICE OF FOUR-YEARS-OLD YOUNG GIRL *[Off Stage]*: Look! There's the water. Granddad, there's the water.

DON: Yes, my darling, it's the water.

VOICE OF FOUR-YEARS-OLD YOUNG GIRL *[Off Stage]*: It's where we saw the dragons.

DON: The dragons? Oh, you mean the Dragon Boat Races. Yes, that's right, my darling, that is where we saw the Dragon Boats racing. You are right. We liked them, didn't we? We had a good time that day. We both enjoyed ourselves. The Dragon Boats, yes, we had a good time that day.

Blood, Passion & Self-Sacrifice

[Enter DULCINEA.]

DULCINEA: Are you alright?

DON: What? Yes, yes, of course I am. I was just thinking things over, that's all.

DULCINEA: Don, I have a confession to make.

DON: Then, please, make it.

DULCINEA: I did keep one newspaper clipping that I found. *[DULCINEA produces the clipping.]* It is about the fatality of a five years old girl some fifteen years ago. An awful accident in which her grandfather reversed a lorry without checking behind.

DON: All the executions of all the criminals will not wash the blood from my hands. I hoped to turn my grief to some use. I hoped my actions would be a medicine to ease my mental torment, but they do not soothe me.

DULCINEA: It is because you are trying to wash the blood from your hands with oceans of more blood. You have waded in to the stuff so far you are drowning in it.

DON: Drowning? No. I have not lost sight of the reason I commit these acts; it is all for love, for the love of my deceased granddaughter, always for love. I wanted to do something that will not change the world, but might right a few wrongs and make me feel better.

DULCINEA: You have turned your guilt ridden, hand washing into a form of retribution arbitrarily administered by yourself.

DON: Guilt is a damnable soul mate. It gnaws at the psyche. I can never walk with a light heart. I can never have any peace. Over and over again the afflicted memories of my granddaughter stab like daggers pushed into my mind. The error I made, the blunder I committed, is played out in my senses time and time again. The memory of her beautiful face laced with blood pouring from the breeches in her flesh due to my blunder never leaves me. A young life wasted and all the delicious might-have-beens of joy denied to me because of my blunder. All the happiness swept away in an instant. My mind burns from the painful fever of remembrance. I am ground down by my guilt over and over and over again. I pray for redemption, but I receive no answer, there is just silence, darkness and suffering. Rest assured, God's commands would be done, if only I knew what they were, but God never says a word.

DULCINEA: Self-indulgent, self-pitying rhetoric; you wallow in it. All that rhetoric is important to you, isn't? It is like a cocoon to protect you. You hide inside it. Ultimately, Don, we are human beings and we make mistakes.

DON: The person I am now was created by the action of cause and effect. I committed a fiendish act and I have become a Fiend.

DULCINEA: Life is not to suffer for a crime in this life or some assumed past existence or because one cannot live up to an ideal of behaviour. Celebrate existence. Enjoy life; don't suffer it. You are a good person who made a mistake.

DON: I assure you; I earned my modesty long ago and I embrace my fate. What is done is done. When faced with a clear choice, I chose the wrong one, casually, nonchalantly, thoughtlessly, and that decision destroyed all my happiness;

but, ultimately, there is one positive feeling I cherish, after all my self-recrimination and self-imposed hurt, I know my granddaughter loved me.

DULCINEA: Then, let her be your salvation.

DON: The problem is in life we learn our lessons from experience and so after the event, after the lessons are of any use to us. We cannot go back to change the events of the past in order to correct our mistakes.

DULCINEA: So, you live in a world of might-have-beens, if-onlys and regrets. They are daydreams you nurture. Don, a lot occurs in life that we would prefer did not.

DON: My granddaughter is dead. I killed her when she was only 5 years old. I did not invent or dream that.

DULCINEA: No, but the rest. You still image her to be in the nursery, like some kind of Peter Pan. *[DULCINEA picks up the photograph of DON'S granddaughter off the coffee table.]* This photograph you keep of her in a tutu, why is this one so special? Her mother dressed her little girl in a ballet costume, just as many mothers do to their daughters at that age. My mother dressed me in a tutu for my 5-year-old birthday party. Don, why is this picture so special to you?

DON: My granddaughter loved to dance. At her 5th birthday party, she was dressed in a tutu. That photograph was taken three minutes before I killed her.

DULCINEA: Do you still image your granddaughter at twenty years of age in a ballet tutu that she last wore when she was 5 years old?

DON: Well, I imagine her at twenty, quite the young lady, all grown up.

DULCINEA: A twenty years old young woman dressed in a ballet tutu she got on her fifth birthday. You refuse to let her grow up in your mind's eye, refuse to dare to imagine your granddaughter with faults, flaws, problems just like any other young adult.

DON: She never got that chance; I deprived her of the opportunity.

DULCINEA: By accident, yes, of course you did, but, think about it, would she like you to regard her as a young adult like this?

DON: It is the picture etched into my soul.

DULCINEA: You have created the perfect companion in your head. A benevolent phantom who is always the perfect little Miss.

DON: My imaginary realm of romantic adventure makes existence bearable. I have always preferred the infinite world of dreams removed from the temporal reality of mundane day-to-day living. In my dreams, I feel more real. They make me feel complete. My fantasies are as real to me as the news one sees on a television screen or reads in a newspaper; to me they are as real as day-to-day life.

DULCINEA: Your image of your granddaughter says more about you than about her. It is a twee, idealised mannequin that can exist nowhere but in your head. She was a thinking, breathing human being. She deserves better than this, and, frankly, so does your memory of her. Don, it is time to change the fantasy.

DON: You never knew her, never heard her laugh, giggle, or talk, never pushed her on the swing in the park or showed her the boats sailing on the water at the marina.

DULCINEA: Then, why don't you tell me about her, bring her to life for me?

DON: To what value?

DULCINEA: Because I'm curious. Because I'm asking you to tell me about her. What other value need there be? Do you have any other photographs of her?

DON: Of course, I have hundreds of them.

DULCINEA: Then, show them to me.

DON: I warn you; I shall bore you for hours with my memories.

DULCINEA: I'm not going anywhere until tomorrow. Don, I would like to hear about your granddaughter, all about her.

DON: Very well then, but be forewarned, there are an awful lot them.

DULCINEA: I'd love to see the photos, to share those golden moments, those memories, with you. Go and get them and show me what your granddaughter really was like rather than being presented with this fiction of her you have woven in your mind.

DON: Ok, I will get the albums and show you.

[DON exits to get the photo albums. While he is away, DULCINEA takes her mobile phone from her pocket and dials a number on auto dial.]

DULCINEA: Hello, it's me, is everything still in place for tomorrow? Excellent. There's three of them, is that still correct? Magnificent. Just use holiday visas to get into the country as agreed, I shall do the rest. Your money is safe, ready and waiting for you; a straight cash deal. Sure, you almost certainly could get more for them in secret auction on the open market, but you risk getting caught. Remember, most of the gang is either dead or in prison already. Good, I'm glad you see things my way. I shall see you tomorrow as we arranged. Do not ring or text this number in case phone hackers are intercepting the messages, remember, silence is our best protection. I must go now.

[DULCINEA ends the call. DON enters carrying a number of large photograph albums. DULCINEA gives him a warm smile.]

DON: I warn you; I will keep you up for hours looking at these. You must tell me if I bore you.

DULCINEA: I promise I will not be bored. We have hours and hours until morning.

[Music. DON opens the albums and they look through them. He smiles as he looks at the pictures. The BALLERINA enters. She has changed her costume to modern dress; it is the same costume that DULCINEA is wearing. She dances. The music ends. The BALLERINA remains on stage. DULCINEA kisses DON gently on the forehead and DULCINEA exits. DON picks up a sprig pressed and placed in one of the albums.]

DON: Here's rosemary, that's for remembrance. I placed that in this album 15 years ago as a symbol of remembrance and love. All those years ago, all those fond memories now revisited and now enjoyed afresh. *[DON kisses the sprig and replaces it in the photograph album.]* Life was good once long ago. Its resonance was kind and I was happy. All those years ago the sun never stopped shining and I woke up looking forward to every new day. My daughter and my granddaughter were my reasons for living, life was fine and it seemed the summer would never end. Suddenly, all the happiness finished in an instant. After that, I fantasised over all the infinite might-of-beens, knowing that they can never happen and, so, my memories turned to bitterness and regret. Yet, this young girl has changed all that. She has shown me the warmth in the years I had with my granddaughter, helped me to experience the happiness once more, and aided me to find in all those memories that fed my bitterness the reason why I was happy in the first place and why, all those years ago, life was worth living. She has turned the recollections soured by guilt into reminiscences warmed by love. I cannot stop smiling. I feel good about myself, about life, about everything. I know I shall sleep tonight without fear of nightmares. I shall look forward to tomorrow. She has given back to me a reason to be alive, shown me the joy my granddaughter had for life and I can celebrate her life and the pleasure I shared in it. I know I shall wake up tomorrow with a lighter heart. I think I will contact my daughter. Yes, for the first time in years, I will contact my daughter to see if she will meet me. I actually feel happy. Yes, happy. I actually feel happy.

VOICE OF FOUR-YEARS-OLD YOUNG GIRL *[Off Stage]*: Look at all the snow, Granddad.

DON: Yes, my darling, it is everywhere.

VOICE OF FOUR-YEARS-OLD YOUNG GIRL *[Off Stage]*: My wellies go right into it.

DON: The snow is deep.

VOICE OF FOUR-YEARS-OLD YOUNG GIRL *[Off Stage]*: Will we go fast down the hill, Granddad?

DON: On the sledge? Yes, we will go very fast down the hill. Now, you sit in front and I will hold on tight to you. Here we go!

VOICE OF FOUR-YEARS-OLD YOUNG GIRL *[Off Stage]*: Oooooh!

[THE YOUNG GIRL giggles uncontrollably as the sledge slides down the slope.]

DON: Where have all those years gone? Have I been in a deep sleep all this time? Thank you, my dear Dulcinea for waking me up to the joy I had with my granddaughter, thank you.

[Music. DON kisses the picture of his granddaughter. The BALLERINA and DON dance. Music ends. The BALLERINA and DON exit. DULCINEA enters. She is talking into her mobile phone.]

DULCINEA: Good morning. I'm ringing to confirm the agreement. I shall definitely procure them today. All three as agreed. I told you I couldn't keep them even for a few days because I have nowhere safe to store them. As agreed, you shall have them providing the money is given up front. A straight exchange, I shall collect them from the airport and providing you give me the money when we meet this afternoon, they are all yours.

[There is a noise off stage of a door opening.]

Blood, Passion & Self-Sacrifice

DULCINEA: I must go now; I shall see you this afternoon as arranged.

[DULCINEA ends the telephone call. DON enters.]

DON: Good morning.

DULCINEA: Good morning. My, you're looking cheerful this morning.

DON: When I went to bed last night, I slept peacefully for the first time for – well, for -

DULCINEA: For fifteen years?

DON: Yes. I actually dreamt of swimming at a leisurely crawl through warm water with a cool breeze on my face. It was very refreshing, even tranquil. Thank you, my Dulcinea, my friend. I thought I would make us a breakfast, with eggs done sunny side up.

DULCINEA: Sounds perfect.

DON: We were fated to meet. Fated to have this time together.

DULCINEA: I enjoyed hearing your reminiscences, sharing your memories. You kept them locked in a dungeon deep in the recesses of your heart. I just helped you to release them, to enjoy them, to turn the memories feeding bitterness and regret into happiness and nostalgia.

DON: 'So, shines a good deed in a naughty world.' You were the balm to remove the anguish and pain from my sick mind and ease my heart. God answered my prayer. He sent you to me. A celestial emissary in human form.

DULCINEA: I'm hardly an angel.

DON: But a celestial emissary nonetheless. In classical Greece there was a word for a spirit who acted as an intermediate between Gods and men; they called that spirit a 'Daemon'. They existed partway between the heaven and the earth. A Daemon could be good or evil. They were regarded as the messengers of the Gods and often they would take on human form. You, my Daemon, have come in answer to my prayers; knowingly or otherwise.

DULCINEA: I grant you I may be a 'Fallen Angel'. We are both innocents.

DON: I want to believe that you are an innocent.

DULCINEA: I am. Like you, I am a victim.

DON: Then, tell me, my Fallen Angel, my Daemon, why do you need to hide here? What mess are you in?

DULCINEA: If I tell you, will you promise to help me? I'm all alone. I have nobody else to help me.

DON: I promise to help you if I can.

DULCINEA: Very well, then I shall tell you. You will be doing a great deal of good, believe me. At 15:30 Greenwich Mean Time today a plane arriving from South Africa will carry on it a precious cargo. It is the stolen Johansen diamonds. The three diamonds will be smuggled through Heathrow airport. Each diamond is worth a King's ransom. They have been cut to perfection and their value as jewellery is equivalent to a large lottery win, but their value in either commercial or military application is incalculable. It is essential that those diamonds become the property of the British government and are not procured by a foreign hostile power. I intend to go to Heathrow airport today and I shall point out to the authorities the smuggler. The authorities will be able to do the rest.

DON: Why don't you go to the police now?

DULCINEA: To go to the police before the diamonds can be recovered? I cannot do that. You see, on the night of the robbery, I left South Africa for England, and since then I have found out that my former boss and his wife have been killed. Also, since I arrived in London, I have been connected with four more deaths. If I go to the police now, they would arrest me. I only just managed to avoid arrest by fleeing South Africa on a flight to England. I am running for my life. The three men on the Thames Embankment who are dead were after me and then the fourth man I asked you to follow is also dead.

DON: Six deaths: your boss, his wife and the four men in England.

DULCINEA: Exactly. You see why I am frightened and I need your help. Oh, I do not think that the diamonds are cursed or anything like that, but they are worth a lot of money.

DON: How did you get involved in all this?

DULCINEA: I told you, I am not a bad person, but I have hardly led the life of a nun. When I lived in South Africa, I worked as the Personal Assistant to the Head of Security at the Johansen Foundation, one of Africa's leading diamond organisations.

DON: You worked as a Personal Assistant?

DULCINEA: That is correct.

DON: How personal?

DULCINEA: Very personal; his marriage had gone stale. One afternoon, whilst he slept, I mused myself surfing the Internet on his personal computer and by chance I came across some personal files protected by a password.

DON: On the Internet?

DULCINEA: Yes.

DON: And you came across these personally protected files by chance?

DULCINEA: All right, perhaps, they were not on the Internet and, perhaps, I did not come across them by chance, but I found them all the same. Well, I knew Teddy, my employer, well enough, so it was not hard to guess at the passwords he had used. I did it out of a lover's prurient curiously, nothing more; the kind of thing a lover would do to know all about their sweetheart, but what I found shocked me. They were the plans to steal three of the most expensive diamonds in the Johansen collection from their bank vault the very next week. It was all there: the dates, the contact numbers, the means of escape and the buyers. Everything.

DON: What did you do?

Blood, Passion & Self-Sacrifice

DULCINEA: I closed the computer down immediately. I knew Teddy was getting into something way over his head despite the money he would be paid for his part in the job. The Johansen Foundation would never give up looking for him. He had signed his own death warrant and, even worse, he may have signed mine too because of my relationship with him. I resolved to return to England right away to get myself out of the mess. However, the same night I left South Africa for England the robbery took place. The dates on the computer must have been purposely set one week ahead, presumably by Teddy as a security precaution. However, worse still, the night I left South Africa, Teddy and his wife died in an automobile accident that could not have been a coincidence. So, don't you see, I worked for the Johansen Foundation in their security section, my boss, who was my lover, and his wife die and I leave South Africa on the same night the diamonds are stolen. I am innocent, I swear to you, but you see how it looks? You see how I'm implicated? To help the authorities recover the diamonds and then tell them my story is my only hope. Will you help me? I'm depending on you.

DON: So, this is all about diamonds?

DULCINEA: Yes. That is why I needed you to hide me, just until today.

DON: Until today?

DULCINEA: The plane arrives from South Africa carrying the smuggler and the three diamonds today. This afternoon, I will go to the airport, point out the smuggler to the Customs and Excise people and give myself up to the police. By allowing me to stay here until this afternoon, you will be doing a good deed for society and helping me.

DON: If this is just about some diamonds, then it's hardly a cataclysmic perturbation in nature. How could I refuse? You are my redemption. Of course, I shall help you. If it aids you to capture the diamond thieves and exonerate yourself, then let us, 'Cry Havoc and let slip the dogs of war!'

DULCINEA [laughs]: You are funny at times; I like you.

DON: I have my moments. Right, well, that's settled, now, first things first, breakfast with eggs done sunny side up?

DULCINEA: Excellent idea. I knew I could trust you. You are my friend, my Guardian, my Don Quixoté.

[DULCINEA goes to DON and she lovingly pecks him on the forehead. It is a filial kiss, not that of a lover.]

DULCINEA: Let us go and make breakfast together.

DON: I'd like that.

DULCINEA: I love the smell of toast, especially when it has been slightly burnt.

DON: Then, slightly burnt toast you shall have.

[They exit. Music. The BALLERINA enters. She dances. Enter DON. The BALLERINA and DON embrace and they move together in unison to the music. The BALLERINA exits.]

DON: Time to tidy up, whilst my Dulcinea is at the airport.

[DON begins to clear away the photo albums. DON picks up the bin with the ashes in it. DON goes to clear away the bin. DON notices a partly charred piece of paper in the bin. DON picks it up. DON reads it.]

DON: Ghana? This is part of an airplane ticket. She came to England from Ghana not from South Africa? Ghana? She said she arrived from South Africa by plane. Please, God, no, not this, not what I think. She came from Ghana not South Africa. I prayed for help, I prayed and prayed. I thought God had abandoned me, but I was wrong, on the contrary, the Almighty sent to me one of his most powerful angels, a Daemon, a Fallen Angel. Her magic certainly worked on me; for the first time since my granddaughter died, I was happy. She arrived from Ghana not South Africa. Sometimes God punishes us by granting us our wishes, for they are granted at too high a price. She arrived from Ghana. I wanted to think that my Dulcinea is how my granddaughter might have been all grown up and a lovely, young lady. Was I deluded by an evil Daemon, an instrument of darkness? Have I had my eyes open, but my senses shut? I must look at the world head on, free myself from my daydreams. Time to wake up; time to leave the security of my dark cave, this bliss of ignorance, and step into the stark sunlight of the world. I must go to the airport. I must find out. Please, God, don't let my fears about her be right. I really don't want this dream to end, at least, not this way. She arrived from Ghana not South Africa. I must go to the airport. I must know what she is.

[Music. The BALLERINA enters. The BALLERINA embraces DON. Images on the screen of DULCINEA at the airport with three young children, DON using a mobile phone, the police, DULCINEA running. On stage, the BALLERINA kisses DON on the forehead. The music ends. The BALLERINA remains on stage for the rest of the play.]

DON: In the entire universe, I should have known that the only person who could save me was my granddaughter. As to my Dulcinea, the brightest Angel who fell from grace, the picture is now complete; I have glimpsed behind her mask and the spell is broken. She helped me to find the joy in the memories of my granddaughter, but the price she asked me to pay was to aid her in an abomination. The choice that she presented to me was to either betray our friendship or to ignore an anathema. But if my friend turns out to be a Daemon with dark intent, if she saved me only to exploit our friendship to aid her to commit an abominable crime, if she fed me a dream to serve her own prurient purposes? True, it was a dream I wanted to live in. She gave me the world how I would like it to be. It was seductive and I was bitten. My soul soared high with expectation, but it was due to the manipulation of a Devil that came out of the dark to trap me with equivocation, untruth and false affection. If only the world could be the just and happy place of our desires. Perhaps earth is Hell because one can never live up to the person one would like to be. Strange how one's most noble of actions end up being a broken promise and a betrayal of the person one trusted.

[Enter DULCINEA. She is panting and distraught.]

DULCINEA: I had to come back.

DON: I'm glad you did.

DULCINEA: I couldn't go through with it.

DON: You mean you nearly got caught.

DULCINEA: What? What are you saying?

DON: We haven't got time for this damsel in distress performance anymore. The police will be here shortly and you are facing imprisonment for child trafficking and six counts of murder.

DULCINEA: Please, don't talk to me like that. You know that inwardly I'm a good person who has led a bad life. I need your help.

DON: I have something to tell you; it is a sorrowful story of trust exploited and love abused. I went to the airport. You were there to collect something coming through the passenger terminal, not to identify a diamond struggler. The items are precious, far more precious than diamonds, they were three eight-year-old children you had procured and manage to keep when the police broke up the Ghana child sex ring. The reason the police at the airport accosted you when you took charge of the three children was because I telephoned the airport police and informed them.

DULCINEA: You did that? I was counting on your devotion; on your belief in me. You promised to help me!

DON: To procure diamonds, not children.

DULCINEA: I only just managed to escape. You misunderstand; I was saving those children from sex slavery not procuring them into it.

DON: You were saving them for your own nefarious interests. The three men you met on the Thames Embankment that are now dead. You did not meet them by chance; it was prearranged. They were part of the Ghana child sex slavery gang. When they met you, they recognized you as a member of the gang, you were just a young woman alone, and so they would relax their guard. It was easy for you to draw a gun on them, disarm them, make them kneel in front of you and then coldly execute them in the style of the London serial killer. Therefore, as soon as the police discovered that the three men were child traffickers the executions would be accredited to the London serial killer. Brilliant. Really brilliant reasoning. What went wrong? Did the third man try to knock the gun out of your hand as you shot him rendering you unconscious on the ground?

DULCINEA: Not quite.

DON: But quite near enough to what happened. Then, who should come along to help you but the London serial killer himself? Of all the luck, sic friat crustulum, thus the cookie crumbles, but even that you worked to your advantage.

DULCINEA: You make me the villain of the piece, yet I have done nothing more than yourself. I executed criminals escaping justice for crimes against children.

DON: You disposed of people in your way. You did not need them anymore. You have the European contacts list you stole off Teddy. That is why Teddy and his wife had to die isn't it? Why you had to kill them? You stole the contacts list off his computer. It is possible that it was you who informed the police in Ghana about the child sex ring to rid yourself of them. They had served their purpose.

DULCINEA: Supposition. All supposition.

DON: But right, nonetheless. Then, there was the fourth murder in England; the man you said was blackmailing you. He wasn't a Blackmailer; he was another member of the Ghana set up, another person in the way you no longer needed, another person to be got rid of. You could hardly kill him in your flat so you had me follow him to see where he lived and you executed him in his own flat again in the style of the London serial killer. Very clever; cold, ruthless, clever.

Blood, Passion & Self-Sacrifice

DULCINEA: If that is all true then how alike we are, fallen angels seeking redemption.

DON: If desire for redemption lingers within your heart, hand the contact list to the police.

DULCINEA: There is no contact list; otherwise, I would give it to them.

DON: That's a lie. If you intended redemption, then you would not have bolted at the airport after you took charge of the three children when the authorities accosted you. You could have given the police the contact list and told them the explanation you have given to me. I would have granted you the executions of the four men in London as committed by me, the London serial killer. Teddy and his wife's death in a car crash need never be questioned as anything more than an automobile accident and you would have walked from the court free for helping the authorities break up the Ghana child sex trafficking ring. I can still save you, but you must give me the contact list.

DULCINEA: There isn't one!

[Off stage, there is a knock on the front door.]

DON: That will be the police. Let me save you, give me the contact list.

DULCINEA: There isn't one! For possibly the first time since we have met, I am actually telling you the truth! You're my Don Quixoté; please, help me. If you ever felt anything for me, please, help me to escape!

DON: For you, life is just lying and ambition. You will follow the Devil's road to your doom. I can save you, but only from yourself. Give me the contact list.

[The knocking on the front door is louder. DULCINEA makes to go, but DON blocks DULCINEA'S exit. DULCINEA is near panic. DULCINEA produces a gun.]

DULCINEA: Please, don't make me use this. Please! Just let me go!

DON: You know I can't let you go; that is not the promised end. We were fated to meet. I have been praying to meet you for a long time.

DULCINEA: We met purely by chance.

DON: If you believe in God, there is no such thing as chance, just the illusion of chance. I have executed many criminals, but there is one criminal that I cannot execute, however, you can.

DULCINEA: Who? You?

DON: You can end my suffering. I called on the spirits for help and they sent me one of God's once greatest Angels. 'De profundis clamavi ad te domine.' Out of the depths I cried out to you, O Lord, and you answered me by sending me a Fallen Angel.

DULCINEA: I cannot kill you. I like you. You're my friend.

DON: I'm an impediment in your way.

DULCINEA: You're my friend!

DON: I'm an obstacle preventing you from achieving your objective. Yet, you may do some good despite yourself. Unnatural deeds breed unnatural acts; if it's to be done, best do it quickly.

[DON goes to take the gun.]

DULCINEA: No, please, I can't go to jail. It would kill me. Just let me go. Don, please, don't make me do this. I beg you, please!

[DULCINEA shots the gun. Pause.]

DON: Exitus acta probat; the end justifies the means. Thank you. You are my salvation.

DULCINEA: No, oh, no. I didn't mean it. Oh, Don, why wouldn't you just let me go? Why? Don, I did not mean to shoot you!

[DULCINEA helps DON to the settee. DULCINEA holds DON'S hand. The BALLERINA goes to DON. The sound of hammering on the front door is louder.]

DON: 'Here's a knocking, indeed!' If it is the door to heaven then I shall join my granddaughter. If it's to hell, then my suffering continues. But, if there is nothing beyond the door, then this is the end and I'm free from the pain.

DULCINEA: Don, I didn't mean it. Don, I did not mean to shoot you.

DON: I know. For the first time, you have actually told me the truth and, perhaps, there lies your salvation. You are a celestial emissary fulfilling your destiny; you are free from guilt. I prayed for help and I received it. Be careful for what you pray for because sometimes the Gods answer one's prayers in ways one cannot imagine. In return, I may have helped you to redemption despite yourself my damsel in distress. Your lies to the police are useless now. I'm glad we met. I have no regrets, I asked for help and you came. There are no regrets. Vale et tibi gratias ago, farewell and I thank you, my Fallen Angel, my heaven-sent Daemon, my Redeemer, my Dulcinea.

[DON dies. DULCINEA is crying. DULCINEA kisses DON'S forehead and hand. DULCINEA embraces DON. The BALLERINA kneels by DON and embraces him also. Sound of the front door being smashed in.

The lights fade to blackout.]

Heroes of Yesterday

A comedy.

M C Sanders

List of Characters:

Sebastian Hardwick - a sixty something Professor of Drama and an ex-actor

Young Sebastian - Sebastian Hardwick aged twenty something

Dolores DeWinter - a sixty something actress

Young Dolores - Dolores DeWinter aged twenty something

Elizabeth - Sebastian's granddaughter. A university student reading English.

Rex - Dolores' agent.

Dr Marion Davis - the Head of the Faculty where Sebastian teaches.

Sylvia - Elizabeth's friend at university.

Head villain & his three henchmen

Three students - 1 girl & 2 boys.

An everyman to play: TV Presenter, TV voice-over, the Major of Solihull & the Major of Wigan.

[Other minor characters are played by members of the cast.]

Blood, Passion & Self-Sacrifice

1st Scene

TV PRESENTER [*Voice off*]: Now whatever you do, don't change channels. Because here on Channel 47 we return to the television series that we guarantee is about to take the nation by storm. Another chance to see those derring-do, romantic adventures of old starring Sebastian Hardwick and Dolores DeWinter. Films made for TV that entertained our mums and dads all those years ago, I mean, of course, our series called, *Heroes of Yesterday*.

[*Into the film. Set in medieval England. Enter YOUNG SEBASTIAN swinging in on a vine as Robin Hood. There is dramatic incidental music throughout.*]

YOUNG SEBASTIAN: Little John and Friar Tuck take that food we took off the High Sheriff of Nottingham and distribute it to the poor, honest citizens of England!

VOICES OFF: Aye, Aye, Robin!

YOUNG SEBASTIAN: So, this is the castle of the sinister and deceitful Sir Guy of Gisbourne, is it?

[*Enter YOUNG DOLORES as Maid Marion*]

YOUNG DOLORES: Robin, what are you doing here in the castle? If you're caught you will be killed instantly.

YOUNG SEBASTIAN: Marion, I had to come to see if you were safe from the treacherous Prince John and his henchman, the evil Sir Guy of Gisbourne.

YOUNG DOLORES: Oh, Robin, you're so valiant and reckless; yet so gentle and caring.

[They kiss.]

YOUNG SEBASTIAN: Marion, will you come back with me to Sherwood Forest? I can offer you naught but a future of good, clean living and danger, but we will be together and we are in love. You do love me, Marion, don't you?

YOUNG DOLORES: It is because I love you, Robin, that I shall come with you. We can face any thing together. Oh, Robin, every day since you went away to fight for freedom in the forest my soul has been in torment thinking that something terrible might happen to you and that you would never know that I loved you. There, I have said the word, 'love'. Your love has pierced my heart with an arrow as deadly as any that Cupid may fire. Before, I was too proud and a fool, a fool, a fool, but now I have said the word, 'love'.

YOUNG SEBASTIAN: It does not worry you that you are a noble Norman by birth and that I am a mere Saxon?

YOUNG DOLORES: There is no such thing as Normans and Saxons in England, but Englishmen and Englishwomen fighting to live in a free world.

[Enter SIR GUY OF GISBOURNE & HIS 3 HENCHMEN.]

YOUNG DOLORES: Ooh, Robin, it is the wicked Sir Guy of Gisbourne and his henchmen, we are doomed!

SIR GUY: Robin Hood, you will never leave Nottingham Castle alive and return to your beloved Sherwood Forest and to freedom. Just behind that door there are ten thousand marauding Norman soldiers waiting for my command to kill you. You are my prisoner and the whole of England will be under the tyrannical rule of my beloved leader, Prince John!

YOUNG SEBASTIAN: Ah, you forget, Sir Guy, that I am the deadliest bowman and the greatest swordsman in the whole of England. Fifty gold sovereigns say that I can trim the whiskers on my Lord High Sheriff's beard!

[YOUNG SEBASTIAN *throws a purse onto the floor. He has a sword fight with* SIR GUY & THE 3 HENCHMEN. *YOUNG SEBASTIAN wins the fight and a kiss from YOUNG DOLORES.* SIR GUY & THE 3 HENCHMEN *lay dead on the floor.*]

YOUNG DOLORES: Listen to me, my love, England is mightier than mere Normans and Saxons. It belongs to us all to live peacefully together as free people mutually respecting each other's rights.

YOUNG SEBASTIAN: Then, Marion, come with me to Sherwood Forest and fight with the merry men and I against the treacherous Prince John, hoping for the time when our noble King Richard returns from fighting in the Holy Lands to restore peace and freedom throughout this land of ours. We can get Friar Tuck to marry us.

YOUNG DOLORES: So, off we go to save England and to freedom. Oh, Robin, please, lead us to victory!

YOUNG SEBASTIAN: Then let us cry: God for King Richard, England and St. George!

[*They race off. The incidental music builds to a crescendo.*]

M C Sanders

2nd Scene

[The office of Dolores' theatrical agent. Reviews and schedules are scattered across a desk. REX, her agent, reads aloud. DOLORES listens intently.]

REX: And here's a really good one! This is the best of the lot. *[Reading from a newspaper]* 'Best on the Box. The best thing to hit our tele screens in years. Miss. Dolores DeWinter, veteran actress' -

DOLORES: Veteran actress!!

REX: Just bear with me Dolores and listen. 'Miss. Dolores DeWinter, veteran actress of stage and screen, shines in these popular classics of old as she and her on screen partner, Sebastian Hardwick, battle against dastardly villains to find love and romance in times gone by. Great stuff for both young and old and propelling Miss. DeWinter and Mr Hardwick back into the celebrity firmament where they both rightly belong.'

DOLORES: 'Back into the celebrity firmament where they both rightly belong.'

REX: And you know what that means, Dolores, don't you?

DOLORES: Lots of money.

REX: Exactly. And listen to this one, 'Delicious Dolores' –

DOLORES: Now, that's more like it.

REX: 'Delicious Dolores battles in love to win all our hearts in these rediscovered gems shown on Channel 47 under the title *Heroes of Yesterday*. With her on screen partner Sebastian

Blood, Passion & Self-Sacrifice

Hardwick, Miss. DeWinter shows that the fight for love and noble causes is just as popular now as ever before. Set the TV recorder if you're going out, these are not to be missed.' And here's another one, 'Another riveting performance from Dolores DeWinter -'

DOLORES: '- riveting performance', they must think that I work in a shipyard. All these lovely reviews in the press are marvellous; I get the picture, Rex. This is amazing! I didn't even know that Channel 47 existed until you rang me up and told me which button to push on the remote control.

REX: According to the ratings, Dolores, last night twenty million viewers watched you and Seb in *Robin Hood, quest for Freedom* and that is expected to rise next week to twenty-five million viewers for *Buccaneers in Love.* Twenty-five million. That's more than will watch any other TV channel.

DOLORES: Last night, twenty million viewers knew which button to press on their remote control to watch Channel 47. How?

REX: It's mentioned on Internet sites, in celeb magazines, even in the popular press.

DOLORES: I must start buying a newspaper.

REX: Dolores it's different nowadays from when you and Seb made these films. Back then there were only two television channels, both in black and white and both on for just a few hours each night.

DOLORES: Where now, there are so many channels that I doubt if anybody is sad enough to be able to name all of them and the channels broadcast endlessly.

REX: More important, it's the stuff that the television stations are broadcasting. Not one of them is making programmes that provide people with romantic heroes or role models who triumph over adversity, who right the wrong and win the love of their desire.

DOLORES: And twenty million viewers took the trouble to find out which button to press on their remote control to watch a load of old rubbish I made decades ago.

REX: A load of old rubbish? Dolores, modern classics, please.

DOLORES: Modern classics!

REX: Dolores all the forecasts show that twenty million is just the beginning. This is going to grow and grow kiddo. Now then, my dear, we really need to exploit this, to grab it by the bollocks and run with it.

DOLORES: Rex, I can always trust in you to find just the right metaphor to sum up any situation.

REX: We will maintain the artistic integrity of these modern classics, of course, that goes without saying - which is why I didn't say it.

DOLORES: Rex, can we get to the point.

REX: The point being, Dolores, is that this is our big lottery win, our gravy train arriving in the station, our - my - pension plan. We're already talking about world rights syndication including America. I've booked you in for the circuit of chat show appearances on all the TV and radio channels. Every newspaper wants to interview you, special features in their magazines, big spreads.

Blood, Passion & Self-Sacrifice

DOLORES: This is bizarre! All those wonderful roles I have performed on the stage: Juliet, Phaedra, Hecuba, Medea, Lady Macbeth, Cleopatra, the Duchess of Malfi, to mention but a few, and it's a load of old codswallop that I made decades ago that will make me famous. You know, at the time, when Seb and I made these shows, they enjoyed a certain popularity sure and we were recognised when we went to places, but it didn't last very long after the series had finished and we were no longer on the television. Twenty million viewers watched us last night and it is already anticipated that even more viewers will watch us next week? That means that we are more popular now than when the series was first shown on the television all those years ago. Madness. Absolute madness. *[Pause.]* So, how much money are we going to make out of all this?

REX: That's more like it. The whole thing is still up in the air, my dear, but I reckon we could be talking millions.

DOLORES: Millions of pounds? You're joking.

REX: Dolores, kiddo, you know me, I don't do funny when taking money.

DOLORES: Seb and I only made those television shows in the first place because we were both out of work at the time and we never really made that much money out of them, but now we're talking millions! It will seem strange being a celebrity in the popular press again after all these years. Indeed, one feels an almost erotic frisson about it.

REX: I knew you'd like it, girl.

DOLORES: I'm hooked.

REX: Also, there's a company interested in you doing a commercial to advertise their new soap.

DOLORES: Soap?

REX: Why not? It pays well. Apparently, the new product has a brand name similar to your surname. It's called 'Delovely'.

DOLORES: Delovely DeWinter. Whatever.

REX: And, I have commissioned someone to write your autobiography.

DOLORES: What?

REX: Not mentioning deeply personal details such as your date of birth and so on. No, no, no, no, no, it will stress more your professional career, lots of big, glossy pictures of you from your successful stage and screen appearances as: Juliet, Phaedra, Medea, Hecuba, Lady Macbeth, Cleopatra, the Duchess of Malfi, and all.

DOLORES: That sounds good. Places these 'modern classics' in perspective with my stage performances. I like that. And you have commissioned someone to write my autobiography? Well, I'll look forward to reading it.

REX: We'll have it ready to be in the shops by Christmas. Oh, Dolores, kiddo, it's all going to be marvellous!

DOLORES: It's all going to be financially lucrative, you mean. This is all so sudden - no time to consult my Cosmetic Surgeon, I'll have to rely on my Beautician, and I'll need a whole new wardrobe, of course. Rex, darling, it all sounds great!

REX: It certainly does, kiddo! I'll make the arrangements with the television chat shows, the newspapers, the radio stations and the soap company.

DOLORES: And I'll look absolutely drop dead gorgeous. Let the show and the money roll on!

[They exit]

3rd Scene

[SEBASTIAN & ELIZABETH in the study of their home. SEBASTIAN is reading and occasionally consults his notes. ELIZABETH is ready to go out to her friends].

ELIZABETH: Granddad, I'm going around to see my friend, Sylvia, for the evening.

SEBASTIAN: Oh, excellent. I could do with the house to myself to finish my lecture notes.

ELIZABETH: Is there anything you want before I leave?

SEBASTIAN: No, no, no, you go and enjoy yourself. I'm spending the evening reading this paper on, 'The Freudian analysis of infanticide in Euripides' latter tragedies' in preparation for my lecture tomorrow to my final year students.

ELIZABETH: Euripides. We have chosen a Euripides play to do for the University Drama Festival. The one to help raise money for the new University Theatre.

SEBASTIAN: The one to be performed in front of Prince William?

ELIZABETH: Yes. It was good of him to agree to come along, so we thought that we would choose a play that would be of interest to him.

SEBASTIAN: Excellent. And you have chosen Euripides. Well, which one of the great Greek master's plays did you choose?

ELIZABETH: *Medea.*

SEBASTIAN: You have chosen *Medea?*

ELIZABETH: Yes.

SEBASTIAN: *Medea* is a marvellous play. Although, a very difficult play for a young cast to do. The emotional range demanded by the story of a beautiful princess who is betrayed in love by her husband for another woman and so gets her sons, the young princes, to murder her husband's lover and - hold on! You're going to do this play in front of Prince William?

ELIZABETH: Yes. We thought it might be socially relevant and of interest of them.

SEBASTIAN: Of interest of him - yes! Socially relevant to him - yes! Especially, considering that his mother, the Princess of Wales, a beautiful princess almost certainly would have considered herself betrayed in love by her husband for another woman. But, it's hardly appropriate, Elizabeth, is it?

ELIZABETH: You have always said that drama should be provocative and relevant to its audience.

Blood, Passion & Self-Sacrifice

SEBASTIAN: Elizabeth, you will be lucky that he doesn't have you arrested for treason and locked away in the Tower.

ELIZABETH: Well, at least, that would get us a headline in the newspapers and the money to build the new University Theatre.

SEBASTIAN: Why can't you do *Mary Poppins* like you did last year? It's a lovely musical and everybody enjoyed it.

ELIZABETH: You fell asleep partway through it.

SEBASTIAN: I did not fall asleep; I was merely resting my eyes.

ELIZABETH: Granddad, you were snoring.

SEBASTIAN: I was not snoring.

ELIZABETH: The whole theatre heard you.

SEBASTIAN: I'd had a hard day lecturing and taking several tutorials. I admit that my attention may have drifted - momentarily.

ELIZABETH: Whatever. Anyway, this year the University Drama Group has decided to do Euripides' *Medea,* the story of a beautiful princess who avenges her husband's infidelity by getting her sons, the young princes, to kill his lover on their wedding day; I'm sure Prince William will love it. *[She kisses him on the cheek.]* Now, I'm off out. Good luck with the lecture notes. See you later.

SEBASTIAN: Elizabeth I really think that we need to discuss this.

[The front door slams shut. Exit SEBASTIAN].

4th Scene

[ELIZABETH arrives at friends' house. SYLVIA is watching the TV.

ELIZABETH: You have the television on?

SYLVIA: Yes, there's a new series on that everyone is talking about, *Heroes of Yesterday.* They're repeats of old TV films and they're great! Unfortunately, you've missed part of it. They're broken for the commercials.

ELIZABETH: Watching repeats of old TV films? Well, if we must.

SYLVIA: They're fantastic. Elizabeth, you'll love them. The commercials have nearly finished.

[A commercial. Enter DOLORES].

TV VOICE OVER *[Voice off]*: We asked actress Miss. Dolores DeWinter why her skin is still so soft and lovely. Well, Dolores what's the secret?

ELIZABETH: Oh, I know her. She's a famous stage actress.

DOLORES: Being a professional actress it is important to look after your skin. So, I wash every day in - Delovely.

[Chorus off echoing 'Delovely'.]

DOLORES: Frankly, it's a girl's best friend.

Blood, Passion & Self-Sacrifice

TV VOICE OVER *[Voice off]*: Well, Dolores, I think we would all agree that it - certainly works.

DOLORES: Thank you.

[Chorus off echoing 'Delovely'. Exit DOLORES. Commercial ends].

TV PRESENTER *[Voice off]*: And now continuing our series on Channel 47 of *Heroes of Yesterday*. Another chance to see those films made for TV that entertained our mums and dads all those years ago.

[Into the film. There is dramatic incidental music throughout. Set in Elizabethan times. Enter YOUNG DOLORES. She waits nervously expecting her lover to arrive.]

YOUNG DOLORES: How can my heart be at peace when my love, the valiant Englishman, Captain Drake, is to fight the overwhelming might of my country's dreaded war fleet, the Spanish Armada?

[Enter YOUNG SEBASTIAN swinging in on a rope as swashbuckling hero.]

YOUNG SEBASTIAN: Mr Smee!

VOICE OFF: Aye, Aye, Captain!

YOUNG SEBASTIAN: Make ready the mizzenmast, Mr Smee! We set sail with the noonday tide!

VOICE OFF: Aye, aye, Captain!

YOUNG DOLORES: Captain Drake, thank the heavens that you are safe!

YOUNG SEBASTIAN: My love, we have so little time together before my battle with the might of the Spanish Armada begins.

[They embrace.]

YOUNG DOLORES: Oh, Captain Drake every time you sail away to fight for freedom my soul is wracked like a bark tossed in a gale at sea thinking that something awful has happened to you and that you will never know that I love you. There, I have said the word 'love' and nailed my colours to the mast. Before, I was too proud and a fool, a fool, a fool, but now I have said the word, 'love'.

SYLVIA: Ooh, it's so romantic.

ELIZABETH: Oh, please! Just hand me the puke bucket.

YOUNG SEBASTIAN: Nothing will ever separate us again, not race, not pride, not war, not prejudices. In a monastery in the New World there is a statute that the priests call 'La Dama de Rosa' - the Lady of the Rose - that is how I have always thought of you.

ELIZABETH: Hold on! That's my grandfather!

SYLVIA: What? The Professor!

ELIZABETH: Yes! That's my grandfather!

SYLVIA: Ooh, so it is!!!

[Sylvia starts laughing. Enter SPANISH ADMIRAL & HIS 3 HENCHMEN.]

Blood, Passion & Self-Sacrifice

YOUNG DOLORES: The Spanish Admiral in charge of the mighty Spanish Armada, Captain Drake, we are doomed!

SPANISH ADMIRAL: Captain Drake, you will never leave these Spanish waters alive and return to your beloved England and to freedom. Just behind that door there are ten thousand marauding Conquistadors awaiting my command to kill you. You are my prisoner!

YOUNG SEBASTIAN: Ah! Fifty Pieces-of-Eight says that I can cut the plumes off the Spanish Admiral's hat.

[YOUNG SEBASTIAN throws a purse full of money onto the floor and he has a swordfight with the four villains.]

ELIZABETH: What the hell's my grandfather doing in trash like this?! He told me that when he was a professional actor that he used to do Shakespeare and Greek Tragedy! He explained to me how difficult it was to master French Alexandrine rhyming couplets in Racine! He would talk at length about the textual problems of translating Cervantes into English for a modern audience!

SYLVIA: Well, the villains in this are Spanish.

[YOUNG SEBASTIAN wins the fight and a kiss from YOUNG DOLORES].

YOUNG DOLORES: It doesn't seem to matter that I am Spanish and you are English and that our countries are at war.

YOUNG SEBASTIAN: Condesa, this isn't merely one country verses another. This is freedom verses tyranny. This is liberty liberating democracy. Our battle is the fight of all freedom loving people.

YOUNG DOLORES: Oh, Captain Drake, how right you are. So, off we go to save England and the new world from the tyrannical threat to freedom. Come, Captain Drake, lead us to victory!

[They race off. The incidental music builds to a crescendo.]

5th Scene

[SEBASTIAN & ELIZABETH in the study of their home.]

ELIZABETH: But, Granddad, why didn't you tell me?

SEBASTIAN: Because it didn't seem important, Elizabeth. When your grandmother was alive, I did work in the legitimate theatre performing Shakespeare, Racine, Tennessee Williams, Moliere, Euripides and the rest, but as a professional actor you have to go where the work is and so you do other things as well.

ELIZABETH: Like hack, romantic melodrama on the television?

SEBASTIAN: Of course. Most of which I would point out, young lady, is to an excellent standard and is superb drama. We faced all that kind of prudery and prejudice at the time, thank you very much, when some critics didn't even regard television drama as proper acting.

ELIZABETH: It's hardly Shakespeare though, is it?

SEBASTIAN: Nobody ever argued that it was. Although remember in its day Shakespeare was popular drama; it was later generations that regarded it as art. Those television melodramas in their day were regarded as ephemeral pieces of popular entertainment to be shown once and once only. They were never made to be repeated several times in one week, examined and studied, placed on DVDs, or what-have-you, to be shown over and over again with every nuance of the thing examined and dissected. They were never regarded as art.

ELIZABETH: Granddad, I'm worried over your reputation and standing in the University as a prominent professor and classical actor. These television shows will change everything.

SEBASTIAN: Elizabeth, there is really no need to worry. Those old films had a certain popularity and notoriety in their day, but that's all. One was recognised in the street by people when the programmes were actually being shown on the television, but as soon as they were off the air one was quickly forgotten. Now as then, I will be forgotten within a few weeks of being off the air just like the first time that they were shown. Within a month nobody will remember them or for that matter remember me.

ELIZABETH: Granddad, times have changed. Nowadays, programmes are repeated over and over again on the television and available on the Internet.

SEBASTIAN: Who would want to watch that dross more than once? Times haven't changed that much. You'll see, you mark my words. If anybody bothers to watch them nowadays, they will dismiss them for the rubbish they are.

[They exit]

M C Sanders

6th Scene

[DOLORES and the MAYOR of SOLIHULL. They wear raincoats and hold umbrellas. There is the noise of torrential rain and the odd thunderclap.]

DOLORES: Ladies and Gentleman I feel blessed that, as a professional actress I am given an opportunity like this to help to make a difference in the community and to be able to contribute in some albeit small way by giving something back to the community and to the many, many fans who have given me such marvellous support throughout my professional career. I am deeply moved that so many wonderful warm and loving people remember me for my performances in *Heroes of Yesterday* and that I am so warmly regarded and revered by you all. I am especially touched that so many of you have turned out to see me on such a cold and rain swept day as today. I count it as a rare privilege and an honour to be invited here to this shopping centre in the heart of Solihull to launch what I know will become an integral part of the local community in the years to come. So, if I can ask the Mayor of Solihull to hold my umbrella while I take the scissors to cut the ribbon. Thank you. It is with great pleasure that I declare this new Fish and Chip shop open!

7th Scene

[SEBASTIAN and Dr DAVIS, THE HEAD OF THE FACULTY, sit either side of a desk in her office.]

SEBASTIAN: I hate to play the role of telling tales out of school, but I really do think that this play that the students have chosen to perform to help raise money to build a new University Theatre is not really suitable to be performed in front of Prince William.

Blood, Passion & Self-Sacrifice

Dr DAVIS: Euripides' *Medea?*

SEBASTIAN: Yes. And as you are the Head of the Faculty, Dr Davis, I thought that I had better make you privy to my reservations about performing this particular play by Euripides in front of Prince William.

Dr DAVIS: *Medea.* Apart from the children murdering their father's lover, isn't that the one where the mother, Medea, murders her children at the end?

SEBASTIAN: Yes, yes, it is.

Dr DAVIS: It's excellent stuff. I really enjoyed that part of the play. It's one of my favourites. Didn't the BBC soap opera, *The Eastenders,* use it for one of their plots a few months ago?

SEBASTIAN: Probably.

Dr DAVIS: Killing the kids; it really is excellent stuff, but *The Eastenders* did not do the story as well as Euripides.

SEBASTIAN: That's because a television scriptwriter does not have as much time to write a scene as a theatre playwright. There's much more pressure on them to deliver the script quickly than there is in the theatre, so the chances are that it is not going to be as good.

Dr DAVIS: I see, Professor. You know, after a long, hard, tiring, mentally exhausting, even gruelling, day teaching the bright, young, agile little shits we call 'students' here at the University, there is nothing that I like better then to relax watching a good drama like *Medea.* Isn't there another play by Euripides where they kill the kids?

SEBASTIAN: Yes. *Hecuba.*

Dr DAVIS: Ooh, now that is a good one. That is a good one. Hecuba kills somebody else's children in that, doesn't she?

SEBASTIAN: Yes, she does.

Dr DAVIS: Excellent. Isn't that the play where they bake the children into a pie and serve it to their mother to eat?

SEBASTIAN: No. I think, Dr Davis, you're getting it confused with Shakespeare's *Titus Andronicus.*

Dr DAVIS: Yes, of course. Now that is a good play. The students did that play for us a couple of years ago, didn't they?

SEBASTIAN: Yes, two years ago.

Dr DAVIS: I dearly enjoyed that scene in the kitchen when they are preparing the pie with the actress imitating the popular television chief, Fanny Craddock.

SEBASTIAN: The students added that scene; it's not in the original Shakespearian text.

Dr DAVIS: Ah, the little dears. You know, even now, if I'm at home in my kitchen stuffing a chicken, I still have a private, little chuckle at that line, 'And all our children are reared on organically home-grown food'. It still makes me smile.

SEBASTIAN: Dr Davis, if I could bring you back to the point.

Dr DAVIS: Yes, Professor, of course. *[Pause]*. Just remind me, what was the point?

SEBASTIAN: *Medea* and Prince William.

Dr DAVIS: Well, I am certainly not going to tell the students that they cannot perform a play because it may offend somebody.

SEBASTIAN: I totally agree.

Dr DAVIS: Heavens above, if I went down that road, we would end up never doing any plays at all. Even last year when the students performed *Mary Poppins,* I received complaints from people in the audience about somebody snoring.

SEBASTIAN: Snoring. The offender had probably had a hard day lecturing and taking several tutorials. That's assuming it was one of the professors or, indeed, that they even worked for the University. Whoever it was, I, personally, did not hear anybody snoring.

Dr DAVIS: You must have been the only one who didn't. Anyway, Professor, regarding the performing of *Medea,* what I shall do is get in touch with our contact at the Palace and explain what play the students are going to perform and, then, it is up to the Palace whether they decide to attend or not.

SEBASTIAN: Good idea.

Dr DAVIS: After all, we only invited them because we thought it might raise a bit more money to help build the new University Theatre. It was good of them to offer to attend, but if they change their minds then so be it.

SEBASTIAN: We can always ask another celebrity to come.

Dr DAVIS: Exactly. Indeed, Professor Hardwick, nowadays you are something of a celebrity yourself with your recent appearances on television.

SEBASTIAN: Oh, I'd hardly call myself a celebrity, Dr Davis.

Dr DAVIS: I feel you're being too modest.

SEBASTIAN: I have not watched any of these repeats of my old television films.

Dr DAVIS: I have, Professor, and they are excellent.

SEBASTIAN: Or taken any interest in the trivia and tittle-tattle surrounding them.

Dr DAVIS: Then, perhaps you should. How are your students reacting to all this?

SEBASTIAN: I think that my newly required fame is a bit of a novelty and a bit of a distraction for the students. For example, yesterday, I was giving a lecture to the second-year students on the German playwright Friedrich Schiller and the relationship of his plays to Goethe and Sturm und Drang drama in Weimar classicism. When I had finished the lecture and I invited questions from the floor, the first question that I was asked was, 'Is it true that you were once short-listed for the part of James Bond?'.

Blood, Passion & Self-Sacrifice

Dr DAVIS: Really? I have not heard that bit of gossip before.

SEBASTIAN: It is all ephemeral nonsense and it will disappear on the wind as soon as the series has ended. Then, we can all get back to concentrating on work that is more worthwhile.

Dr DAVIS: Quite; but is it true, Professor, where you once short-listed for the part of James Bond?

SEBASTIAN: Of course, it is not tr- well, it was all a long time ago, you understand? One auditioned for many parts during one's career.

Dr DAVIS: Really?! Then, Professor, which James Bond was it that you were replacing?

SEBASTIAN: Which James Bond?

Dr DAVIS: I mean which actor?

SEBASTIAN: Sean Connery

Dr DAVIS: Wasn't he replaced by that rather handsome Australian chap?

SEBASTIAN: Yes. George Lazenby.

Dr DAVIS: Who, according to the press, couldn't act.

SEBASTIAN: That was a vicious critique circulated by the press; of course, he could act and performed very well in the part.

Dr DAVIS: But you, an established Shakespearian classical actor with the National Theatre and the Royal Shakespeare Company, you auditioned for James Bond and didn't get the part; whilst an Australian actor, whose acting career at that time amounted to carrying an empty cardboard box off a boat in a thirty second television commercial advertising chocolate bars, also auditioned for the part and got it.

SEBASTIAN: Yes.

Dr DAVIS: So, you a Shakespearian actor failed to get the part because he was better than you in the audition.

SEBASTIAN: Those parts are not selected purely on acting ability!

Dr DAVIS: But you were on the short-list.

SEBASTIAN: On the short-list? One doesn't like to boost.

Dr DAVIS: Who else was on the short-list with you?

SEBASTIAN: I don't know; it was a very long short-list.

Dr DAVIS: But, nevertheless, Professor, you were on it. And, certainly, your erstwhile Leading Lady, Dolores DeWinter, seems to have liked you. *[She takes a magazine out of the drawer of her desk.]* In this television magazine she says and I quote, 'Sometimes to work with, he was impossibly handsome.'

SEBASTIAN: Dolores said that about me?

Dr DAVIS: 'Sometimes to work with, he was impossibly handsome.' Look for yourself.

Blood, Passion & Self-Sacrifice

[She hands him the magazine].

SEBASTIAN: Where? It's just all pictures.

Dr DAVIS: No, it's not, there's a bit of writing at the bottom of the page.

SEBASTIAN: Oh, yes, 'Dolores DeWinter shares her Secrets of Romance'. What the hell did Dolores ever know about romance?

Dr DAVIS: Professor, just read a little further down the page on what she says about you.

SEBASTIAN: 'On co-star Sebastian Hardwick'.

Dr DAVIS: That's it.

SEBASTIAN: 'On co-star Sebastian Hardwick: Sometimes to work with, he was impossibly handsome.' *[Pauses to come to terms with it.]* I haven't seen Dolores in decades. I doubt that I would even recognise her now.

Dr DAVIS: There's a picture of what she looks like nowadays in the magazine. She looks a little older perhaps, but other than that she has hardly changed in forty years. If, as she says in the television commercial, it is due to the type of soap that she uses then I must start using it myself. You may keep the magazine, Professor. She obviously knows you.

SEBASTIAN: Obviously. *[He reads it again.]* 'Sometimes to work with, he was impossibly handsome.' It isn't even good grammar.

Dr DAVIS: I think we all know what she means.

SEBASTIAN: Strange world. During my days as an actor, I played: Romeo, Hamlet, Tartuffe, Oedipus, Algernon Moncrieff and Jimmy Porter all to great acclaim and people are more interested in this trivia.

Dr DAVIS: I am sure all those performances were excellent, Professor, but I'm afraid that I did not see them and neither did the vast majority of the population; however, most people, including myself, have seen *Heroes of Yesterday*.

SEBASTIAN: I'll make a point of watching the series myself. If only to see what all the fuss is about.

Dr DAVIS: That's good, because tonight's film sounds a really good one.

[SEBASTIAN searches through the magazine and reads. The scene changes as SEBASTIAN reads.]

SEBASTIAN: *'General Custer, death, love and glory,* Sebastian Hardwick and Dolores DeWinter face thousands of marauding Indians as General & Mrs George Armstrong Custer in this romantic adventure yarn about the massacre at the Little Big Horn.'

[Exit Dr DAVIS & SEBASTIAN.]

8th Scene

[Into the film. Enter YOUNG DOLORES. She is a Southern Belle of the mid. 19th century. There is dramatic incidental music throughout.]

YOUNG DOLORES: Can it really be four long years since I last saw my love, General George Armstrong Custer?

Blood, Passion & Self-Sacrifice

[YOUNG SEBASTIAN enters dressed as General Custer.]

YOUNG SEBASTIAN: Scarlet, my darling!

YOUNG DOLORES: George, please tell me that my eyes do not deceive me.

YOUNG SEBASTIAN: Scarlet, my darling, they do not!

YOUNG DOLORES: George, you're home at last. I've been waiting for so long for your return.

[They kiss.]

YOUNG SEBASTIAN: I'm sorry my darling for leaving you waiting all these long years whilst I was away fighting for freedom. Please forgive me, but even now I cannot stay long. On the way here I called in to see the President.

YOUNG DOLORES: The President of the United States of America?

YOUNG SEBASTIAN: Yes.

YOUNG DOLORES: But what could he want from you, George?

YOUNG SEBASTIAN: He wants me to re-join my regiment tonight.

YOUNG DOLORES: George, this is awful.

YOUNG SEBASTIAN: It's worse than awful.

YOUNG DOLORES: Why, George? Why? To where is the regiment riding?

YOUNG SEBASTIAN: To hell or to glory. It's perhaps the same thing.

YOUNG DOLORES: But that can mean only one thing, George; you're taking the regiment into the Black Hills to face 10,000 marauding Red Indians.

YOUNG SEBASTIAN: Yes. Six hundred of us to face ten thousand of them.

[There is the sound of arrows being fired and above their heads stuck in the wood appear several arrows.]

YOUNG SEBASTIAN: Indians!

[The RED INDIAN CHIEF & HIS THREE HENCHMEN enter.]

RED INDIAN CHIEF: So, this is the house of General Custer's squaw. We must kill General Custer and his noble band of six hundred soldiers and then the whole of the free world will be our slaves. General Custer you will never leave Fort Lincoln alive. Just behind that door there are ten thousand marauding Red Indians waiting for my command to kill you. You are my prisoner!

YOUNG SEBASTIAN: Fifty dollars says that I can cut off all the feathers from the Red Indian Chief's headdress.

[YOUNG SEBASTIAN throws a purse full of money onto the floor. He draws his sabre and pistols. They fight. The RED INDIAN CHIEF AND HIS 3 HENCHMEN are killed.]

Blood, Passion & Self-Sacrifice

YOUNG DOLORES: Oh, George, will your sacrifice at the Little Big Horn really save America and freedom?

YOUNG SEBASTIAN: Scarlet, this isn't merely a tribe of marauding Red Indians verse the United States of America. This is freedom verses tyranny. This is liberty liberating democracy. Our battle is the fight of all freedom loving people. For, it is the right of all free men to fight for the freedom of the land they love.

YOUNG DOLORES: George, every time that you have led a military campaign my soul has been wracked by the barbarous arrows of uncertainty thinking that something awful might happen to you and that you would never know that I love you. There, I have said the word 'love' and rallied around the flag for one glorious last stand. Before I was a fool, a fool, a fool, but now I have said the word, 'love'. Now you know that I love you. Yet, now you must go to sacrifice yourself so that others may live in freedom.

YOUNG SEBASTIAN: Oh, Scarlet, frankly, my dear, I don't give a damn about the Red Indians, but I am mighty pleased that we rode life's path together.

YOUNG DOLORES: But now I must journey through life alone.

YOUNG SEBASTIAN: And I go and lead the regiment into history.

[They kiss. The incidental music builds to a dramatic crescendo. YOUNG SEBASTIAN exits. YOUNG DOLORES swoons to the ground. Lights down, exit YOUNG DOLORES. A commercial. Enter MISS. DOLORES DEWINTER].

TV VOICE OVER *[Voice off]*: We asked the actress Miss. Dolores DeWinter why her skin is still so soft and lovely. Well, Dolores what's the secret?

DOLORES: Being a professional actress it is important to look after your skin. So, I wash every day in - Delovely.

[Chorus off echoing 'Delovely'.]

DOLORES: Frankly, it's a girl's best friend.

TV VOICE OVER *[Voice off]*: Well, Delores, I think we would all agree that it - certainly works.

DELORES: Thank you.

[Chorus off echoing 'Delovely'. Exit DOLORES.]

9th Scene

[A group of students hug around a tabloid newspaper. There are at least 2 girls and 2 boys; one of them is SYLVIA. They are reacting with a giggle of excitement to what they are reading. One boy has a rolled-up paper, which he uses with great enthusiasm to demonstrate certain points he is making during the scene.]

1st BOY STUDENT *[reads from the newspaper]*: "The reason Sebastian Hardwick was much loved for his film and stage work is possibly that he not only knew his onions when it came to acting, but in the carrot and onion department, or should we say the cucumber and onions lunchbox, he had the nickname, 'Cucumber-man'. This came about when in one play he had to wear tights for the part of the Roman General, Marc Anthony, much to the awe and amusement of everybody back stage who gave him the honorary title of 'Cucumber-man' when they saw the size of our warrior's weapon - and we don't mean his sword. But, before the censor reaches for his editing blade, this is one of his talents that was seen on stage only and it has not been seen on screen.'

[They laugh.]

SYLVIA: But if it were that long he'd have to have special trousers made, otherwise, where would it go?

[The boys look at each other for an answer.]

2nd BOY STUDENT: Erm, he could strap it down his leg, I suppose.

SYLVIA: Wouldn't that be uncomfortable?

2nd BOY STUDENT: Only when he crossed his legs.

2nd GIRL STUDENT: It all sounds so vulgar and distinguishing. I can just imagine it.

1st BOY STUDENT: Exactly, surely you would notice. It's never struck me that the Professor has got a big dick - not that I have specifically looked.

SYLVIA: I have and he doesn't.

1st BOY STUDENT: Maybe you're looking on the wrong side of his trousers. He's right-handed, so he probably dresses on the right.

SYLVIA: How do you work that one out? Phil, here, is right-handed and he doesn't dress on the right.

[Phil covers his pelvic area in embarrassment.]

2nd GIRL STUDENT: I think that the whole thing sounds so disgusting, yet strangely, I find myself compelled, intrigued, fascinated, absorbed, attracted, beguiled, bewitched, captivated, engrossed, riveted, enthralled, entranced, smitten, intoxicated, *[Pause.]* spellbound, excited, aroused, impassioned, inflamed and quite interested actually by the whole idea.

SYLVIA: At his next lecture, then, we'll have to contrive to find out.

1st BOY STUDENT: How are we going to do that?

SYLVIA: By asking him subtle questions at the end of the lecture that will draw him out.

2nd BOY STUDENT: What, you mean such as, 'Excuse me, Professor, but it is rumoured that you are hung like a cucumber, is it true?'

SYLVIA: Well, I was thinking of more subtle questions than that.

1st BOY STUDENT: What we can do is observe him closely during the lecture and then compare notes afterwards. So, who thinks that he dresses on the right?

[The boys raise their hands.]

1st BOY STUDENT: And the left?

[SYLVIA raises her hand. The 2nd girl has not voted.]

2nd GIRL STUDENT: I'm still undecided. I need more time to think.

1st BOY STUDENT: Right, ok. So, most of us think that he dresses on the right, with one don't know.

[They exit.]

10th Scene

[DOLORES and the MAYOR of WIGAN. They wear raincoats and hold umbrellas. There is the noise of torrential rain and the odd thunderclap.]

DOLORES: Ladies and Gentleman I feel blessed that, as a professional actress I am given an opportunity like this to help to make a difference in the community and to be able to contribute in some albeit small way by giving something back to the community and to the many, many fans who have given me such marvellous support throughout my professional career. I am deeply moved that so many wonderful warm and loving people remember me for my performances in *Heroes of Yesterday* and that I am so warmly regarded and revered by you all. I am especially touched that so many of you have turned out to see me on such a cold and rain swept day as today. I count it as a rare privilege and an honour to be invited here to this shopping centre in the heart of Wigan to launch what I know will become an integral part of the local community in the years to come. If I can ask the Mayor of Wigan to hand me the scissors to cut the ribbon. Thank you. So, it is with great pleasure that I declare this new Special Discount Canine Saloon, Nail Pairing, Dog Bath and Poodle Parlour open.

11th Scene

[The scene changes to a lecture hall. SEBASTIAN talks whilst the students crane their necks to study his upper legs. He moves around as

M C Sanders

he talks and the students move their heads in unison watching avidly for evidence of 'the cucumber'. The chair next to the 2nd GIRL STUDENT is empty.]

SEBASTIAN: A play without an audience is like a world without a God. It is essential that there is an auditor listening to the stage character, watching their actions and making moral judgements on them; just as God watches our actions and makes moral judgements on us in real life. The relationship is actor - performance - auditor. In this sense a play must always exist within a world where God exists, where every word, every action and every stage effect has a meaning and so has a significance that the auditor, playing the role of God, can interpret and pass a moral judgement thereupon.

Theatre, therefore, must always be a communal activity in which all the parties involved, the actors, the writers, the artistic director, the producers, the production crew, the front of house staff and, of course, the audience, all share a set of given values and standards by which the play is judged. In essence, we still practice today the tribal art form of theatre found in ancient classical Greece and, to go even further back in time, by anthropological tribal communities.

Without the all-important auditor, the performance of the play is rendered to merely a repetition, in the sense described by the artistic director Peter Brook in his excellent book, *The Empty Space,* the deadly, spiritually empty repeating of a text devoid of any significance; whereas, with the introduction of the auditor, the actor is assisted to achieve a performance that is always fresh and imbued with a moral sense and meaning.

The stage is a reflection of life, but this artificially created life portrayed on the stage cannot be relived without a working system based on observing certain values and making value judgements. The auditor makes moral decisions on every aspect of the play either consciously or unconsciously on everything on stage; be it: the position and height of a chair, the texture of the costumes, the actor's movements, the method of expression used by the actors, etc, etc.

All forms of theatre need an audience. The auditor completes the steps of creation with the actor and the production team to produce that unique sense of the moment. The audience is indivisible to the action on stage and it is an active part of the event.

In this fashion, Samuel Beckett's two famous tramps in *Waiting for Godot* exist within an internal contradiction. Whilst they wait for Godot and search for things to occupy their time in order to keep themselves amused, the all-important auditor, by observing every movement and nuance on stage, is assisting the actor to realise a performance at each individual moment of the play, and so is imbuing meaning into the meaningless universe of the characters.

Right, are there any questions?

1st BOY STUDENT: So, Professor on the stage any movement of say a limb has significance?

SEBASTIAN: Yes, if I move my arm, so, it does not necessary mean anything in real life but in a play, it might be a metaphor of great significance.

SYLVIA: What about if you moved a larger limb? *[The others look at her]*. I mean like a leg, or something, your left leg perhaps?

SEBASTIAN: Well, if I walk. *[He walks across to them.]* Again, it has no real meaning in real life, but on stage it may. Likewise, if I lift my left leg, high into the air, like this. *[The students stare in concentration.]* Once again, it has no real meaning in real life, but on stage it may. Right, so are there any further questions?

[SEBASTIAN places his left foot on the empty chair by the 2nd GIRL STUDENT. She cries 'Oooh!' as she watches him, her eyes fixed on the upper part of his left leg and then she swoons into a faint. SEBASTIAN starts in surprise. The others fuss around her.]

SYLVIA: No, Professor, I think you're just answered all our questions for the moment, thank you.

[Blackout.]

INTERVAL

12th Scene

[The office of Dolores' theatrical agent. DOLORES and REX are in the room.]

DOLORES: Every television chat show I appear on, every newspaper and every magazine I'm interviewed for, every radio station I'm a guest on, even people I meet in the street, they all ask where is Sebastian Hardwick? I'm getting a bit tired - no, I'm getting a bit sick to bloody death of replying, 'Well, we haven't seen each other for an awfully long time now, understand?' Rex, will you find him?

REX: Dolores, my dear, I have looked and looked and looked without success.

Blood, Passion & Self-Sacrifice

DOLORES: Then, look again, for heaven's sake! We need him.

REX: I have scoured all the theatrical agencies. He is definitely not working in the profession either in this country or internationally. Dolores, can't you give me some indication of what might have happened to him?

DOLORES: I haven't seen him in decades. I'm not sure whether I would even recognise him now. It's all so long ago. He could have left the country. Rex, he could be dead for all I know.

REX: Let's hope for our sake that he's not dead. Dead doesn't look good in print. It doesn't make for nice reading. Think, Dolores, when was the last time you saw him?

DOLORES: That would have been just after the funeral of his wife Elizabeth. She died in childbirth. It was a big shock to everybody. Poor Seb was devastated. We lost touch with each other shortly after that. I remember the baby survived though. Yes, that's right. Elizabeth gave birth to a daughter and Seb called the baby girl after his wife, Elizabeth. She must be in her early forties now. She was called Elizabeth, after her mother, yes, that was her name.

REX: That would all fit in with the fact that he disappears off the theatrical map around then.

DOLORES: He must have left the profession to bring up his daughter. Yes, of course. That's what he has done. I feel awful for not keeping in contact with him if he was bringing up the little girl by himself. You know, I really do feel quite annoyed with myself over that.

REX: *[Hands her a handkerchief]*: Do you need a handkerchief, my dear?

DOLORES: No, I bloody well don't. You've been watching too many of my old romantic, adventure movies. I said that I felt 'quite annoyed with myself' not emotionally laid waste by the turbulent, impersonal forces of fate.

[REX blows his nose on the handkerchief and puts it back into his pocket.]

DOLORES: Oh, Rex!

REX: The daughter, Elizabeth, may explain why he left the profession, but it doesn't tell us where he is.

DOLORES: Can't we hire a private detective, or someone, to locate Seb? I'm sure he can't be that difficult to find.

REX: Private detectives cost money. There is a cheaper and better option open to us.

DOLORES: Pray do explain.

REX: We shall ask the media to find him for us. The television, newspaper and radio people like that sort thing. A noble crusade in which they can get their viewers, readership or listeners involved. A nice human-interest story that shouldn't run for too long. Hopefully, a story with a happy ending. And, more important for us, lots more free publicity.

DOLORES: Rex, at times, you do verge on the genius.

REX: I have my moments, my dear. Now, I'll make a few phone calls to set up the interviews for you.

Blood, Passion & Self-Sacrifice

DOLORES: Whilst I pay a quick visit to my Beautician.

REX: And I'm sure we will see Miss. Dolores DeWinter and Mr Sebastian Hardwick acting out a big reunion scene for the benefit of the public in the very near future.

[They exit.]

13ᵗʰ Scene

TV PRESENTER *[Voice off]*: And now continuing our series *Heroes of Yesterday*. Another chance to see Sebastian Hardwick and Dolores DeWinter in those films made for TV that entertained our mums and dads all those years ago.

[Into the film. Enter YOUNG DOLORES. She wears a romantic version of a nurse's uniform of 1854 and she carries a lamp. There is dramatic incidental music throughout.]

YOUNG DOLORES: I must check to see if the consignment of balaclavas has arrived yet. How noble of the women of England to kit them to save our valiant soldiers from the onslaught of another vicious, cruel Russian winter out here in the Crimea.

[YOUNG SEBASTIAN enters dressed as an 1854 cavalry officer of the 27ᵗʰ Lancers]

YOUNG SEBASTIAN: Florence, my darling!

YOUNG DOLORES: Alfred! You're safe from the volley and thunder of the Russian cannons.

YOUNG SEBASTIAN: Florence, my darling, when I first came in, you looked - distracted. What were you thinking?

YOUNG DOLORES: Oh, I was just thinking of mountains green, pleasant pastures, clouded hills, a green and pleasant land, and a host of golden daffodils fluttering and dancing in the breeze.

YOUNG SEBASTIAN: Ah, yes, England. How we would all dearly love to return to that sacred land from this mouth of hell here in the Crimea. However, I must rejoin my regiment tonight.

YOUNG DOLORES: Tonight! But Alfred that can mean only one thing!

YOUNG SEBASTIAN: Yes, we are engaging the enemy. I have a message here from the Chiefs of Staff to the 27th Lancers. We are to charge the Russian artillery positions at Balaklava.

YOUNG DOLORES: Alfred, the Russians have their strongest cannon batteries situated in that valley! A cavalry charge against cannons! It will be suicide! You will be riding into a valley of death!

YOUNG SEBASTIAN: Yes. Six hundred of us to face the iron might of the Russian cannon fire. It will be a wild charge into hell or glory.

YOUNG DOLORES: Someone has blundered. The message must be wrong.

YOUNG SEBASTIAN: If it is then it shall be a magnificent blunder. But, Florence, ours is not to reason why; ours is but to do and die.

[Enter RUSSIAN GENERAL & HIS 3 HENCHMEN.]

Blood, Passion & Self-Sacrifice

YOUNG DOLORES: Alfred, the Russian General in charge of the cannons and his cohorts, we are doomed!

RUSSIAN GENERAL: Alfred, Lord Tennyson, you will never lead that bold charge against our beloved Russian cannons to save England and freedom. Just behind that door there are ten thousand marauding Cossacks awaiting my command to kill you. You are my prisoner!

YOUNG SEBASTIAN: Ah! Fifty guineas say that with a flash and a stroke of my sabre I can cut off the epaulettes from the Russian General's tunic!

[YOUNG SEBASTIAN throws a purse full of money onto the floor. He draws his sabre. They fight. The four Russians are killed.]

YOUNG SEBASTIAN: Ah! Shattered and sundered!

[YOUNG SEBASTIAN & YOUNG DOLORES kiss.]

YOUNG DOLORES: Oh, Alfred, will your wild charge at the Russian cannons really save the free world?

YOUNG SEBASTIAN: Florence, this isn't merely Russia verses England and France. This is freedom verses tyranny. This is liberty liberating democracy. Our battle is the fight of all freedom loving people.

YOUNG DOLORES: Alfred, every time that you have charged into battle my soul has been wracked by the ruthless sabre cuts of uncertainty, thinking that something awful might happen to you and that you would never know that I love you. There, I have said the word 'love' and charged wildly into your heart. Before I was a fool, a fool, a fool, but now I have said the word, 'love'. Now you know that I love you and you must storm into that valley, that mouth of hell, with cannon to the right of you, cannon to the left of you and cannon in front of you so that others may live in freedom.

YOUNG SEBASTIAN: My darling, the distance that we must charge is only half a league, half a league, half a league onward, I shall be back by your side before night fall. *[He gives her a locket.]* Here, I would like you to keep this until I return. It was my mothers.

YOUNG DOLORES: Oh, Alfred, I think that you are one of the most noblest men that I have ever known. When you ride, you shall carry my love with you.

[They kiss].

YOUNG SEBASTIAN: Come, Florence, and forward the Light Brigade! Charge for the guns!!

[They exit. The incidental music builds to a crescendo. A commercial. Enter MISS. DOLORES DEWINTER].

TV VOICE OVER *[Voice off]*: We asked the actress Miss. Dolores DeWinter why her skin is still so soft and lovely. Well, Dolores what's the secret?

DOLORES: Being a professional actress it is important to look after your skin. So, I wash every day in Delovely.

[Chorus off echoing 'Delovely'.]

DOLORES: Frankly, it's a girl's best friend.

TV VOICE OVER *[Voice off]*: Well, Delores, I think we would all agree that it - certainly works.

Blood, Passion & Self-Sacrifice

DELORES: Thank you.

[Chorus off echoing 'Delovely'. Exit DOLORES.]

14th Scene

[SEBASTIAN & ELIZABETH. She holds a tabloid newspaper.]

SEBASTIAN: Elizabeth, it was a cucumber.

ELIZABETH: Don't keep saying that, Granddad, I can read.

SEBASTIAN: It was an actual real cucumber.

ELIZABETH: Granddad, please!!!

SEBASTIAN: Elizabeth, listen to me. It was a vegetable that has the nomenclature of 'cucumber'.

ELIZABETH: What?!

SEBASTIAN: It was meant to be a joke. We were playing in *Anthony and Cleopatra* at the Old Vic. All the men wore very, short Roman tunics, almost like miniskirts. Well, Derrick Hardy, who was playing Enobarbus, a beautiful earthy performance, that stressed the battle-worn facet of the character, yet displayed a soul desperate to be loved -

ELIZABETH: Granddad, can you just get on with it!

SEBASTIAN: He was out shopping in the market across from the theatre just before a matinee performance. He noticed on a vegetable stall these rather large cucumbers and he had this amusing idea that it would be great fun if all the men in the cast wore, backstage, one of these large cucumbers under their Roman tunic. Well, he didn't have very much money on him at the time and you didn't get many of these large cucumbers to the pound.

ELIZABETH: I can image.

SEBASTIAN: So, he could only afford to buy two of them: one for him and one for me. Anyway, we wore these ridiculously large cucumbers backstage under the Roman tunics and everybody thought that it was extremely funny. However, unfortunately, the press got news of the story and blew it out of all proportion. Hence, the sobriquet of -

ELIZABETH: -'Cucumber man'. Granddad, it's such a bizarre explanation that it must be true, but nobody is ever going to believe it.

SEBASTIAN: That is the nature of the beast of the popular press; it always panders to the lowest common denominator and people seem to prefer that to the truth.

ELIZABETH: I'm just going to have to live with this.

SEBASTIAN: No! No, you're not. I don't mind if all this is affecting me only, but if it's affecting you too then that's different. Elizabeth, you and your mother are my only family, and I am not going to stand for this. I thought that the public hype would all blow over, just as it did at the time when these films were first shown, but now it's all gone too far. *[He produces a letter from his pocket.]* I have received a letter from Dolores. They ran some sort of campaign in the media to find me and one of the students must have written to her to tell her where I live. She wants me to appear with her on television and in the press to promote *Heroes of Yesterday*.

Blood, Passion & Self-Sacrifice

Outrageous, but it is time that we met and I had a frank exchange of views with her!

15th Scene

[A meeting room at the University. There is a table with a bowl of fruit on it. There are bananas among the fruit. A waste paper bin stands by the desk. DOLORES and REX are in the room.]

DOLORES: I never thought Seb would go into teaching. University professor. And a very, prestigious university at that.

REX: He's done well for himself, that's for sure.

DOLORES: Yes, he has, which probably means that he won't be too keen to help us to promote, *Heroes of Yesterday.*

REX: I think I'll reserve judgement on that until he sees the paycheque. I didn't come all the way down here to see him for nothing. What was that lecture he was giving when we walked in?

DOLORES: 'The Meaning and Significance of the Dramatic Moment in an Existential Universe.'

REX: Doesn't *Heroes of Yesterday* have meaning and significance?

DOLORES: It has as much or as little as anything else. Academics love to make simple ideas sound complex. In real life any action is arbitrary and its meaning or significance is messy, uncertain or quite possibly non-existent; whilst in a play all actions have some form of meaning because they are written by human beings with something to say to other human beings -

[As she speaks, DOLORES picks up a banana from the bowl of fruit on the table. She holds it at the bottom and starts peeling it. Once she has got it peeled, she looks up and realises that REX is staring at her. He has read far more into her actions than merely peeling a banana. She sighs holding the banana at its base.]

DOLORES: Dream on, lover-boy!

[DOLORES bites a large chunk off the top of the banana. REX cringes. DOLORES dumps the rest of the banana into the waste paper bin.]

REX: I doubt if I shall ever look at a banana quite in the same light ever again. You know, Dolores, I think that you would fit in well at a university. Really, I mean it. After all, you already do guest lectures on acting. In fact, it may well be a lucrative vein of gold to tap into, if you know how to go about it. Definitely something to which I must give a bit more thought.

DOLORES: Thinking about money, now that's the Rex I'm use to.

REX: Ah, and talking of money, here comes Sebastian. He must have finished his lecture. Looks like he has one of his students with him. Now, remember, Dolores, be Miss. Wonderful for him.

DOLORES: Miss. Wonderful?

[Enter SEBASTIAN & ELIZABETH. DOLORES goes to SEBASTIAN to give him a theatrical hug.]

DOLORES: Seb, darling, lovely to see you again after all these years!

SEBASTIAN: Alas, Dolores, the circumstances do not permit me to share that sentiment.

DOLORES: Oh, Seb, darling, so cold.

SEBASTIAN: Well, how would you greet the ghost of Christmas past?

DOLORES: The ghost of Christmas past, well let's see Mr Scrooge if we can get you to repent by the end of the evening.

REX: Sebastian, if I may call you that, Dolores never had anything to do with the airing of *Heroes of Yesterday* or the stories published about you.

SEBASTIAN: Who is this?

DOLORES: This is Rex, my agent.

SEBASTIAN: Your agent! You came here with your agent.

DOLORES: Of course, I came here with my agent. Your letter demanded to see me about the television company showing our old movies, so who else should I have brought?

SEBASTIAN: Ah, I see, sorry, you're right. *[Turning to Rex.]* How do you do?

REX: I do very well, thank you. Something, by the end of this meeting I hope that I can say about all three of us.

SEBASTIAN: I've been out of professional acting for over thirty years. I've worked here as a professor for nearly twenty years. I'm too old to start racing around a media circus of chat shows, press interviews and God knows what.

DOLORES: 'Too old.' I sincerely hope that I never consider myself too old for anything.

SEBASTIAN: Too old, too disinclined, too settled to want all this.

DOLORES: And then a wind of change came tap, tap, tapping at the casement window of your ivory tower to blow away the cobwebs.

SEBASTIAN: Dolores, I am sorry to have brought you and your agent all the way out here, but I thought that you were to blame for all this. If Channel 47 is to blame, then it is to them I need to talk.

DOLORES: Seb, all Channel 47 have done is show a few old movies that have proved to be extraordinarily popular.

SEBASTIAN: Then who am I to blame? I suppose you're going to tell me it's all the fault of the newspapers, the television and the radio chat shows.

DOLORES: If you're looking for someone to blame, Seb, then why don't you start by blaming yourself for making those movies in the first place?

ELIZABETH: Professor Hardwick is a highly respected academic. This is ruining his reputation.

REX: We are not here to ruin reputations, my dear, we are here to make them.

SEBASTIAN: Elizabeth, please, leave this to me.

Blood, Passion & Self-Sacrifice

DOLORES: Elizabeth?

SEBASTIAN: This is Miss. Elizabeth Hardwick, my granddaughter.

DOLORES: Your granddaughter. I see.

SEBASTIAN: My daughter, Dr. Elizabeth Hardwick, is in general practice at her surgery in London. This is her daughter, my granddaughter, Elizabeth. I'm afraid that we were not very imaginative when it came to choosing girl's names in my family.

DOLORES: I understand. My dear, I'm honoured to meet you. Your grandmother and I were good friends.

SEBASTIAN: Elizabeth is staying with me here at the University, temporarily, whilst she is studying for her degree.

DOLORES: I am truly delighted to meet you.

ELIZABETH: To be candid, I was actually quite tense at the thought of meeting you.

DOLORES: Am I really such a dragon? Don't answer that unless the answer is 'no'.

ELIZABETH: Dragon, no; formidable, yes.

DOLORES: Formidable. Well, there's a new word for my CV.

ELIZABETH: I admire you as a classical actress, I really do.

DOLORES: As a classical actress; not, just as an actress? You know, Elizabeth, the difference between high art and popular entertainment isn't as great as certain people would have you believe. Attitudes towards art change with time. One generation's dross is the next generation's art. I'm sure if we could bring William Shakespeare in a time machine into the present day and show him theatre companies doing, *The Merry Wives of Windsor,* he may have a wry smile about why are they doing that piece of old codswallop instead of one of his better plays, but he is not going to stop them performing it, is he? And, if it is regarded as art, nowadays, then so be it.

ELIZABETH: And *Heroes of Yesterday* is your equivalent to *The Merry Wives of Windsor?*

DOLORES: Clever girl. In some ways perhaps it is. Did your grandfather ever tell you about one of our greatest London West End successes? The one for which we both received London Theatre Critic Awards.

SEBASTIAN: We appeared in many plays together.

DOLORES: But *Romeo and Juliet* was probably our greatest hit.

ELIZABETH: You received an acting award for appearing in *Romeo and Juliet* on the West End, Granddad?

SEBASTIAN *[a little uneasy about all this]*: Yes, Elizabeth, yes, I did.

ELIZABETH *[impressed]*: Really!

Blood, Passion & Self-Sacrifice

SEBASTIAN: I was rather good in it, even though I say so myself. We were both given London Theatre Critic Awards for our performances.

ELIZABETH: Granddad, that's marvellous!

DELORES: We won the awards primarily because of our interpretation of the love scenes as I recall.

SEBASTIAN: We approached the play as a romance.

ELIZABETH: A romance? That's fine, that's a quite valid interpretation of the Shakespearian text.

DOLORES: But it was the scenes, or, at least, one scene, that we set in Juliet's bedchamber that really set the town buzzing and clinched the awards for us, wouldn't you agree Seb?

SEBASTIAN: We did emphasize the romantic facets of the characters, Dolores, yes, yes, we did.

ELIZABETH: The scene set in Juliet's bedchamber?

DOLORES: It was given a romantic interpretation; but, a very modern, romantic interpretation. Would you agree, Seb?

SEBASTIAN: For the time it was considered very modern, Dolores, yes.

ELIZABETH: A very modern, romantic interpretation *[The penny drops.]* What, you mean that you did a nude scene together?!

DELORES: It is justified by the Shakespearian text.

ELIZABETH: My grandfather prancing around on stage in the nude justified by a four-hundred-year-old Shakespearian text!

SEBASTIAN: We weren't prancing around, Elizabeth; it was all done very artistically and tastefully. Delores entered –

DELORES: -in the nude-

SEBASTIAN: -from stage left and I entered –

DELORES: - in the nude –

SEBASTIAN: - from stage right –

DELORES: - and we embraced in the middle.

ELIZABETH: In the nude! In public! My grandfather embracing in the nude in public! I suppose that was justified by a four-hundred-year-old Shakespearian text as well was it?

DELORES: It was actually!

SEBASTIAN: Delores, please, you're not helping. Elizabeth, the whole thing was done very tastefully.

DELORES: That's right, it was kept secret until the first night. Even, the production crew did not realise that there was a nude scene in the play until the dress rehearsal.

SEBASTIAN: It was not sensationalist in the least.

DELORES: Not by today's standards, but at the time it was on the front page of every tabloid newspaper the next day and for most of the six-month run of the production. All the free publicity meant that the house was sold out for every performance and we were nominated for several acting awards.

ELIZABETH: Undoubtedly the theatrical success of the season.

DOLORES: Elizabeth, yes, it was! I remember getting a letter off a young man who confessed to me that he thought that my portrayal of Juliet was excellent and that I was the first woman that he had ever seen fully naked. What a sweet boy. Then, he told me that he was entering the priesthood. I do hope that it wasn't the traumatic experience of seeing me in the nude that drove him into celibacy.

SEBASTIAN: Elizabeth, everybody was doing nudes scenes in those days, it was actually fashionable.

ELIZABETH: Fashionable?

SEBASTIAN: Yes, artistic trends go in fashions.

ELIZABETH: I'm not talking about art or fashions; I'm talking about my grandfather on stage in the nude.

DOLORES: And he was very good, may I say.

ELIZABETH: Nobody asked you. In fact, hearing that you have done a nude scene on stage, why am I not surprised?

DOLORES: My! And I'm the one that's meant to be formidable.

ELIZABETH: My grandfather is one of the most respected professors on the campus and all this is making a fool of him.

DOLORES: Oh, Elizabeth, grow up! So, you have discovered that your grandfather had a life when he was young. Well, big deal!

ELIZABETH: I'm not a child!

REX: Elizabeth, we are certainly not calling you a child, but grant me that I probably know more about media spin than the three of you put together. All this need not damage your grandfather's academic reputation; in fact, it could enhance it.

SEBASTIAN & ELIZABETH: Enhance it!

REX: Yes, enhance it, providing all this is managed properly. Sebastian you must remember how media spin works. It all depends on how you sell the product.

SEBASTIAN: I'm just a commodity, am I?

REX: When it comes to marketing, we all are. As for you, one of the most respected academics on the campus and one of the best actors of his generation, frankly, I can't even see why you want to put the genie back into the bottle. But I do think that you need a little help with the marketing. Sebastian, think about it, just think about it and we will chat later. Now, Elizabeth, we need to leave these two to talk.

SEBASTIAN: Dolores and I do need to talk, my dear.

ELIZABETH: All right, then, Granddad.

REX: Why don't you show me around the campus and I'll explain my ideas to you.

Blood, Passion & Self-Sacrifice

ELIZABETH: Did you ever go to university, Rex?

REX: Yes, I've been to Oxford, Cambridge and Yale. Once, I even did a summer show at the Sorbonne.

[Exit ELIZABETH & REX.]

SEBASTIAN: Well, thank you, Dolores for that, you really know how to get up people's noses.

DOLORES: Oh, really, then why didn't you tell her instead of letting her find out from somebody else?

SEBASTIAN: She's still a baby.

DOLORES: You'll be telling me that she is still in nappies next.

SEBASTIAN: She's my grandchild, and I'm worried about the affect all this is having on her.

DOLORES: Seb, can I just make clear to you that I never released anything to the press about you auditioning for James Bond or about that incident with the cucumbers. I didn't have to. All the press had to do is to go through back-issues of their own newspapers to find those stories.

SEBASTIAN: You're right, Dolores. Sorry. Although you did say that, 'Sometimes to work with, I was impossibly handsome'.

DOLORES: No, I didn't. I did tell that magazine that you were handsome.

SEBASTIAN: Oh, thank you.

DOLORES: And I remember saying that as a perfectionist, sometimes you were impossible to work with.

SEBASTIAN: Oh, thank you.

DOLORES: But I never said, 'Sometimes to work with, he was impossibly handsome'. The magazine must have edited the two statements together because they thought it sounded better. Seb, sincerely, how are you coping with your newfound fame?

SEBASTIAN: Remember, I have two other people to think about as well as myself, there are my daughter and my granddaughter. When I first encountered all the rehashed trivia again, I was upset; no, I was annoyed; no, I was angry; no, I was furious.

DOLORES: Seb, you're not writing a dissertation.

SEBASTIAN: Well, my daughter has dealt with my newly acquired fame marvelously. She thinks it's all a hoot.

DOLORES: Good.

SEBASTIAN: It's my granddaughter that I'm worried for. I love her dearly and she is deeply upset by all this.

DOLORES: That young lady, and despite what you may think, she is a young lady, I can assure you is more than capable of handling all this. I learnt that from our brief exchange a few moments ago. She's not a child, Seb; you're being over protective.

SEBASTIAN: Grandfather's prerogative.

DOLORES: I'll have a talk with her.

Blood, Passion & Self-Sacrifice

SEBASTIAN: Dolores, thank you, but I would prefer it if you didn't.

DOLORES: I didn't ask you. Of course, she's having difficulty coming to terms with all this. She is use to seeing you as, as -

SEBASTIAN: What?

DOLORES: - as a bit of an old fogey.

SEBASTIAN: An old fogey!

DOLORES: Well, look at the state of you, and you say that you have been doing the same job for twenty years. When your wife Elizabeth was alive you use to be really dynamic.

SEBASTIAN: I had to sacrifice most of that when Elizabeth died to rear my daughter and then when my granddaughter came along, well, I felt responsible for helping to rear her too.

DOLORES: So, Elizabeth, your granddaughter I mean, has only ever known you living your life through somebody else, either her mother or her, and now that she has learnt that dear Granddad, the old fogey, once long ago had a life himself, she is having difficulty coming to terms with it. No surprises there, I think. I'll have a talk with her. Don't worry, she has more than proved that she is capable of handling me. But, Seb, that's not all, is it?

SEBASTIAN: No. It's me as well, Dolores.

DOLORES: Oh, God, you're not going to tell me that you have some horrible illness with only months to live.

SEBASTIAN: No, no, no, it's nothing like that. It's just - well, look at me, you said it yourself, I'm an old fogey nowadays.

DOLORES: When Elizabeth was alive you were always so positive.

SEBASTIAN: That was all a long time ago, Dolores.

DOLORES: You know, Seb, looking at those old movies of ours now entitled, *Heroes of Yesterday,* when I first started watching them, I laughed at them or wallowed in a little nostalgia about incidents that had happened on the set whilst we were making them, but then I realised as the series unfolded week by week that we were good in them. Truly, Seb, we were good in them. Probably, they are amongst the best work that the pair of us have ever done. Now, I'm actually proud of making them.

SEBASTIAN: I've never been ashamed of them. Never. Sure, I've dismissed them as rubbish compared to Racine or Euripides, but I've never been ashamed of making them, or being associated with them. But you want me to go back to being a third-rate matinee idol and for what - a few thousand pounds.

DOLORES: According to Rex, four million pounds spread over the next two years.

SEBASTIAN: Exactly, four million pounds spread over - what! Four million pounds?!!

DOLORES: Seb, you don't understand. When we made those films there was only two channels on television, BBC and ITV. They were both in black and white and they were on air for only five to six hours a day. Those films were made to be shown once and that was it. Now, it's different. There are countless number of television channels running continuously with hours and hours of air-time to fill, each of those episodes is repeated at least four times during the week on Channel 47, plus shows about the making of the shows, plus DVDs, videos, internet sites and so on. All the companies are desperate for decent material that is not costing them a lot of money but will attract an audience. So, yesterday's ephemeral dross is now marketed as today's modern classics. When we appeared on the television all those years ago, we were genuinely known by most people; now, you can be on the television, be called a celebrity and yet the vast majority of the population have never heard of you. According to Rex, the DVD sales of our films alone will make more money than we were paid to make the entire series. I've even got my autobiography due for publication this Christmas.

SEBASTIAN: I look forward to reading it.

DOLORES: Frankly, so do I.

[They smile conspiratorially.]

SEBASTIAN: I watched this week's episode of *Heroes of Yesterday. They Died Facing the Cannons* - about the disastrous charge of the Light Brigade in the Crimea war. I remember the make-up girl actually had a picture of Alfred Lord Tennyson stuck up on the dressing room mirror to make me up to look like him. Historically, he was the Poet Laureate who wrote the poem about the Charge of the Light Brigade, he wasn't even in Russia when the battle took place, let alone leading the cavalry charge. And you were playing Florence Nightingale trying to ride a horse with that ridiculous lamp.

DOLORES: It was the romantic loves scenes that I found most funny. I must have been out of my mind to agree to do my major speech declaring my undying love for you whilst sitting on a horse charging into battle with cannons going off all around. Still, I did cry at your death scene at the end of the film; it was very moving.

SEBASTIAN: Thank you, Dolores. I appreciate the compliment. They were good times, Dolores.

DOLORES: Yes. Yes, they were.

SEBASTIAN: You know, I could do with a change from here. My status at the University as a professor has changed since the series has been aired. I'm not taken as seriously as I use to be. I do need a change.

DOLORES: For your granddaughter's sake?

SEBASTIAN: No, for mine.

[They link arms and exit.]

16th Scene

TV PRESENTER *[Voice off]*: And now continuing our series *Heroes of Yesterday*. Another chance to see Sebastian Hardwick and Dolores DeWinter in those films made for TV that entertained our mums and dads all those years ago.

[Into the film. Enter YOUNG DOLORES. She wears a full leather trouser suit and high heel boots. Enter YOUNG SEBASTIAN wearing a black tie, evening dress. There is dramatic incidental music throughout.]

YOUNG DOLORES: Good evening, Commander.

YOUNG SEBASTIAN: Miss. Highheels, we're needed. Or, should I call you Honesty?

YOUNG DOLORES: No, Commander, I think we will keep this relationship on a professional basis, don't you? Miss. Highheels will do nicely.

YOUNG SEBASTIAN: Very well, Miss. Highheels it is.

YOUNG DOLORES: So, Commander, you promised to show a girl a good time, why have you brought me here to the perfidious lair of Professor Sin hidden deep under the seabed of the English Channel?

YOUNG SEBASTIAN: On the way here, Miss. Highheels, I called in see Number One.

YOUNG DOLORES: The head of our crack top-secret iron force?

YOUNG SEBASTIAN: Yes.

YOUNG DOLORES: What did he want to see you about, Commander?

YOUNG SEBASTIAN: He wants us to undertake an impossibly, dangerous mission to save the free world from the abomination of an insidious plot being hatched by none other than, Professor Sin.

YOUNG DOLORES: The two of us to face the most, evil diabolical mastermind on the planet?

YOUNG SEBASTIAN: Yes. Professor Sin has stolen a thermonuclear device that will destroy the entire free world if we do not stop him Miss. Highheels.

[Enter PROFESSOR SIN & HIS 3 HENCHMEN.]

PROFESSOR SIN: Commander, and the delectable Miss. Highheels, you will never leave my secret underground base alive and return to your beloved England and to freedom. Just behind that iron curtain there are ten thousand marauding communists awaiting my command to kill you. You are my prisoners!

YOUNG SEBASTIAN: Leave this to me, Miss. Highheels.

YOUNG DOLORES: O contraire, Commander.

PROFESSOR SIN: Kommen, mein Liebling.

[YOUNG DOLORES moves YOUNG SEBASTIAN aside and does some karate moves on PROFESSOR SIN which involves kicking him between the legs and throwing him over her shoulder. The villain lies unconscious on the floor.]

YOUNG SEBASTIAN: Watching that even brought water to my eyes.

[They both fight the 3 HENCHMEN. YOUNG SEBASTIAN & YOUNG DOLORES win. PROFESSOR SIN and HIS 3 HENCHMEN lay unconscious on the floor. YOUNG SEBASTIAN & YOUNG DOLORES kiss.]

YOUNG SEBASTIAN: My God, but I love you when you're angry. There, I have said the word 'love' and given you the secret to my heart. Before, I was too proud and a fool, a fool, a fool, but now I have said the word, 'love'.

YOUNG DOLORES: Together we could face anything, Commander. *[They kiss again.]* So, off we go to save the free world from the communist threat.

YOUNG SEBASTIAN: Miss. Highheels, this isn't merely the West verses the East.

YOUNG DOLORES: This is freedom verses tyranny.

YOUNG SEBASTIAN: Liberty liberating democracy.

YOUNG DOLORES: Indubitably! Let us go and save the world. After you, Commander.

YOUNG SEBASTIAN: No, I insist, after you, Miss. Highheels.

[They race off, guns in hand to face more villains. The incidental music builds to a crescendo.]

17th Scene

[SEBASTIAN and Dr DAVIS sit either side of a desk in her office.]

SEBASTIAN: Thank you, Dr Davis, for supporting me over these past, very difficult months, I do appreciate it.

Dr DAVIS: It's quite all right, Professor, as the Head of the Faculty it was the least that I could do. Indeed, I only wish, Professor, or, if I may, Sebastian, - *[He nods his agreement.]* - that you would come up to see me more often.

SEBASTIAN: Oh, well, that's good of you, Dr Davis -

M C Sanders

Dr DAVIS: Marion, please, Professor, call me, Marion.

SEBASTIAN: - Marion, but I do feel that it would be best if I had a change for a few years. At the moment, on campus, my newfound fame is proving too distracting for both the students and the masters.

Dr DAVIS: Ah, yes, your two-year sabbatical in America. I will miss you.

SEBASTIAN: Yes, well, I'm sure that the whole of the faculty will miss me – er - Marion. Nevertheless, a couple of years away in America doing a mixture of promotions for *Heroes of Yesterday* and guest lectures, I think, will do me a lot of good by giving me the break from here that I have needed for a long time.

Dr DAVIS: I believe that it will be quite financially lucrative for you as well.

SEBASTIAN: Yes, I'm told that it will be.

Dr DAVIS: These rumours circulating in the press about you being short-listed for the part of James Bond and about cucumbers, Sebastian, I don't pay much attention to them myself.

SEBASTIAN: I'm glad to hear it.

Dr DAVIS: I regard you primarily as a wonderful human being with an astute intellect, Sebastian.

SEBASTIAN: Thank you, Marion. I did play a spy in one of those old television films all those years ago and on the back of that performance I did audition for the part of the spy

James Bond when Sean Connery left the part, but to be candid, that is as far as it ever went.

Dr DAVIS: Please, please, Sebastian, no modesty, no modesty. I know that other women, Sebastian, regard you as, 'impossibly handsome'.

SEBASTIAN: Oh, well, that also may have been slightly misquoted.

Dr DAVIS: Do accept that whilst I respect you as a human being, Sebastian, to meet a man who has been short-listed for the part of James Bond and endowed with something attributed to the size of a cucumber, well, you have to understand that I might be a double PhD in philosophy, hold professorships from Oxford, Cambridge, the Sorbonne and Yale, be a member of the Royal Academy, and be sponsored for Dame of the British Empire, but what many people forget is that - *[She takes off her glasses and her hair band to let her hair fall free.]* -I am also a woman - *[She comes to sit on the desk lifting her dress above her knees.]* - and I also have needs like any other woman. Oh God, Sebastian, it's lonely at the top!

SEBASTIAN: It's quite lonely about one third of the way down as well Marion.

[They start a cat and mouse movement around the desk.]

SEBASTIAN: Marion, I respect you as an academic and an intellectual but I have always thought that we had a more plutonic relationship.

Dr DAVIS: Oh, Sebastian, perhaps I do dream dreams of epicurean bliss, especially when my husband is away, but, Sebastian, cannot two people strive to make paradise on this earth? Come to me and be my love, and we will all the pleasures prove.

SEBASTIAN: That sounds very exhausting, Marion.

Dr DAVIS: When a girl is in the presence of an Adonis, she feels capable of striding like an Olympian Goddess over hills and valleys, dales and fields to drink deeply all that the aqua vitae of desire may yield! Come, Sebastian, and quench my flames of passion!

SEBASTIAN: Dr Davis -

Dr DAVIS: Marion.

SEBASTIAN: - Marion, I accept that you obviously find me attractive.

Dr DAVIS: I want to bathe in the waterfall of your caresses!

SEBASTIAN: Well, perhaps, slightly more than just attractive.

Dr DAVIS: We are all victims of fate's fickle, fastidious whims, but occasionally the wind of destiny blows our fortunes in a felicitous and salubrious direction. Ooh, Sebastian, in your presence I stand like Mount Vesuvius about to erupt! Come into my arms, my love, and let us both make that leap of faith without parachutes into the erotic ether so that we may free-fall into an ecstasy of passionate embraces. Oh, God, but I yearn to be released into the giddy weightlessness of our mutual desires and the carnal attractions of your merciless charms. Sebastian, come over here and just take me!

[She sings.]

Falling in love again
Never vanted to
Vhat am I to do?
Can't help it

Love's always been my game
Play it how I may
I vas made that vay
Can't help it

Men cluster to me
Like moths around a flame
And if their vings burn,
I know I'm not to blame

Falling in love again
Never vanted to
Vhat am I to do?
I can't help it.

SEBASTIAN: Marion- Dr Davis - I was rather hoping that we could be just good friends.

Dr DAVIS: Kommen, mein Liebling.

[Dr DAVIS makes to kiss him.]

SEBASTIAN: Oh, my God!

[He exits hurriedly.]

Dr DAVIS: Oh, Sebastian, you are cruel to banish me to the outer darkness of emotional despair without hope of one kiss, one smile, one tender adieu rather than a goodbye. Is it such a crime that I ask for paradise to be ours?

[She exits chasing him.]

18th Scene

[ELIZABETH sits reading a book. There is a small table and two chairs. The table has a pitcher of water and a glass on it. Enter DOLORES.]

DOLORES: Can we talk?

ELIZABETH: Yes, of course.

DOLORES: Your grandfather is a fine actor and I can tell you that in my time I have worked with the best of them as well as more ham than you would fine in a butcher's shop window.

ELIZABETH: I appreciate that. It was just that I was shocked, that was all. Really, I didn't know the full story about my grandfather's acting career.

DOLORES: I can't think why he didn't tell you. We made a good team Seb and I. We were doing something that we wanted to do and we were getting paid for it, not a lot, but it was a very comfortable living, and we entertained a lot of people and made them happy for a few hours, and they may even have learnt something from it. We were very lucky people. You should be proud of your grandfather.

ELIZABETH: I am. Now that I have had time to come to terms with it, I am.

DOLORES: I accept that you feel all those films for television that we made were unworthy of your grandfather's talent.

Blood, Passion & Self-Sacrifice

ELIZABETH: Actually, I think that they're superb.

DOLORES: You do?

ELIZABETH: Yes, and so do all my friends; we are not quite the culture snobs that you think that we are. We can appreciate a bit more than plays written hundreds of years ago.

DOLORES: You patronise me.

ELIZABETH: No. It is possible that we, my friends and I, have a deeper appreciation of those films than you do. We regard them as modern classics; whereas you seem to dismiss them as pieces of dribble that pay well. Sure, the titles are bizarre even surreal: *Robin Hood, quest for Freedom, Buccaneers in Love, General Custer, death, love and glory, They Died Facing the Cannons* - the image of you as Florence Nightingale on a horse carrying a lamp as you ride into battle as part of the charge of the Light Brigade attempting to catch up to your lover so that you may die together is impressed on my mind forever. It was so romantic, and on the line, 'If we must die, then we shall die together,' I actually cried.

DOLORES: Don't remind me, after riding on that horse for a few days, my backside was sore for weeks afterwards.

ELIZABETH: And this week's adventure, *Love behind the Iron Curtain,* for someone who was too young to have lived through the period of history known as The Cold War, it sounds surreal. However, all those films do hold poetic truths. They engage our emotions and they allow us to empathise with noble thoughts, actions and sentiments.

DOLORES: At the time of making them, frankly, Seb and I hardly believed in them or saw them as beautiful, but 'poetic truths' -I like that. May I use it in my next television interview?

ELIZABETH: Of course. Also, you do give superb performances in them.

DOLORES: Thank you.

ELIZABETH: I don't know anybody who does not like them.

DOLORES: Good. *[Pause]*. You know, I use to know your grandmother; we use to be good friends. You're very like her, you know? We use to share all kinds of secrets.

ELIZABETH: Oh, am I about to be adopted?

DOLORES: Adopted? I'm not looking for a surrogate granddaughter. Oh, God, you know, I've only just realised, I'm old enough to have a granddaughter, OF CHILD-BEARING AGE! You'll be calling me 'Granny' next!

[DOLORES places her hand to her head in dismay. ELIZABETH makes to get her a glass of water.]

DOLORES: Don't fuss, dear, I assure you that Granny isn't having one of her funny turns; I'm just trying to remember the telephone number of my cosmetic surgeon.

ELIZABETH: A cosmetic surgeon? Is that really why your skin is so soft and lovely? I thought it was because you use Delovely soap.

Blood, Passion & Self-Sacrifice

DOLORES: Darling, if I had a bar of soap to hand at this moment, I can assure you that I would hit you with it. I am not ready yet to become anybody's grandmother, but I was hoping that we might be friends.

ELIZABETH: I'd like that. I really would.

DOLORES: I'm glad *[Pause]*. What are you reading? *[ELIZABETH shows her the book.] The Secret about Men.* Well, if we could learn that out of a book it would make life a lot easier.

ELIZABETH: I suppose you're going to tell me that you have had more men than hot dinners.

DOLORES: Hot dinners, no; birthdays, yes. Frankly, dear, my experience of men is that they always think with their bollocks. You're a lovely looking girl, so as long as you always bear in mind that the average man is reputed to think about sex every six seconds then you won't go far wrong.

ELIABETH: Well, that piece of older-sister advice in easy enough to remember.

[Pause. They smile.]

DOLORES: I have some pictures and reviews of the plays that your grandfather and I appeared in together, would you like to see them?

ELIZABETH: Yes, yes, I would love to. Thank you, Dolores.

DOLORES: My pleasure.

ELIZABETH: I have been thinking about what to do after I graduate from university. I have decided to go into professional acting. I have been taking drama lessons and my teacher is enthusiastic about my decision. I'm going to apply for Drama School.

DOLORES: I would fully expect you to become a beautiful actress. I would be delighted to help you if I may?

EIZABETH: It would be great, Dolores, if you would. Thank you. I really appreciate that, I do.

DOLORES: My pleasure, my dear.

[They link arms and exit].

19th Scene

[SEBASTIAN is packing to leave. Enter ELIZABETH]

ELIZABETH: Granddad, I'm sorry that I've behaved so prudish over all this, but it was a bit of a shock to discover that your grandfather was quite a catch years ago, when I've always regarded him as, well as -

SEBASTIAN: A bit of an old fogey?

ELIZABETH: Well, yes. Why did you give it all up? Was it for mum?

SEBASTIAN: To be totally honest with you, Elizabeth, the answer is - no, not entirely. Everybody has their day and a time when their acting career is at its height. Dolores will never admit it to you, but she hasn't really done anything of note for quite some time. I freely admit that when I was good, I was very good and it was great fun, but the parts started to dry up. New artistic directors had new ideas and we were the old school. Then, when your grandmother died, well, I thought that it was time to take stock. I did have a child to rear, your mother, and the acting parts weren't coming along as often as they use to do; so, I sat and I thought and it occurred to me that if forty odd years on someone said to me that I hadn't been a great actor, well, I could dismiss it with a shrug and a, 'Everyone's a critic'; but, if someone said to me that I hadn't been a good father or a good grandfather, then, I'd be very, very deeply wounded and profoundly hurt.

[Pause. They embrace.]

SEBASTIAN: It's not easy having children at times, you know?

ELIZABETH: Frankly, Granddad, it's not easy having grandparents at times either. *[Pause]*. You will be away in America for about two years?

SEBASTIAN: Yes. Rex has arranged for me to do a college lecture tour as well as the promotion tour for *Heroes of Yesterday*. It was good of him.

ELIZABETH: Good of him, at 15% of your income.

SEBASTIAN: I don't deny him his money, Elizabeth. We both know that I need to be doing something new. I had started to gather cobwebs being here all these years. Will you be all right sharing a flat with your friend, Sylvia?

ELIZABETH: Yes. Don't worry, Granddad, I'll be fine. Besides, Dolores will be around a lot over the next few years. You know that she is being sponsored to become the next University Chancellor?

SEBASTIAN: Yes, she told me. We will be calling her Dame Dolores before she's through.

ELIZABETH: Do you think that she stands a good chance of getting the Chancellorship?

SEBASTIAN: Considering that she is donating a vast amount of money to build the new University Theatre and that most of the females on campus regard her as a role model, whilst most of the males on campus regard her as a fantasy of the bedroom, I think that she probably stands a pretty good chance, don't you?

ELIZABETH: I hope that she gets it. Also, I've decided on my career when I graduate.

SEBASTIAN: Oh, what?

ELIZABETH: I want to be a professional actress.

SEBASTIAN: My dear, that is wonderful. Perhaps it runs in the blood. A classical actress, I hope?

ELIZABETH: Yes, but I want to do other types of drama as well.

SEBASTIAN: Of course, of course.

ELIZABETH: I've even landed a role as the Leading Lady in our next production in the University Drama Group.

SEBASTIAN: In *Medea?*

ELIZABETH: No. No, we have decided not to do that play.

SEBASTIAN: To be candid, the part of Medea as a role demands an emotional range that is really beyond the emotional experience of a young actress to portray.

ELIZABETH: Well, that as may be. As Prince William is not attending now -

SEBASTIAN: No, I believe the Chancellor of the Exchequer, the Right Honourable Sir Harold Smyth is coming instead.

ELIABETH: Yes, old Horny Harry. So, we have decided to change the choice of play to something that would be of interest to him.

SEBASTIAN: What?

ELIZABETH: We are going to do a Shakespeare.

SEBASTIAN: A Shakespeare. Excellent idea. Well, do tell me with which of the Bard's oeuvre are you going to grace the Right Honourable politician.

ELIZABETH: It's one of the great love stories.

SEBASTIAN: One of the great love stories, excellent choice.

ELIZABETH: I got the idea after talking to Dolores. Oh, Granddad, it's a beauty play and a beautiful idea! Everybody in the Drama Group adores it! Dolores was the Leading Lady in this play, you played the Leading Male, both to much acclaim on the West End and now I'm going to play the Leading Lady as well. And Granddad, guess what?

Delores is going to help me with my interpretation of the role.

SEBASTIAN: Well, you certainly could not have a better mentor. Dolores has played many Shakespearean roles on the London stage. It's one of the great love stories you said?

ELIZABETH: Yes.

SEBASTIAN: Well, Dolores played Viola in *Twelfth Night* to great acclaim, Rosalind in *As You Like It* for which she won a critics award and she has played Juliet in *Romeo and Jul* - Elizabeth, please tell me that I'm not going to regret asking you my next question? Which one of the Shakespearean great love stories are you going to do?

ELIZABETH: It's the one with Romeo in it.

SEBASTIAN: And Dolores is helping you with your interpretation of this play?

ELIZABETH: That's what I said.

SEBASTIAN: Elizabeth, how romantic an interpretation are you giving to this production of *Romeo and Juliet*?

ELIZABETH: For Horny Harry? A very romantic interpretation.

SEBASTIAN: You mean that you're going to do a nude scene in it?

ELIZABETH: Yes. It's justified by the script.

SEBASTIAN: A nude scene justified by a 400-year-old script!

ELIZABETH: Yes. You said so yourself.

SEBASTIAN: Yes, yes, I did!! *[Pause.]* Yes, I did, didn't I?

ELIZABETH: Yes, you did.

SEBASTIAN: But, you're my granddaughter.

ELIZABETH: That's right, Granddad. I'm your granddaughter, a young adult and capable of making up my own mind.

SEBASTIAN: Yes. Yes, you're right. Sorry. But please remember that some of us have been there and done it forty odd years ago. If you wish to avoid the fate of Icarus and avoid melting your wings by flying too near to the sun through intellectual arrogance or hubris, perhaps, you would allow me to give you a little professional advice based on my own experience?

ELIZABETH: Granddad, I would love you to do that.

[They link arms as they start to exit.]

SEBASTIAN: Always remember that the secret of a successful nude scene is titillation regardless of the intellectual pretentiousness of the production; nobody will be listening to the lines properly, it is the visuals that dominate. Rehearse the scene fully clothed to get the interpretation correct, but remember in performance you keep the audience hooked visually.

ELZABETH: I understand, thank you, Granddad, thank you.

M C Sanders

[She gives him a peck of a kiss on the cheek. They exit.

Blackout.]

An Admirer from Afar

A short comedy.

M C Sanders

List of Characters:

Thelma Winslow/Maggie Bradawl – a 60-something actress

Dr Jeffries – a mystic.

Alf – an old man, smartly dressed in a suit, shirt & tie, and a flat cap

Floor Manager/Landlady – [these two minor characters, played by the same person, can be either male or female; in the script I have made them female].

Blood, Passion & Self-Sacrifice

[Introduction – type of music reminiscent of a TV soap opera.
Scene - TV studio, the set is a launderette. A scene is about to be shot.
On stage the FLOOR MANAGER and THELMA as
MAGGIE.]

FLOOR MANAGER: Rolling, and action!

[THELMA as MAGGIE pours a carton of soap power into one of
the washing machines. Then, she walks down the set towards the
camera.]

FLOOR MANAGER *[as a Customer with a northern accent out of*
shot]: Have you some change for the washing machines, luv?

THELMA as MAGGIE: Aye, pet, just a mo while I look in
me purse.

[THELMA takes out her purse to look for some change. ALF
appears in front of her. THELMA faints.]

FLOOR MANAGER: Cut! Cut!

[ALF exits. The FLOOR MANAGER helps THELMA to her
feet.]

FLOOR MANAGER: Are you OK, Thelma?

THELMA: Yes, yes, it was just a dizzy spell – erm, women's
problems, you understand? Nothing more. Give me a
moment. Oh, could I see the take we just did?

FLOOR MANAGER: The take where you fainted?

THELMA: Yes. If you don't mine?

FLOOR MANAGER: Ok. *[Speaks into a microphone attached*

244

to an ear-piece.] Could you just run that take again? Yes, where Thelma fainted.

[We see the take on a screen at the back. It is THELMA as MAGGIE filling the washing machine with power and walking down the set. We hear the dialogue.]

FLOOR MANAGER *[as a Customer with a northern accent out of shot]*: Have you some change for the washing machines, luv?

THELMA as MAGGIE: Aye, pet, just a mo while I look in me purse.

[We see THELMA as MAGGIE fainting. Alf is not in the scene. Scene change to – a doctor's consulting room. Dr JEFFRIES sits at a desk. THELMA sits opposite to him.]

{*The transformation of MAGGIE into THELMA need be nothing more than THELMA donning designer sunglasses, a fur coat over MAGGIE's apron, removing a grey wig to reveal a fashionable hair style and changing flat sensible shoes for high heels and visa-versa to return to MAGGIE.*}

Dr JEFFRIES: And this little, old man appears to you every night, Miss Winslow?

THELMA: Yes, every night at 2 o'clock without fail. Regardless of how many sleeping pills I take, I wake up when I hear him calling, 'Maggie', and there he is.

Dr JEFFRIES: How long have you had these visitations?

THELMA: For about five, no six weeks. The problem is, it's getting worse. He's started to appear to me at the television studio.

Blood, Passion & Self-Sacrifice

Dr JEFFRIES: The first time was yesterday?

THELMA: Yes. I was so shocked I fainted. I lied to the Floor Manager, telling her it was women's problems. God, I hate myself for using that excuse, but I am desperate.

Dr JEFFRIES: Did anybody else see the little, old man?

THELMA: I don't think so. He wasn't even on the video recording of the scene. I managed to see it afterwards.

Dr JEFFRIES: You definitely don't recognize him?

THELMA: Never seen him before in my life.

Dr JEFFRIES: Why should he appear to you at the studio during a scene in your TV show?

THELMA: If the little, old man exists.

Dr JEFFRIES: If the little, old man exists? You feel the entity is a product of your imagination?

THELMA: Doctor Jeffries, I can't sleep properly because he appears to me every night, and now he's following me around. A little, old man, whom nobody else except me can see, is stalking me. If the studio found out, they'd think I was bonkers. It would end my career as an actress. I came to you because you're some sort of expert in mental and psychic phenomena, can you help me?

Dr JEFFRIES: Yes, I think so, Miss Winslow. You're in a soap opera, aren't you? Erm, sorry, I mean television drama series.

THELMA: I have played the part of Maggie Bradawl in the

television drama series, *Gilmoss*, for nine years now. It is a very successful rendition. Maggie is everybody's favourite granny. Maggie even has her own web-page on the *Gilmoss* internet website. I believe what she writes is very good, although, frankly, I've never actually read it myself, but I'm assured it is very good.

Dr JEFFRIES: True stardom, then.

THELMA: Yes.

Dr JEFFRIES: And the spirit appeared to you whilst playing this character?

THELMA: Yes. In the television series, Maggie works part-time in a local launderette. We were shooting a scene on the set of the launderette and the little, old man appeared to me. Nobody else saw him, and he is not on the video recording. God, if the studio found out, they would think that I'm cracking up! Please doctor, can you help me?

Dr JEFFRIES: If it will give you some peace of mind, Miss Winslow, I don't think that you are imagining this. It sounds like the spirit of someone who has passed over, and the spirit wants something from you.

THELMA: From me? What can a ghost possibly want from me?

Dr JEFFRIES: That is what we need to find out, Miss Winslow. This character you play on television -

THELMA: Maggie Bradawl?

Dr JEFFRIES: You told me that the spirit calls you, 'Maggie'.

THELMA: Oh God!

Dr JEFFRIES: The price of fame, I'm afraid. I firmly believe that this *Gilmoss* character is the key to your problem.

THELMA: Maggie Bradawl, a fictitious character, is being stalked by the ghost of a little, old man whom nobody but me, the actress playing Maggie Bradawl, can see.

Dr JEFFRIES: It sounds like an improbable fiction; but the truth so often does. You must ask the spirit what it wants in the character of Maggie Bradawl.

THELMA: What!

Dr JEFFRIES: The spirit's request may not seem to be very much to you, but to this spirit it is important. The solution rests with you, Miss. Winslow. In a way, this is the result of the success of your acting talents, and it is through your acting talents that we can resolve this problem. You must face up to the spirit. I shall be with you.

THELMA: I can resolve this through my own talents as an actress?

Dr JEFFRIES: That is correct, Miss. Winslow.

THELMA: Anything to get rid of this thing. What do I have to do?

[Soap opera music.
Scene change to – THELMA's mid middle-class home. Enter THELMA as MAGGIE and Dr JEFFRIES.]

THELMA: Come into the lounge before anybody in the

street sees me dressed like this. I know some people think that *Gilmoss* actually exists, but this is surreal.

Dr JEFFRIES: Please, dim the lights.

[THELMA dims the lights.]

THELMA: What happens now?'

Dr JEFFRIES: Now, we wait. I shall link with my spirit guides to ask them for protection for both of us. *[Dr JEFFRIES adopts a lotus position. He makes some mystic signs as he incants the lyrics of Daisy Bell/Bicycle Built for Two.]*

> Daisy, Daisy,
> Give me your answer, do!
> I'm half crazy,
> All for the love of you!
> It won't be a stylish marriage,
> I can't afford a carriage,
> But you'll look sweet on the seat
> Of a bicycle built for two!

[Dr JEFFRIES explains] My spirit guides were very keen peregrinators in the 1880s. They travelled everywhere on their velocipedes.

THELMA: Dr Jeffries, no further explanation is required.

[An elegant, carriage clock chimes 2 am.]

THELMA: Two o'clock.

Dr JEFFRIES: It has gone very cold.

THELMA: It always starts like this.

Blood, Passion & Self-Sacrifice

[ALF enters. Dr JEFFRIES moves to stand behind THELMA and places a firm, reassuring hand on her shoulder to give her moral support.]

Dr JEFFRIES: Do and say exactly as I tell you. Send love to the spirit.

THELMA: Love? How the hell am I supposed to do that?

Dr JEFFRIES: Just think nice thoughts.

ALF: Maggie, sweetheart! Maggie, sweetheart!'

Dr JEFFRIES: Answer him in character.

THELMA as MAGGIE: Yes, chuck, what do yer want, luv?

ALF: I need to talk to yer, sweetheart, private like.

Dr JEFFRIES: Tell it I'm a confidant.

THELMA as MAGGIE: This is a friend. It's alright, luv, nothing will get past these four walls.

THELMA *[in an aside to Dr JEFFRIES]*: Oh, God, did I really say that?

Dr JEFFRIES: Just stay in character.

ALF: Well, it's like this; I need yer to do me a favour. I know you're always doing favours for folk who come into the launderette in *Gilmoss*. I wouldn't ask if it wasn't important, but would you be an angel and do something for me?

THELMA as MAGGIE: Of course, luv. What?

ALF: I owe the local Grocer on the corner £5. Would you be a pet and go to me lodgings and find me wallet, which I keep hidden under me bed. Take the £5, and then go to the Grocer and pay him for me? I know it's only £5, but I hate leaving a debt unpaid. Sorry, sweetheart, but there's nobody else that I can ask.

THELMA as MAGGIE: Of course, I will, luv.

Dr JEFFRIES: Get the address where he used to live.

THELMA as MAGGIE: Erm, luv, have yer got your address for me?

ALF: You should know that, sweetheart. You've replied to all the letters that I have written to you over the years. You even sent me a signed photo of yer-self last time after I told you in me last letter how much I luv you.

THELMA [*in an aside to Dr JEFFRIES*]: Damn that fan club!

Dr JEFFRIES: Do not let it become anxious, but try to get the address.

ALF: I've often mentioned in me letters to you, Maggie, that you're always welcome at my house. I luv *Gilmoss* and you are my favourite. I have always had a soft-spot for you, sweetheart. Anytime you're passing, you just pop in for a cuppa.

Dr JEFFRIES: Say something to it! Don't allow it to become vexed.

THELMA [*in an aside to Dr JEFFRIES*]: Say what?

Dr JEFFRIES *[places both hands on her shoulders to give her reassurance]*: Stay in character and think!

THELMA as MAGGIE: I would have come, luv, but you know what it's like in the launderette, I'm always run off me feet.

ALF: But you've got me address, haven't you, sweetheart? As I told you in me last letter, I luv you.

THELMA as MAGGIE *[in inspiration]*: Well, of course, I've got your address, pet; it would just save me looking it up, that's all. Yer know what I'm like, I can't remember a thing from one day to the next. Why, I'd forget me head if it wasn't screwed on properly.

Dr JEFFRIES: Well done!

ALF *[laughs]*: Aye, I know what yer like, Maggie, that's why I luv you so much. You're as bad as me. It's Victoria Street, just off Grimshaw Road, No. 3, just say that Alf sent yer. OK, sweetheart?

Dr JEFFRIES: Reassure it that you will do what it asks.

THELMA as MAGGIE: Don't worry, luv, I'll do that favour for yer. You rest easy now.

ALF: You're a goodun, Maggie, that's why I luv yer. I know you will not let me down. *[As ALF exits.]* - Good-bye, sweetheart, and thank you. Thank you. You'll take a load off me mind if you do that for me. Good-bye, sweetheart. Good-bye.

Dr JEFFRIES: God bless you, Alf. *[Dr JEFFRIES sings*

Daisy Bell/Bicycle Built for Two as makes some mystic signs.] Thank-you spirit guides for your help and protection. *[Pause.]* He's gone.

THELMA: Yes, you're right. He's gone. He kept saying that he loved, Maggie. That is sweet. He was actually in love with her. Poor, dear soul. Poor, dear Alf.

Dr JEFFRIES: This is still not resolved. I'm afraid that we have failed.

THELMA *[Removes her wig.]*: Failed! I admit that extempore is not one of my fortes as an actress, and it was a little touch and go back there, although it is always like that when one is improvising; however, let me just say that I gave a competent performance, Dr Jeffries, even if I have to say so myself.

Dr JEFFRIES: I mean that we have failed because we did not get the *full* address. So, it is still not resolved. No.3 Victoria Street, off Grimshaw Road, - well, it could be anywhere.

THELMA: It's in Oldham.

Dr JEFFRIES: Oldham?

THELMA: Dr Jeffries, please, grant me the respect that, as an actress, I know, and I can recognise, my provincial accents!

Dr JEFFRIES: My apologies, Miss Winslow. Then, tomorrow we shall go to Oldham.

[Soap opera music.
Scene change to – ALF's room. A basic bedroom with a single bed

and a large picture of MAGGIE BRADAWL on the wall. Enter the LANDLADY, Dr JEFFRIES and THELMA.]

LANDLADY: This is Alf's old room. Alf really loved you, you know? He definitely had a soft-spot for you. Oh, sorry, I mean Maggie, of course. I don't think he would have liked you. Frankly, you're a bit posh for him; nothing personal like, you understand, but he really loved Maggie. Down-to-earth, you see. Mind you, we all like Maggie. Nothing personal, you understand, I'm sure you're a lovely person as well.

[Dr JEFFERIES looks under the mattress of the bed. Dr JEFFRIES finds ALF's wallet and holds it up.]

LANDLADY: That's Alf's wallet! Well, I never! I wondered where that had got to. I looked everywhere for it.

[Dr JEFFERIES opens it. Dr JEFFRIES takes out of the wallet a folded photo and unfolds it to reveal a large picture of MAGGIE BRADAWL signed by THELMA. Then, he takes out a £5 note. He holds it up.]

Dr JEFFRIES: £5.

THELMA: Do you know whether Alf had an account with a local Grocer, as I believe he was saving that money to pay an outstanding debt.

LANDLADY: Alf was a stickler for paying his debts. He wouldn't rest in peace knowing he owed anybody anything. There's a Grocer on the corner of the street that Alf used, and, yes, he owed him £5 when he died. The three of us could go together and pay it.

Dr JEFFRIES & THELMA: Good idea.

[Scene change to – ALF's grave. THELMA holds a wreath for the grave. Enter Dr JEFFRIES.]

THELMA: Thank you for meeting me here. I thought placing a wreath on Alf's grave seemed an appropriate gesture.

Dr JEFFRIES: It is very thoughtful of you. No further visitations, I hope?

THELMA: Since we paid Alf's £5 dept to the Grocer, thankfully, none whatsoever. I had to tell my Producer about the haunting. She was pressing me for an explanation. It was either let her assume that I was suffering from a neurosis due to over-work or tell her the truth. So, I told her the truth.

Dr JEFFRIES: Good.

THELMA: Not really, she still assumed that I was suffering from a neurosis due to over-work. Anyway, she wants to use the idea in the show. Maggie Bradawl haunted by a ghost who is in love with her. She thinks it will make a good plot line. Do you mind?

Dr JEFFRIES: I do not mind at all, and I'm sure that Alf, your ardent admirer, will regard it as a very, great honour.

THELMA: Good.

Dr JEFFRIES: Indeed, I suspect Alf will feel that, now, he is always in your debt.

THELMA: What!!!
[Blackout.]

Vissi d'arte

Maria Callas - her life, her art and her loves.

A one act monologue.

M C Sanders

This is a play about one of the greatest sopranos of our age, indeed, some people would say of all time, Maria Callas. Maria successfully revived the myth of the operatic diva and became one of the most famous Greeks since Plato. One of her finest performances was as Tosca in the opera of the same name by Giacomo Puccini. In Act II, Tosca sings the magnificent aria, Vissi d'arte. It is Italian, and a literal translation is, 'I lived for art'. As this is a one act monologue for a 50-something Maria Callas, whom during the piece reflexes on her life, the name of the aria seemed an appropriate enough title for the play. There is no singing in the play; it is purely a dramatic piece. Maria Callas' life was as colourful, tragic, grand and fascinating as the operas in which she appeared. She was certainly a passionate person who sacrificed everything for her art. The monologue strives to capture all of this. The play was first performed on Saturday, 6th May, 2006, at the studio theatre above The Salisbury public house in St Martin's Lane, London, by Miss Cindy Wells. Since then, Cindy has given over 60 performances of the piece at various venues across England. With Cindy's help, I have made amendments to the play over the years. Fortunately, the performances of the play have always been well received. An interesting, entertaining and fine tribute to a great lady? Well, I shall leave that for you to decide.

Blood, Passion & Self-Sacrifice

[Maria is aged fifty-something. She is sharp, glamorous, commanding, flamboyant, intelligent, fiery and funny.

Open with the aria Casta diva from 'Norma' by Vincenzo Bellini & the librettist Felice Romani.

Maria is sitting at her dressing table. She is preparing herself for a media interview.]

MARIA: The English artist, L S Lowry, used to paint whilst listening to a recording of me singing. His favourite aria was Casta diva from *Norma*; one of my greatest and one of my favourite bel canto rôles. I performed it over 90 times. Once, Maestro Lowry painted a portrait of his girlfriend, whom he called *Ann*. Yet, when I saw the portrait, I thought that it looked like me. Interesting, that the mysterious Ann in the portrait has never been found, despite Maestro Lowry insisting that she exists; the dear man, blest him.

My mother never liked me; she adored Maria Callas, but she never liked me, Mary Kalogeropoulos. After the death of my brother, Vassily, when he was just two-years-old, my dear papa went to an astrologer to ask when was the best time to make love for him and his wife to have another son. My mother prayed for a boy and my parents were convinced that God would give them a son with beautiful blonde hair. They would christen him, Patrois; they never even thought of a girl's name. Mother even knitted a set of blue baby clothes for Patrois. When I was born the following year, dark-haired and female, my mother was so disappointed that she would not even look at me for four days.

I was always the second child to my older sister, Yakinthi, who always looked magnificent; so nice and slim, so socially adept and so elegant, and she always had boyfriends. In my youth, I was fat, spotty and short-sighted. Mother thought that I looked like a Greek peasant. If that was not enough, my mother found that Yakinthi could sing. So, my mother decided that we both could sing and enrolled us in singing and piano lessons. I was made to sing when I was only five-years-old to fulfil mother's dreams of stardom via her daughters. Fat, spotty, short-sighted and made to sing in public; no wonder I hid behind a mask that later became Maria Callas. Yakinthi proved good at playing the piano, whilst I excelled at singing. 'You might be fat, short-sighted and look like a peasant, but at least you have your voice.' My mother's words still ring in my ears. It is a cruel thing to make a child think they are an ugly duckling. But at least I could sing. When mother realized I was good at something, she pushed and pushed and pushed me, wanting the celebrity stardom through me that she had yearned for in her youth.

Shortly before I was born, my parents gave up a profitable pharmacy in Greece to move to New York. They could not speak a word of English, but they were spurred on by dreams of a new beginning in a new country. I was actually born in Brooklyn. My parents wanted us all to become American. So, in the USA, they changed our family name. After all, who outside the Greek community could pronounce, Kalogeropoulos, let alone spell it? So, my lovely papa changed it to, Kalos, which the New Yorkers pronounced, Callas. My mother wanted us all to have American names. My sister, Yakinthi, named after the hyacinth flower, started to call herself, Jackie. Jackie, a name that has haunted me ever since. Whilst my mother started to call me the American version of Maria, Mary. Mary Callas; I ask you, honestly, what type of name is Mary Callas for La Divina, the Divine one, a Goddess of the stage, a high priestess of the opera world, the Prima Dona Absoluta, one of the most famous Greeks since Plato? Where's the exotic mystic in Mary? Where's the allure?

Blood, Passion & Self-Sacrifice

During those days in New York, my lovely papa and my mother argued constantly in front of Yakinthi and me, especially after papa lost his pharmacy business in the 1929 Stock Market crash. We had hardly any money, so we lived in a small apartment in Queens. Yakinthi and I listened to the constant bickering of our parents echoing off the walls of our small home. According to mother, papa's failed business was all papa's fault. He was useless. She, the daughter of a Colonel in the Greek army, had dared to marry beneath her for love to a mere pharmacist. Mother insisted that her father, the Colonel, had been right; dear papa was not worthy of her. Our mother would not let Yakinthi and I talk to the working-class children in our neighbourhood. Our clothes, table manners and etiquette always had to be socially correct; after all, we were the granddaughters of a Colonel in the Greek army. Mother bought a pianola and played classical arias to Yakinthi and me. We went to the New York City Library every week after school to read classical literature and we had piano and singing lessons. Mother insisted that we were middle-class girls. My only friends in those days of childhood so long ago were my music and my three canaries: David, Elmina and Stephanakos. My canaries taught me how to sing; they knew the secret of bel canto. Dear papa had made a good living from his pharmacy business until the Stock Market crash. Even after that he made a steady income as a Travelling Salesman selling medical supplies. Alas, mother was never satisfied. At least his job as a Travelling Salesman took the poor man away from mother's constant nagging. But when he returned home, mother would start nagging at him again. Eventually, my mother decided to return to Greece. When she told my dear papa, I remember him saying, 'At last, my God, you have pitied me.' Unfortunately, mother took Yakinthi and myself with her. It was 1937 and we lived in central Athens. I took my three dear, little canaries with me;

after all, David, Elmina and Stephanakos were my only friends. Money was always short, yet my mother never worked. She persuaded Yakinthi to take a wealthy older lover, Milton, the son of a shipping magnate. He was generous to us, blest him. I saw my first full opera in 1938, at the Lyric Theatre, in Athens, because Milton bought the tickets for us. It was *La Traviata*. The production was appalling; but I loved it.

One good thing my mother did do for me was to enrol me into the Greek National Conservatoire and she persuaded Madame Maria Trivella to tutor me. At thirteen, I was the youngest student at the Conservatoire. Mother and Madame Trivella had to lie about my age, stating that I was 16-years-old, so that I could get a scholarship. Madame Trivella thought I was a soprano, not a contralto as my mother had said. There were other teachers my mother took me to see, such as the lovely Spanish soprano, Maestra Elvira de Hidalgo, a gentle creature who gave with all her heart. At first, when she saw a fat, spotty, short-sighted girl standing in front of her, she said she could not teach me; then, she heard me sing and she adopted me as her surrogate daughter. The training was strict and uncompromising, often five hours a day, but I loved it and it saved me being at home and listening to mother moan. I thought that Maestra de Hidalgo was like a proper mother to me. She knew that we were short of money, so she secured for me supporting rôles at the Greek National Opera, blest her. The other singers were jealous of my voice and my ability to act, so they made horrible remarks about me, but I ignored them. Fortunately, because of my myopia, I couldn't see them in the wings mocking me in any case.

By 1939 I had risen through the chorus to secure the lead rôle of Santuzza in *Cavalleria Rusticana*. At 16, I was the youngest person in the cast. The jealousy and the back-biting in the company was terrible, but my mother had toughened me up well; it was her harshness that instilled in me a selfish, aggressive streak which enabled me to climb to the top. So, I proved more than capable of dealing with that load of mediocre no-hopers at the Greek National Opera.

During World War Two, the Italians occupied Greece; everything was in short supply except Italian soldiers. I always found the Italian officers to be gentlemen. Mother took an Italian officer as a lover; a lovely man called, Colonel Bonalti; after all, her father had been a Colonel in the Greek army, so as far as she was concerned, he was in the same social class as us. Colonel Bonalti adored my singing. He was very kind to us, blest him.

During the occupation, I did go out with an Italian opera lover myself, dear Major di Stasio. He was not a Colonel, but he was a senior army officer and so in our social class, therefore mother approved. He always insisted that I call him 'Major', not 'Uncle'. Dear Major di Stasio; oh, I do hope the Germans didn't shoot him when they caught him after the Italians left the war. In those days, I sang in concerts to raise money for the poor of Athens. I sang for the Italians and I sang for the Germans. What did I do in those far away days during World War II? I sang. What else was I expected to do? When I returned home from the Conservatoire, our apartment rang with my vocalising and constant repetition of phrases. Then, each night, I went down to the air raid shelter with my three, dear, little canaries. Fortunately, the British and the Americans never bombed Athens because they did not want to risk damaging the Acropolis; strange how buildings are considered to be more important than people.

Then, I secured the rôle of Tosca. I distinctly remember it was 27th August, 1942. World War II raged around us, and I sang *Tosca*. The Greek critics enthused that I possessed a rare dramatic and musical gift, and that I was a new star in the Greek firmament. They said that Mary Kalogeropoulos would be a name everybody would remember. The dears, how were they to know that outside of Greece, nobody could pronounce Kalogeropoulos, yet alone spell it. So, my mother's plump, spotty, young peasant girl, who had to wear glasses due to her myopia, did actually become a success. I have my mother to thank for that; I don't deny it. I thought that mother would like me now. After all, I was earning money for the family and I was a celebrity.

When the Italians left the war, the Germans took over the occupation for a short while. I sang in *Fidelio*, which was conducted by Hans Weiner, Commander in Chief of the Wehrmacht; an odd choice of opera considering the story is about the freedom and the brotherhood of man, hardly a politically correct Nazi theme, but it is good and it is German, which is probably why the Nazis permitted it to be performed. Der Oberbefehlshaber Weiner was very strict and authoritative in rehearsals. He expected lines to be learnt before the first rehearsal; oddly enough, I rather liked that, blest him; I regarded it as being very professional. After that, I performed in 1944 at the Herodes Atticus amphitheatre at the foot of the Acropolis. It was a beautiful, sultry evening in August in the open-air of our capital city, Athens. A German critic extolled that I gave bud, blossom and fruit to the harmony of sound that ennobled the art of the prima donna; blest him. Oh, I do hope the British didn't shoot him when they caught him after the war.

Once the occupation ended, I lost my scholarship at the Conservatoire and my job at the Athens opera; they accused me of fraternizing with the emery. Fraternizing! Me! My mother actually hid two British soldiers in our apartment for two weeks during the occupation at grave personal risk to ourselves. I actually sang to them. Sure, I did sing for the

Italians and the Germans as well, but who else could I sing for? I sang to raise money for the poor of Athens. I sang to the British when they arrived. I'm a singer. Sure, I did have an Italian officer as a lover, oh dear Major di Stasio, I do sincerely hope that neither the Germans nor the British shot him for being an Italian officer. But fraternizing? Never! Really! Never! Well, hardly ever. And I did have a Greek lover as well at that time. One of my fellow singers, dear Evangelos Mangeneros. He wanted me to marry him. He was 15 years older than me and already had children to two other women, both of whom he financially supported. Mother thought he was an unsuitable match for me. I thought that he was good in bed, but marriage, well, mother was probably right on that occasion. I told him, 'You cannot ask me for my life; for the time being I want only to be married to my art.' One of my better lines, I think; it made the dear man cry, blest him.

After the war, dear Maestra de Hidalgo advised me to go to Italy where my voice would be adored, but they had been the occupying force in Greece and I only just escaped persecution and arrest because we had hidden two British soldiers during the occupation and I had sung to raise money for the Athenian poor. I needed to distance myself from the Italians, so I returned to New York and to my lovely, sweet papa. But, the star of Athens was considered a non-entity in the USA. All The Met could offer me was *Madama Butterfly* and *Fidelio* to be sung in English; in English! I ask you, seriously? Dear Maestra de Hidalgo was right, I needed to go to Italy.

Fortunately, Giovanni Zenatello, the great tenor, yes, the great Giovanni Zenatello was auditioning in New York for a production of *La Gioconda* to be performed in Verona at its huge amphitheatre seating 25,000 people. When I auditioned for him, dear Giovanni was so enamoured with my voice

that he jumped up and we sang a duet together. He took me
to Italy, where I sang for the Maestro Tullio Serafin, yes, the
great Serafin, a Music Director at La Scala. He fell in love
with my bel canto voice, the dear man. I knew that I was in a
place where I would be loved. Maestro Serafin became my
mentor and supporter. I drank deep from his well of
knowledge; he taught me that in music there must always be
expression and justification. If you do not persuade the
public with the gestures and your belief in the interpretation
of the rôle then your performance is wrong. Opera must be
dramatic or it becomes a sleeping pill. An opera can be the
silliest thing; I actually remember once performing with
Hans Beirer in Wagner's *Parsifal*; he sang in German and the
rest of us sang in Italian, ludicrous, but the audience loved it.
One gives the public a world of illusions and something
more colourful than life; nevertheless, a good opera
expresses a real truth, exaggerated, but true.

Maestro Serafin's Svengali influence was to push, push, push
me to sing until I was exhausted; but still, I assert that I am
my own creation. I made a decision to become a bel canto
diva. It was my decision. Bel canto is the way I express
myself; it is my universe. When I sing, I am no longer a fat,
spotty, short-sighted girl; I am La Callas. I feel whole, I feel
complete, and when I get my performance right, it makes me
feel - elated. Maestro Serafin explained to me that a bel
canto diva must look beautiful and interesting all the time
she is on the stage, beautiful costumes, beautiful jewellery,
beautiful make-up; the vision, like the music, should be
harmonious and beautiful. Well, that takes money and
determination. So, I married a man who owned twelve
factories and was old enough to be my father, Giovanni
Battista Meneghini. Poor Titta, he idolized me and took the
blame for my excessive workload; but I worked feverishly
before I met him and I continued to work feverishly when I
lived with him at our beautiful apartments in Milan and

Blood, Passion & Self-Sacrifice

Verona. I. My decision. *[She stamps the table.]* I was determined to become a diva. I remember Titta and I met over dinner in Verona in 1947. It was my first night in Italy. He was a director of the Arena in Verona where I was to perform *La Gioconda*. The theatre company took us all to dinner. He ordered a veal chop, but the restaurant had run out, so I offered him mine. Our eyes met. The next day he took me to Venice and two days later we dined at Lake Garda and we became an item. On stage, I could control the emotions of a 25,000 strong audience with a phrase of music or a gesture of my hand. Yet, off stage, I was just a lonely, myopic, overweight, young singer. One night, whilst coming off the stage at the Arena, I managed to fall down one of the open chutes leading underneath the stage and sprain my ankle; in the subdued light in the off-stage area, I simply didn't see the opening with my poor eye-sight. I was vulnerable, alone and short-sighted. However, myopic or not, I saw in this wealthy, older man, who had made a fortune making bricks and who adored me, a bank balance that would pay for my career during my apprenticeship in Italy. I could not find work for five months after *La Gioconda*, I was told that I was not Italian enough in my diction and my voice was weak in the higher registers. Titta paid for the two years I needed to correct all that before the money started to roll in, and he helped me to change into a diva; to become a vision of refined elegance in elaborate expensive make-up and designer clothes that looked chic and foreboding.

After all, being able to sing is only part of becoming a successful diva. I remember when mother took us back to Greece, I was walking along a street in Athens with my sister, Yakinthi, and a group of boys shouted over at us, 'Look there's Laurel and Hardy'. That night, I cried in bed. I had to look right. 'It isn't over until the fat lady sings,' was definitely not going to be my epitaph. I recall losing 80 pounds in weight, thus turning myself into the most beautiful lady on the stage, moving with elegance and charm. People wondered how I did it. I always insisted that I simply ate a special diet sans pasta and potatoes, and kept the slimming drugs well and truly out of sight. My weight loss made my voice lighter, less dark and deep, and the public loved it. I blossomed into a diva, a Goddess of the stage. And, if the excessive weight loss affected my voice in later life, well the brightest stars all shine for least.

If my mother did not love me, then Titta did. It was love at first sight. After all, we were both in love with the same person, La Callas. We made a good team; Titta was infatuated by my fame and I was besotted with singing and celebrity. He became my agent, covered all my expenses during my apprenticeship in Italy and haggled with the theatre companies for larger and larger fees, whilst I was free to concentrate on my singing and my looks. Titta gave me a new piece of jewellery on every first night. Blest him. He bought me a little painting of the Madonna, the Madonnina, which I took everywhere with me like a good luck charm. But more important was now, like my older sister, Yakinthi, or Violetta in *La Traviata*, I could live for love, whilst a wealthy, older man took care of me. My older sister, Yakinthi, visited us, and she was shocked to find her younger sister in bed with a middle-aged man. Considering her own lover was a wealthy shipping owner who was much older than her, I found her reaction rather surprising. However, I was able to use my sister's reaction to persuade Titta to marry me. Blest her. But, when one of Titta's middle-aged friends fancied Yakinthi, and, even worse, thought that she was my younger sister! *[She stamps the table in anger.]* I pointed out that Yakinthi was six years older than me, and I told Yakinthi to go home; sisterly love is one thing, but harvesting my cabbage patch is quite another. Titta and I married in Verona in the charmingly petite,

Blood, Passion & Self-Sacrifice

Cappella Pellegrini. It was 21st April, 1949, and the summer that year was beautiful. That night, I sailed for Buenos Aires alone; a strange way to spend one's honeymoon you may think, but Titta explained that I could claim it on expenses because I was booked to do a summer season there. I sent both my parents a telegraph telling them of my marriage. It read, 'Siamo sposati e felici.' We are married and we are happy. I'm sure when mother got it translated from Italian she was furious, but I didn't need her anymore. Thanks to mother, like her, I am able to cast people aside once they have served their purpose. Ironically, I was only doing what she had taught me. After all, the only thing that counted was my career. For twelve years, my husband, not my mother, my husband was my trouble-shooter, protector, hard-nosed negotiator and factotum; he even gave up his bricks to manage my career, blest him. In Buenos Aires, when I sang Casta diva during my performance in *Norma*, everyone was in tears. I was extremely pleased at that. The ugly duckling, Mary Kalogeropoulos, was dead and the divine Goddess of the stage, Maria Callas, was born. Callas, a name everybody could pronounce; Maria, a name worthy of a Goddess of the stage. And if most people think that I'm Italian and not American; well, é la vita. In Milan, my designer clothes, contact lenses, jewellery and elegant apartment all had to be perfect for the cameras. Like mother and my beautiful older sister, Yakinthi, I always ensured that my clothes and my apartment were perfect and, frankly, much, much more expensive than theirs. Now, I was like my sister: thin, elegant, chic, classy and effortlessly beautiful. I loved it, and I didn't need mother anymore.

However, every girl grows out of the protection of her daddy, even of her sugar-daddy, and in September,1957, a Greek sailed into my life, a modern Odysseus, Aristotle Onassis. Sexually, I never got anything out of my marriage. I spent my youth without a satisfying sex-life; well, some of it anyway. But Aristo could physically satisfy me, and, of course, pay for my rather expensive penchant for café society; that world of wealth and privilege. Titta and I could never have children despite trying, yet suddenly I needed a divorce because I was six months pregnant with Aristo's baby. Titta cast himself as the wronged husband, spurned by a truculent younger wife and purposely made things difficult for me to get a divorce. Poor Titta, he never did understand why I left him. The fame went to his head like too much wine. He had stopped protecting me in his pursuit of the fame and the money but, ultimately, his little girl had grown up and wanted to leave home. He turned our house, Sirmione in Verona, into a shrine to me and he lives there with his memories; blest him.

But I get ahead of myself. It was in 1949 in Venice at the Teatro La Fenice when I came to international acclaim. I was singing Brünnhilde in *Die Walküre*; yes, all six hours of it. When God was kind to me and, in the opera following mine, rendered the soprano, Margarita Cairo, too ill to sing. The production was, Vincenzo Bellini's *I Puritani*, and it was the major rôle of Elvira. I had only six days to learn the part. I thought it was an impossible task to master the part in six days, but Maestro Serafin pushed me to do it. I thought that if Maestro Serafin thinks that I can do it, then maybe I can. Under his Svengali influence, I surprised myself at my ability to learn the rôle so fast. The work was excessive, but I was young and my voice seemed to take the strain. The critics loved it. An artist performing a Brünnhilde and an Elvira to such a high competency within days of each other; they loved me. They called my performance, a miracle full of splendid high notes from a beautiful poised voice. Maestro Serafin, bless him, taught me how to juxtaposition dramatic soprano arias with coloratura pieces and how to learn a rôle quickly yet competently. The parts and the money poured in. Two years later, God helped me again when Renata Tebaldi was too ill to perform in the lead of *Aïda* at La Scala. So, I made my debut at La Scala, even though that horrible, little moron, Antonio Ghiringhelli, its Superintendent, disliked me because Titta demanded more money and I demanded more rehearsal time. Titta, blest him, was never a diplomat in his negotiations with the theatres; but thanks to him, I earned more money than the other singers, however, my God, I paid the consequences for it as I was considered to be awkward. I am a perfectionist, constantly striving to be better; that is why people think that I am nasty and vitriolic at times; I do not take fools gladly. But it is what made me one of the greatest singers in the world. After *Aïda*, on a chilly December evening in 1951 at La Scala, with the house full, I performed Giuseppe Verdi's beautiful opera *I Vespri Siciliani*. The production was a huge success. I took encore after encore, after encore. After the show, we dined at Servino's ristorante and La Scala became my spiritual home. At La Scala, Maestro Luchino Visconti told me that he only started to direct opera to work with me; blest him. He was a spoilt aristocrat and a communist, and although I can never forgive the Greek communists for killing my three pet canaries when they shot into our Athens' apartment during the civil war at the end of the German occupation, poor David, poor Elmina and poor Stephanakos, blest them *[She crosses herself three times in the style of the Greek Orthodox Church]*; Luchino was not Greek but Italian and he adored La Callas, adored helping to create the diva, adored moulding me into the star of La Scala. We became the dream-team at La Scala. People said that he was gay, but I could not believe that, even when told me himself. I said, Luchino, surely, you're jesting with me. I'm sure that you are always a gentleman with me because you know I am married.

Alas, 1951 was a year of ups and downs for me. I did make a big effort to be reconciled with my mother. I invited her to come on tour with me when I visited Mexico. Titta persuaded me that if my mother and I went away together as adults, we might be able to enjoy a loving relationship. After all, I was now the daughter she had aspired to create; even thinner than my older sister, Yakinthi, more chic, wealthier and more successful. However, we got off on the wrong foot. My mother had returned to my father by this time, leaving Yakinthi in Athens. When I arrived in New York on my way to Mexico, I found mother in hospital with an eye complaint and my lovely papa ill with a heart condition. I visited papa in his apartment with my friend and fellow singer, Giulietta Simionato. Giulietta was thirsty, so my sweet papa gave her a bottle of soda that he found in the fridge. Shortly after, Giulietta was violently sick and rushed into hospital. Apparently, mother kept insecticide in a soda bottle in the fridge unbeknown to my papa. Mother and father were not getting on very well yet again. Fortunately, Giulietta survived. When mother left hospital, she joined me on tour, and she basked in the celebrity life-style with fresh flowers in her hotel suite every day and fêted at receptions in every city. I even bought her a fur coat. It was meant to be a thank-you and a goodbye present; after all, I had my husband, Titta, to care for me now. However, mother told me that as she had sacrificed all to make me a star, I owed everything to her, which she would never let me forget. She said that if I did not do as she asked then she would expose me to the newspapers. Blackmail. I don't like blackmail. So, I cut her off. She carried out her threat. She told the press that I had left her to starve and that I had told her to jump in the lake. As if I would ever do anything like that. I do remember writing to her in a fit of anger telling her to go and jump in the river, but never a lake – not one of my better decisions. I was depressed; I had just returned from a rather gruelling tour of Brazil where I was sacked by the administrator of the tour after he dropped me from *Tosca* because he thought that my performance was lousy, and so in a fit of temper I kneed him in the bollocks. The press reported that I caught him in the lower abdomen. At the time, I thought that the newspapers were being euphemistic, but in retrospect, they were probably right, I don't think that he had any balls. But I digress. After my contretemps with mother, my mother and I have never spoken to each other since, never. I send her a monthly allowance, but I never speak to her. Perhaps, I am more like my mother than I shall care to admit; after all, she herself had not spoken to her mother, my grandmother, for seven years after they argued, and even then, she only went to see the old lady because my grandmother was on her deathbed.

That was in 1951. It was also the year that Renata Tebaldi, my fellow soprano at La Scala, and I fell out. We were in Rio de Janeiro at a music recital and we agreed not to perform encores. I did my set of songs and went off stage; Renata performed her set of songs, and then did two encores! *[She stamps the table in anger.]* The double-crossing bitch! And then I arrive home to another begging letter off mother! So, I told mother to go and jump in the river; but I never said, 'lake'. As to Renata, we were never enemies. We were never friends, but we did actually admire each other's singing, even though I thought that her operatic performances were more relaxing than taking a sleeping pill. Our style of singing is very different; I prefer lyric theatre whilst she merely performs concerts in costume. We tend to sing different repertoires; as I said to the press, we are as different as Champagne and Cognac. I never said as different as Champagne and Coca Cola as one newspaper reported. Maestro Toscanini, one of my favourite music directors at La Scala, called Renata's voice, 'La voce d'angelo', the voice of an angel; but it was to me that he offered the lead rôle in a new opera, *The Consul*, written by his favourite protégé, Gian Carlo Menotti; not Renata. Blest him. I am a dramatic soprano who is capable of singing music written for light and agile coloratura sopranos whose range I extended through training, willpower, and bloody hard work.

To find the right interpretation for a rôle, Maestro Serafin taught me to simply listen to the music; one will find every gesture and expression there. How to sing the words, interpret the score and decide on a gesture, it's all there in listening to the music. That is where the truth and the intentions of the composer will be found. The music makes every gesture and every expression meaningful.

I love rôles that render powerful, moving performances like Violetta in *La Traviata,* or Norma, or Tosca; beautiful, successful, competent women who sacrifice everything for love.

The public love my renditions of those rôles and in the 1950s I was at the summit of my career. In 1956 I returned to New York to make my debut at The Met. I performed one of my favourite rôles, Norma. Whilst I was in America, I helped to establish opera houses in Chicago and Dallas. The Americans love me, but they also love scandal and gossip. A year earlier a paparazzo had photographed me after an exhausting performance of *Madama Butterfly* in Chicago when I was screaming at a Chicago Sherriff who had just handed me a writ from a greedy little moron called Eddie Bagarozy. He used to be my agent and my lover when I returned to live with my dear, lovely papa in New York. Now, he demanded ten percent of all my earnings because I had signed a ten-year contract with him before I left for Italy. I thought my reaction was quite reasonable considering how preposterous the allegation was that I owed him money. Unfortunately, I had to settle with him out of court. When I first went to Italy with Zenatello, I wrote four letters to Eddie explaining how well I was getting on with his wife, who was appearing with me in *La Gioconda*, I told him that I still loved him and I asked him should I marry this generous, kind old man, Titta, whom I had met and who wanted to bankroll my career. Titta was very flattered by my description of him in the letters, blest him. Bagarozy threatened to publish the letters, so I had to pay him off to avoid the scandal, but the hissing snakes in the press still christened me a 'Tigress'. Then, *Time* magazine published bitter stories fed to them by mother because I wouldn't give her more money; she accused me of having a temper. Me! A temper! When all I do is speak my mind. Rather vehemently at times, perhaps. And rather passionately at times, also. But, a temper? Really? The morons! *[She stamps the table in anger.]* And talking of morons, Rudolf Bing at The Met in New York cancelled my contract after I refused to perform two operas without a proper rehearsal time and on tired old sets that The Met had had hanging around in their store room for years! *[She stamps the table in anger.]* I cannot do lousy performances! La Scala and dear Maestro Serafin would never have treated me like that! What does Rudolf Bing know about preparing for an opera? He's an impresario; he isn't even an Artistic Director! He wears an English bowler hat everywhere he goes in New York and he isn't even English, he's Austrian for heaven's sake! The moron! However, by Rudolf cancelling my contract with The Met, he did free me to perform for The American Opera Society in Vincenzo Bellini's *Il Pirata*, for which my beautiful performance won all the critics to my side. Rudolf Bing did say that I was the most intelligent singer that he had ever worked with and he did admire my singing. In 1965, Rudolf invited me back to The Met to sing *Tosca* with my favourite tenor, Franco Corelli, and with that lovely baritone, Tito Gobbi. Rudolf Bing, you eccentric old dear; blest him. Actually, in retrospect, I do quite like the label, 'Tigress'.

It is a pity that I did not behave like a tigress when I appeared at the Edinburgh Festival in 1957 in the La Scala production of Vincenzo Bellini's beautiful opera, *La Sonnambula*. I had agreed to do four shows and four shows only. As I explained to them at the time, I was going straight after the fourth performance to a party in Venice given in my honour, yes, given in my honour, by the gossip columnist Elsa Maxwell. I had already refused to attend one party that Elsa wanted to throw in my honour due to work. So, I promised her that I would attend this one and I did not want to let her down again. However, the production in Edinburgh was so successful that La Scala and the Edinburgh Festival decided to put on a fifth performance. I told them I could not do it! I told them that I had promised to go to a party in Venice and that I could not get out of attending it! But the morons went ahead in any case, telling everyone that I was going to appear! When I told them that I wasn't! I was accused of walking out on both La Scala and the Edinburgh Festival, when I had fulfilled my contract; the four performances that I had agreed to do. *[She stamps the table in anger.]* The morons! Elsa had hired two orchestras and invited half of European society to her party in my honour. I remember singing, *Stormy Weather* with Elsa at the party, for alas, the price I paid for not staying to perform in Edinburgh was that La Scala ceased to be my spiritual home. But there were compensations; Aristo was at Elsa's party.

Aristotle Onassis, Aristo, my Greek Adonis, my modern Odysseus, The Other Greek, who paid to have a bed of roses for me to walk upon when we were in Madrid.

Aristo and I were both married, but alas not to each other. Let's face it, what's two pieces of paper when one is in love. I was reluctant at first, cheating on one's husband isn't something I do lightly and, frankly, I was afraid that I might actually enjoy it; but Aristo pestered Titta and me to go for a holiday on his yacht. Sir Winston Churchill was one of his guests. He brought his wife and his little dog with him. His dog was named Toby; I forget the name of his wife. Titta was keen to go because I had been advised to take the sea air for my health, and going on Aristo's yacht was cheaper than hiring a boat for ourselves. However, I knew Aristo's true intentions. One night, after Titta and I had one of our long and irritating arguments, I went up on deck in tears, and there was Aristo sitting alone, contemplating the dark Aegean Sea. He comforted me. My modern Odysseus. The Other Greek. When we left his yacht, *Christina*, I knew that my marriage was over. Aristo waltzed me through café society, which I adored, money was no object to him; unlike Titta, he was never petty with money. We lived on *Christina*, a floating palace where each room is named after a Greek island and adorned with gilded fittings and crystal glass. His crew of 64 pampered me. In Monaco, Princess Grace became my friend. Aristo wanted to dedicate the Monaco opera house to me. I felt relaxed. I started to stay up late. I even tried smoking. If I did not pursue my singing career as frequently as I used to do, it was because I was too busy being a woman, and I loved it. I thought when I met a man that I loved, I would not need to sing any more. When one falls in love, one exists only for the other person. The most important thing is to focus on making each other happy and having a family; I dreamt of having twins. However, during our intense relationship, I still sang. Once, when I was flying off to London to perform and I was still fatigued after a series of demanding performances, Aristo said to me, 'Why do you bother to sing, I've got plenty of money?' Blest him. I think he meant it quite sincerely despite his love of the fame that I brought to him. My modern Odysseus. The Other Greek. I loved his energy and his toughness. I loved his charming, spontaneous magnetic personality. His boyish mischievousness made him irresistible. He called me son petit canari, his little canary. I loved my three, little canaries when I was young. Now, I was a little canary with somebody to care for me. At the Epidaurus amphitheatre, Aristo and I were caught on camara holding hands. Epidaurus, where later in 1961, I would take 17 encores for my performance in *Medea*. At Epidaurus, Aristo and I met a Greek Orthodox priest who blest us both. I felt that I had come home. Everything seemed like cloudless skies with beautiful flowers in full bloom. Strange how my sister, Yakinthi, and I both ended up the unmarried lovers of wealthy shipping owners who were a lot older than us; perhaps, we both needed wealthy older men to pamper us and to take care of us.

I filed for divorce from Titta, but he contested every move in the Italian courts. He gave interviews to the press about us against my wishes. I was furious with him. I phoned him and I told him, 'Be careful, Battista, one day I'm going to arrive at Sirmione with a revolver and I'm going to kill you!' He replied, 'Fine, I'll be waiting to machine gun you down.' We never spoke again. Eventually, to be free of him, I decided to renounce my American citizenship in favour of becoming a Greek citizen because, under Greek law, if one's marriage has not been consecrated by an Orthodox Greek priest, then one is not officially married. It was 1966 and I was free. Aristo had divorced also. He cheated on me, I knew that, but he always came back to me. I waited in my rooms paid for my him at The Ritz in Paris like a modern Penelope waiting for her modern Odysseus to return. So, even when he took Jackie Kennedy on *Christina* for a summer holiday, I thought that he would return to me and the good times would begin again. Alas, like Tosca, I was fooling myself, living in a dream world of fanciful expectation, and, like her, I had a cruel trick played on me. Just two years later, when I thought all was set for us to marry, I read in the newspapers that Aristo had married Jackie Kennedy. Jackie. That bloody name again. It haunts me. Aristo was never in love with Jackie, so why did he marry her? Even ten days after his wedding to her, he came secretly to see me in Paris. At first, I would not let him in.

Blood, Passion & Self-Sacrifice

So, he stood in the street and whistled to me as the boys use to do in Greece to their sweethearts in our youth. I was so angry with him! *[She stamps the table in anger.]* To learn that he had got married from a newspaper! After nearly nine years of knowing each other, he did not even have the guts to tell me he was getting married! He would not go away from my window, so, eventually, I relented and I let him in to avoid the paparazzi seeing him waiting outside. I told him that he was irresponsible and a fool. He admitted to me that his marriage to Jackie was a mistake. He looked like a little boy lost. I realized that I still loved him, and so I let him stay. Love is noble, but very difficult and you pay a heavy price.

Interesting, I always seem to need a dominant figure in my life; my elder sister, Yakinthi, provided a rôle model when I was a child, then mother moulded me into a hard, ambitious diva, then Titta gave me, a struggling starlet, the protection and the money that I needed, and then Aristo made me fall in love with him and waltzed me through café society.

Yet, I suspect that like mother and Titta, Aristo loved me only for the fame that I could give to him. I knew we would never be an item again, but I became his close friend and confidante. He respected me because he could always trust me to tell him the truth and to keep his secrets. At least now as friends we had nothing to prove to each other, and we never argued after that moment.

I remember performing at The Met in 1965, and Jackie Kennedy was in the audience. After the assassination of her husband, President John F. Kennedy, she was the toast of America, but I received a five-minute standing ovation and Jackie had to politely stand there through it. In retrospect, that was very, very satisfying; even if she did get her revenge later by marrying my lover.

M C Sanders

Jackie and I may have been the prize jewels in Aristo's collection of affairs with famous ladies, but I was his favourite. He still needed son petit canari. After the death of his son, Alexander, in a plane crash in 1973, it was to me that Aristo came for comfort; not to his wife, Jackie. He was a broken man. He had lost the will to live. I comforted him and, as we talked, I remember saying to him, 'If only our son had lived. If only our son had lived'.

[Maria produces a photograph from her purse.]

He was born on 30th March, 1960. I needed a Caesarean operation. We called him, Oneiro, which is a Greek word meaning, 'dream'. The little angel had breathing problems. He died just a few hours after birth. Aristo and I buried our little boy in North Milan, in the Brescia cemetery where I use to meet Aristo secretly in our first years together. I always carry this photograph of him with me; it is all I have of him, blest him.

[She crosses herself in the style of the Greek Orthodox Church & she kisses the photograph.]

I remember when Aristo lay dying in the American hospital in Paris. I went to visit him; Jackie didn't. His security guards were not going to let me see him at first, but I called to him, 'Aristo, c'est moi; ton petit canari.' He heard my voice. He heard my voice and he told them to allow me to enter. He had taken only one precious item with him into the hospital, a red blanket that I had given to him years before. We held hands. We sat in silence. We did not reminisce. As I made to leave, he said to me, 'I loved you, not always well but as much and to the best that I was capable of. I tried my best.' My affair with Aristo was a failure; but our friendship was a great success. We kissed for the last time; for the last time.

Blood, Passion & Self-Sacrifice

Time takes care of all things. But, alas, nothing lasts forever, neither in love nor in art.

[Maria replaces the photograph back in her purse.]

On 19th December, 1958, I gave my first concert in Paris. It was to mark the ending of the 4th Republic. It was broadcast live on France's only television channel and afterwards a banquet for 450 people was held in my honour. The whole of French society was there to see me, an opera Goddess. Officially, the gala was a fund-raising event for La Légion d'Honneur; I was engaged for five million francs, the highest fee ever paid to an opera singer; I donated the fee to the benefit. It was the height of my career; yet, I started to have problems with my voice in the same year. I couldn't continue a performance of *Norma* in Rome in front of the President of Italy, of all people, due to bronchitis. The mezzo-soprano, Fedora Barbieri, had already been replaced due to losing her voice. I warned the administrators the day before the performance that I too was feeling unwell and that they might have to replace me also. I received a message from the director saying that no one can replace Maria Callas. I was so touched. The dear man, blest him. He knew how to play to my vanity. With the help of several doctors, I thought I could sustain myself through the show just as I had done in my youth, but I could not go on for the second half of the performance because my voice was slipping away. I had to cancel the rest of the show with the President of Italy in the audience and the production being broadcast live on Italian radio. The press accused me of insulting the whole of the Italian nation. They presented me as a temperamental prima donna and opera houses in Italy were threatened with losing their grants if they employed me; but I was ill, I actually did have bronchitis. My voice was exhausted; I was doing too much. Fortunately, I had already been contracted to perform in two productions at La Scala. However, at the opening night of the first production, which was *Anna Bolena*, the carabinieri had to guard the theatre to protect me from an angry mob. Once again, it was my performance and my voice that won the press and the Italian people back to my side despite the political pressure not to hire me, and at the last performance of the second production, which was *Il Pirata*, I received a thirty-minute standing ovation; everybody knew that it would be the last time that I would ever appear at La Scala. In Rome, I had not vilified the audience, or the institutions, or the President, or the theatre, or the nation; I simply had bronchitis.

Perhaps, I did escape into café society with Aristo because I was losing confidence in my voice. Ultimately, donkeys bray and think that they can sing. But I was ill, despite pursuing my new desire to be a socialite. In my profession, one is not allowed to have a weakness. Also, there is always the fear of not succeeding, of not being true to your art. If my voice sounds good, then I am happy; but if I know that my voice is sounding bad, I find it irritating *[She stamps the table.]* when the public are still telling me that I am singing well.

In Paris on a cold evening in April, 1964, during a performance of *Norma*, my voice cracked. That was worse than in May a year later when I collapsed backstage, again in Paris and again during a production of *Norma*.

The brightest stars shine for least. It was with my dear friend, Tito Gobbi, that I gave my last stage performance in an opera. It was in *Tosca* directed by another dear friend, Maestro Franco Zeffirelli. I remember it was a lovely warm summer evening in July, 1965, at The Royal Opera House, Covent Garden, in London, in front of the English Queen, Elizabeth II. The audience gave me a stony cold reception when I first walked onto the stage because I had to cancel three of the four performances I was contracted to do because I knew that my voice would not sustain me through them. Better to give one magnificent performance than four bad ones, I thought. By the end of the show, I had won the English audience over and took encore after encore. I always enjoyed a love affair with the Garden. It started in 1952 with a production of *Norma,* and I always love returning there. Norma, the high priestess who roars like a lion but is forgiving and passionate and sacrifices all for love. How like me.

After that performance in *Tosca* at Covent Garden, I knew that my voice sounded tired. I knew that my voice was changing. One doctor said it was the heavy workload that I had undertaken in my early years which weakened my diaphragm leading to an unsteadiness in the high notes. A voice can wear out if over used. Another doctor blamed my efforts to keep my weight down, which resulted in a loss of physical strength. Yet another doctor said it was due to my early menopause. Does a woman sing with her ovaries? I was under a lot of stress after Aristo deserted me. I was taking medication. Once, I took too many pills and ended up in hospital. It was not a suicide attempt; I just got confused. The press was as cruel as ever; the rôle of the tragic heroine is that of self-sacrifice, she will go to die with the man she loves. *[Pause.]* I just got confused; but it all took its toll on my voice and my health.

So, I have stopped singing for 18 months to rest my voice. Your soul and your energy simply burn out. I achieved more than I could have ever dreamed of achieving. So, in that respect, I am happy. My nerves are calm now and I am at peace. The public is happy with my singing, but I am not. Dear Luciano Pavarotti wants me to record *La Traviata* with him and my dear friend Maestro Luchino Visconti has asked me to perform at La Scala. The critics say that I have lost confidence in my voice to sustain it through a full opera and beg me to perform, blest them, but I know that I can no longer give the great performances that I use to give. I always strive to be better; it is what made me whom I am and it is the realization that I can no longer achieve the same standard of performance any more that prevents me from singing.

Although I can speak six languages, music is really the only language that I know. I express myself through music and when I get it right, I feel - elated.

Was it all worth it? All the hard work and the turbulent life I chose? If mother had not denied me a childhood in her desire for fame, I may have grown up into an ordinary woman with a normal life and the children that I so dearly wanted. It is more difficult to run a good family than a career and there is no greater wealth on earth than a family. Had Oneiro lived, Aristo and I may have married. However, I take the package God handed to me, for better or for worse. I always say a prayer, 'God help me, give me what you want good or bad, but also give me the strength to overcome it'. My mother chose the life of a singer for me and it is that life that I have but, ultimately, it was my choice to become a diva. My sister, Yakinthi, could sing, some say as well as me, but she had no determination or ambition to succeed. I did. The voice and the myth dominate and what I do, I do by desire and by love; it was never my mother, nor Serafin, nor Titta, nor Aristo, it was always me. It is something embedded deep within me to sing as well as I can, and when I get it right, I feel - elated.

Time to meet the media.

[Maria stands up. She checks herself in a full-length mirror.]

Excellent.

Blood, Passion & Self-Sacrifice

[Maria turns to the audience.]

Fame, like music is illusive. Music is to be listened to and then it disappears into the air in the moment; all that remains is the memory. It is the voice and the myth that made me famous, and it is the voice and the myth that has made me whom you think I am.

[Maria goes to the door. She straightens herself, opens the door and she stands in the doorway. Camera flashbulbs flare from off-stage on the other side of the door.]

Oh, boys, if I had known that the photographers were going to be present then I would have made myself up for the occasion. As it is, you will have to show me as I really am.

[She throws a cheeky knowing glance back towards the audience. Maria exits. Music – Maria singing Giuseppe Verdi's I Vespri Siciliani.]

M C Sanders

Printed in Great Britain
by Amazon

11392116R00164